ASPHALT MOON

ASPHALT MOON

A Deets Shanahan Mystery

Ron Tierney

This first world edition published in Great Britain 2007 by
SEVERN HOUSE PUBLISHERS LTD of
9–15 High Street, Sutton, Surrey SM1 1DF.
This first world edition published in the USA 2007 by
SEVERN HOUSE PUBLISHERS INC of
595 Madison Avenue, New York, N.Y. 10022.

British Library Cataloguing in Publication Data

Tierney, Ronald
    Asphalt moon. - (The Deets Shanahan mysteries)
    1.   Shanahan, Deets (Fictitious character) - Fiction
    2.   Private investigators - Indiana - Indianapolis - Fiction
    3.   Detective and mystery stories
    I.   Title
    813.5'4 [F]

    ISBN-13: 978-0-7278-6493-2

All Severn House titles are printed on acid-free paper.

Typeset by Palimpsest Book Production Ltd.,
Grangemouth, Stirlingshire, Scotland.
Printed and bound in Great Britain by
MPG Books Ltd., Bodmin, Cornwall.

To Casey & Einstein

'The coma was nice. But I'm not in a coma now. This place is boring, the food is terrible and,' he said, pulling a bottle from underneath the pillow, 'the beer is warm.'

Shanahan to the doctor as he checked himself out of the hospital

One

Dietrich Shanahan listened to the phone message three more times to try to catch the number at the end of a long, barely audible, ghostlike monologue.

Finally, he was fairly certain he'd jotted down the correct number and called back.

The voice on the answering machine – more distinct, but less informative – told him what numbers he had dialed and nothing else except the tone.

'This is Shanahan. I returned the call,' he said, and placed the phone back in the receiver.

What he had heard was garbled. He wasn't sure whether it was a potential client or just someone complaining about something. Perhaps a prank or a wrong number.

If they didn't connect, it was no big deal. Shanahan had his army-retirement and social security checks. And Howie Cross, another private investigator, had recently paid him for the work he did on a case. The problem was: Shanahan had time on his hands. It was late October. Not a lot to do in the garden. The house he and Maureen had just purchased was in good shape. She was busier than usual selling and listing Eastside homes. His old dog and ancient cat spent most of their time sleeping. Unfortunately, as he aged, Shanahan slept less, not more. He had time. He wouldn't mind something to keep him busy.

'Once upon a time there was a booky man, you know a booky man?'

'You mean boogie man?'

'No, he don't dance.'

When Howie Cross got home, he found the little girl on his front porch. She said she was five. She had blonde hair. She said her mother's name was Mommy.

What was a forty-something man, who lived alone, who never in his life had to deal with children once he wasn't one himself, supposed to do with a little girl?

'When is your mommy coming back?'

The girl shook her head. She had no idea.

'You have a daddy?' Cross asked her.

'No.'

'What's your name?'

'Maya.'

'What's your last name?'

'Maya.'

'No, last name. Like Wilson or Jones. You are Maya who?'

'No,' she said.

'Maya, Maya, oh Maya,' he said. What was the cliché? He was getting nowhere fast. 'What does your mom look like?'

Cross could tell she was seeing her mother in her mind, but she couldn't figure out a way to describe her.

'Where did your mommy go?' he asked.

That's when she got into the story of the booky man. Her mother went to find the booky man. Or she was running away from the booky man. Maya somehow made it seem like both.

The sun was leaving. A chilled wind came out of nowhere. The girl was in a cotton dress. Cross looked around as if a solution lived in some corner of the yard. How long ago had the girl been deposited there? He knew he had to take her inside, but adult men who live alone, and little girls? He was an ex-vice cop. He knew how that looked. This sort of thing made him nervous. He'd take her inside, call the police right away.

'C'mon.' He took her hand, led her across the lawn. The maple that towered over his small home had begun to shed and the gold leaves crunched beneath their feet.

Once inside, Cross went to the larger of the few rooms in his home, one of the oldest in the neighborhood and once a chauffeur's quarters. The main house was either never built or destroyed. He had converted the two-car garage connected to what was probably a small sleeping room into a living room. There was a small kitchen and bath, and some owner before him had added a bedroom. In the living room, Cross had had a fireplace built, not just for coziness, but for warmth. There was no insulation. The floor was made of concrete. And in Indiana winters were cold.

Cross decided to start a fire, have a sip of whiskey – just a sip – and call one of his old friends on the force. There were still a couple who'd talk to him even after he was less than cordially invited to leave the department.

'How long have you been waiting?' Cross asked the girl.

She shrugged her tiny shoulders.

Cross brought her a blanket, sat her down on the sofa. He threw some logs in the fireplace, wadded old newspapers and stuffed them under the wood, and lit them. The fire grew large quickly and slowly lost its ferocity. Cross stuffed more paper in and the flames leapt out. Cross jumped back.

He looked at Maya. Her eyes opened wide.

'Have you ever seen a fireplace?'

She shook her head.

'It will make you warm,' Cross said. He started toward the small middle room, which had become his office, for the phone. 'Stay away from the flames. I'll be right back.'

'You see the doctor?' Maureen asked Shanahan as she came into the kitchen and dropped her real estate book and brief-case on the counter.

'I've been probed, pricked, poked, and pinched,' he said.

She smiled. Her eyes twinkled. He knew he didn't deserve her.

'You have all the fun,' she said.

He threw the pieces of sausage into the pan with the chunks of browned potatoes and then threw in a hefty amount of loosely chopped onions.

'And?' she asked.

'And I'll live. I'm thinking maybe I'll hit a hundred forty since I've cut down on my drinking.'

She pulled a bottle of red wine from the cupboard.

'So you're telling me the good doctor went where no other man has gone before?'

Shanahan wasn't talking.

Casey, Shanahan's sixty-pound hound of the Catahoula

variety, moved across the floor, wanting to go out. One St. Patrick's Day, long before he met Maureen, the dog appeared on his front porch without a collar let alone a license. He didn't want to leave. He was an easy dog to get along with as long as he didn't get the scent of something wild. Unfortunately, he wasn't fond of kids, other animals, or strangers. For that reason, Shanahan left him in the fenced backyard when he went for his afternoon dirty-clubs game at Harry's.

Little did Shanahan know that the dog would climb the fence after Shanahan left and return before Shanahan returned. The old detective didn't know how long that had been going on before someone called him to tell him the story. These days, at Casey's advanced age, he'd be climbing no fences, but Shanahan was reluctant to let him off the leash when they went for a walk by the creek. If he caught the scent of a raccoon, he'd be gone.

The onions, potatoes, and sausage sizzled. He opened a can of white beans, drained off the liquid, and poured them into the pan. Another of his one-pan wonders, quick dinners he'd learned to cook for himself during the decades before he met Maureen.

Cross came back with the phone. There was nothing for the little girl to do. He had no toys, no appropriate books or magazines. He had nothing for her to eat and nothing for her to drink, except tap water – that is unless she was a beer and stale potato chips kind of girl. He was about to punch in the numbers when he noticed something.

'What do you have in your hand?' he asked the little girl.

She said nothing, but her eyes said something else.

'Maya, what do you have?' Cross put the phone back on the table and knelt down in front of her. He nodded toward her left hand, which was closed tight.

'Nothing.'

'Would you let me see nothing? I've never seen nothing before.'

She shook her head.

'Please, Maya. I promise I just want to look.' Cross set the phone down and gently grasped her wrist. 'I won't take anything.' She clenched her tiny fingers as tight as she could. Her fingertips were white. He gently forced open her grip.

A thin gold chain with a small red stone pendant.

He held it up. 'Margot,' Cross said. 'You're mother's name is Margot, isn't it?'

She looked at him directly, thought about it for a moment, and nodded.

He didn't know Margot had a kid. Then again, there was a lot about Margot he didn't know.

Now what would he do? Calling the police might not be the wise thing to do. 'Might not' were the operative words.

What he did know about Margot was that she was a little crazy, a little dangerous, and mightily independent. She wouldn't have just dropped off little Maya like this just to get a babysitter. Seemed as if she had found trouble somewhere and was trying to protect the kid.

Cross didn't like what he was thinking.

He handed her back the pendant. 'Why don't we go shopping, Maya?'

There was a small supermarket a couple of blocks away on Illinois and 56th. He'd get some cereal, some soup, some orange juice and milk. He guessed that was what little girls ate.

After dinner Maureen went to an evening appointment. Shanahan didn't like her showing houses after dark, but for a real-estate agent, that comes with the territory. She assured him that the owners would be there as well as the prospective buyers. That helped.

Again, he felt lost, bored. He had no hobbies. The house felt empty though there were co-inhabitants – Casey, and the quite elderly cat, Einstein. The bony, frail feline took no guff from anyone or anything, including the dog. But these days, the only time he moved was to find a warmer spot to nap.

In Shanahan's mind, there were three old dogs and one beautiful lady. Today, the lady was busy. Today, and most days, he wasn't. Before meeting Maureen, his afternoon and evening hours were spent at a bar on 10th Street. It was tempting. He looked at his watch. He'd steal an hour, a beer, and a shot of J. W. Dant bourbon.

Outside, he stopped before he got to the driveway. He looked across the street at the shadows and silhouettes of scraggly bushes and nearly leafless trees that grew alongside the creek. The moon was out, getting stronger.

He stood for maybe ten minutes. Afterward, he wasn't sure what had gone through his mind. If anything. Something haunting. The way he felt after listening to that strange phone call.

Something unpleasant tugged at him.

There was never so much food in Cross's house, certainly never as much healthy food. Oranges, apples, milk, cereal, and soup. Whole-wheat bread at Maya's insistence, sliced ham, and mild American cheese. When he returned, Cross was in no mood to cook.

Thank God for peanut butter and jelly. It worked. Maya was quietly eating her sandwich, munching on corn curls, and sipping a glass of milk while Cross tried to figure out whether he was played a fool or if the girl's mother was really in trouble. Should he worry about her? About himself? Or should he be pissed?

He tried to get Maya interested in the TV so he could make some calls. The hospitals. He could also check with the club where Margot danced when she was in town. Unfortunately, he didn't know if the club management was involved in some way. Certainly, some of these places had questionable ties to larger crime operations.

There was nothing on television at this time of evening that seemed suitable, let alone interesting to a girl he guessed to be five. He fixed her bed on the sofa in the living room. He'd gladly give up his bedroom, but that's where his ground-line phone was connected and that was the number Margot had. She might try to reach him. He hoped she would.

But there were other reasons keep the little girl out of his bedroom. If Maya was going to go rummaging around, she might uncover some vintage *Playboys*. Despite what her mom did for a living, he didn't want to be responsible for anything untoward. Besides, he had only one clean sheet, large enough to serve as bottom and top for the little girl. Chivalrous or not, it had to be the sofa.

Other problems he'd face tomorrow, if he were still care-taking. Problems like bathing. She was only five, sure, but . . . This was going to be more complicated than he imagined.

He should have bought her a toothbrush and other things little girls need. A doll? Toys. Books. Tomorrow. Tonight, he'd make the calls. Cross had no choice but to try to find the girl's mother.

He laughed when he thought of Margot's last words to him. They were in a letter. He went to his bedroom and retrieved it as if it might yield something beyond goodbye.

> Howie
>   A short note to let you know that on average we had fun times. I think we helped each other for a while. But this last round was a little painful for both of us. You have to know by now that I'm pretty bad at being good. I'll be back through Indianapolis from time to time, at least until I get too old for the circuit. If we happen to run into each other, let us just smile and wave and keep on going. It will be better that way.
>   Love
>   M

Yeah, Cross thought. This wasn't part of the deal. Remember, a smile. Just a smile, Margot? You did keep on going.

Shanahan never made it to the bar. Too much effort. He had the makings of a stiff drink with a chaser just a few feet away. He went back inside, poured himself a shot of J. W. Dant bourbon and followed it with a beer. He waited nervously for Maureen to come home, so he could rest, perhaps go to bed early, get this strange day over with.

Two

S hanahan slept in fits and starts. When he was awake he heard Maureen's breathing rise and fall. Sometimes she fell so silent he was frightened that she'd died. She hadn't. Later, she would mumble something in a dream. He was jealous of her dreams.

He was fully awake in the early gray morning. He felt like crap. The sun was still hidden but produced enough light so that he could maneuver about only half-blind.

He got out of bed as the first glow of light slipped through the half-drawn blinds. Einstein moved ahead of him, not scurrying as he did when he was younger, but slowly, cautiously, toward the kitchen. Shanahan could hear him better than see him.

The seventy-year-old detective was cautious in his movement too. He and Maureen moved here a couple of months earlier and he was less familiar with the floor plan than he was his previous home, where he'd lived for decades. Nonetheless, he made it into the kitchen. He flicked on the light and went to the sink to fill the coffee pot.

He felt something strike his forehead before he heard the sound. The sound of a backfire or gunshot and breaking glass. He touched his forehead, saw blood, dropped quickly to the floor as another gunshot sounded, shattering one of the small clay pots on the windowsill.

Shanahan crawled back toward the hall that led to the bedroom, where he kept his .45. Maureen was up, coming toward him.

'Back in the bedroom! Now!'

'Are you all right?'

'Go!'

Once in the hallway, he got to his feet, uneasily it seemed.

In the bedroom, he went to the bedside table, pulled out his .45.

'Please go sit in that corner. Please.'

'Your face is bleeding,' she said, not budging.

'Go sit, Maureen. I mean it.' He handed her the phone. 'Call 911.'

Shanahan went back into the kitchen carefully, glanced out of the window. He saw no one. Slowly, he went to each window. In the living room, he saw a person in a long black coat get into a car. The car was gone. Because of the dim light and the distance, Shanahan wouldn't recognize the man if he saw him again, or the car for that matter.

Maya was up with the birds, content to watch television. Fortunately, with a responsibility to the little girl, Cross had had only three drinks the previous night – too cold for margaritas, but not too cold for tequila – instead of his usual evening binge, and was unusually sharp for this time of day. Sharp enough to take notice of how easily Maya adjusted. She had turned on the television, fixed herself a bowl of some weirdly named cereal, and poured herself a glass of orange juice.

She smiled as he came into the room, then went back to her cereal and TV.

He was glad she wasn't anxious. But was this usual? Maybe this wasn't all that unusual for her. Maybe she spent a lot of time in different houses with strangers. Cross thought that at five he'd be scared having to stay with some strange man.

His calls last night had revealed nothing. Margot hadn't danced at the Palace of Gold in months and as far as the bartender knew, she wasn't scheduled for anytime soon.

'She usually dances the races,' the bartender volunteered, referring to the Indy 500 in May and NASCAR in August.

Nobody named Margot in the area hospitals. No woman fitting her description was admitted, if the information was right. He called the morgue. No Margots. No Jane Does lately. So if Margot was dead, she wasn't found. If she was hurt, she probably wasn't getting it treated. Maybe Margot and Mr Booky Man were on some beach in the Caribbean and he'd hear from her when she was done with her tan.

'We are in the same place we were yesterday,' Cross told Maya, who looked up momentarily, smiled again, and returned again to her cereal and TV.

'Here we are,' Maureen said, dabbing at the small cuts from the flying glass with cotton and peroxide, 'me playing a fawning Florence Nightingale and you playing big, tough John Wayne . . .' She had already bandaged the crease a bullet made on his cheek.

'I'm glad it was my face,' Shanahan said. 'Nothing to lose here. Anyway, there was only one gun. You can be the Duke next time.'

'You mean if I had a gun, I'd have been your partner.'

'I've seen you with a gun. Remember? So, yes.'

'Full partner, not just a sidekick. I don't like being a sidekick.'

'Equal billing, we would have been Butch Cassidy and the Sundance Kiddo.'

'You being the "kiddo", right?' she asked.

The conversation and medical treatment came to an end when the knock came.

'Only one cop on the force these days?' Shanahan asked when Maureen led Lieutenant Swann into the living room.

'Thanks, nice seeing you too,' Swann said. He wore a dark suit and a flat-top, his hairstyle of the last twenty or thirty years. His form of rebellion, Shanahan thought. A decent guy, a good cop. 'I heard the call come in. They said Shanahan but I didn't recognize the address. New digs?'

Shanahan nodded.

'Somebody got the change-of-address form,' Swann said. 'You know who?'

'No,' Shanahan said. He felt a little light-headed. He sat at the kitchen table. Swann followed and went to the window, pulling out his notebook.

'Hunting accident? Some poor fool tried to shoot a bird?' Swann asked.

'You mean a tipsy vice-president? Not in this neighborhood. Not an accident.'

'Why do you say that?'

'Two gunshots, both targeting my head.'

'You made any recent enemies?'

'Can't think of any.'

'Old enemies?'

'Got a few of those.'

'You nosing around in somebody's business?'

'I don't have a job.'

'You've told me that before,' Swann said.

'I never really lied to you,' Shanahan said.

Swann nodded. 'Not really, huh?'

The front door opened and Casey left the kitchen to investigate. He barked ominously. Maureen followed.

'It's probably Taylor. I had him looking around outside,' Swann said.

Shanahan heard Maureen trying to calm the dog.

'Uniformed, right?' Shanahan asked Swann.

Swann nodded.

'Dog doesn't like uniforms.'

'Takes after his old man,' Swann said. 'You see the guy?'

'Not even sure it was a guy, but probably. Dressed like a guy. Too dark for anything else. The car, too. I couldn't even get the make or the year. It was a dark something . . . gray, green, blue. Not black.'

Swann stood, looked at the window, looked at the opposite wall for where the bullets hit.

'I'll get some guys out here, check the angle of the trajectories, root around in the yard. You should stay out of the yard until we're done.'

'OK,' Shanahan said.

'Taylor and I will check the neighbors, see if they saw anything. Is there a place you can go? He could come back.'

'Here's fine,' Shanahan said, but his mind was thinking about Maureen. Maybe she could go somewhere, but he knew better.

'I knew that,' Swann said. 'If he shows up again, try to get him in the house if you're going to shoot him. Sits better in an investigation.'

'Sure, we'll invite him in, maybe have dinner before we shoot him.'

'Are we going trick-or-treating?' Maya asked, suddenly appearing between the television set and Howie Cross.

'What?' He heard her. It surprised him so much he was trying to buy a moment or two before he answered.

'Halloween.' She smiled. Her grin was her mother's grin. It was a 'why don't you know that?' grin. Everybody else does.

'Well . . . I don't . . . know. Yeah. Halloween, isn't it?' he struggled. 'Maya, where were you living before you moved here?'

'A house.'

'Yes. Good. Where was that house?'

She thought for a moment. 'Near the school.'

'What school?'

'The one I went to.'

'Right. I should have known all that. Were you living here in Indianapolis?'

She shrugged. 'Do you have a costume?'

'For me or for you?'

'You?' She giggled. 'You're too big.'

'We'll get you a costume today and some clothes.'

Finding Margot. There was nothing to go on unless he could get Maya to say something more about where her mother went, who Mr Booky Man was, or where Margot lived when she wasn't on the road. She had to have a home base somewhere. He was pretty sure it wasn't Indianapolis or he would have known that. What other clubs were on the circuit? What cities might she go to?

It was mind-boggling what he didn't know about the woman he'd slept with so many times.

He looked at Maya as she gathered her bowl and glass and headed for the kitchen.

Why would Margot bring Maya to Indianapolis if that's not where they lived? She didn't bring her along when she did these tours. But what did he know? Margot talked little about her private life. She didn't talk much about anyone or anything. It was a charming trait in the beginning.

'Who left you here?' Cross asked, suddenly aware that he had assumed that this man and Margot dropped her off.

'Mommy,' Maya said.

'And was Mr Booky Man with her?'

She shook her head.

'What did Mommy say to you when she dropped you off?'

Maya thought for a moment. 'She told me there was a nice man who lived there.'

'Did she knock at the door?'

'No. She said to go up the steps and knock on the door. When nobody answered I went to tell her, but she was gone.'

'In a car?'

'Yes.'

'What kind of car?'

'A red one.'

'And was anyone else in the car?'

'No. Just Mommy. She was in a hurry. Can I be Cinderella?'

'I don't know.' Cross sat down on the sofa. 'Come here a minute. Let's talk.'

She stood in front of him. He grabbed her tiny hands. It amazed him that she was so delicate.

'I need your help. I need to know more about Mr Booky Man.'

She cocked her head for a moment. Her eyes opened wide. She was waiting.

'Is he taller than your mommy?'

She shook her head again.

'What kind of clothes does he wear?'

She looked puzzled.

'Does he dress like me?' Cross asked. He wore a sweat-shirt and jeans.

She shook her head.

'Does he wear a suit and tie?'

She nodded.

'Is he older than me?'

She nodded again.

'Is he nice to you?'

'Sort of.'

'What do you mean? He's not nice sometimes?'

'He's grumpy.'

'Does he stay with your mom? I mean does he sleep at your house?'

'Sometimes.'

'Is he nice to your mom?'

'Not any more,' she said.

'What does he do? Yell at her?'

She nodded.

'Does he hurt her?'

She didn't answer for a moment. 'She left him.'

'She did? She's going to get him?'

She nodded.

'OK, enough for now. Thank you for helping me, Maya. Let's go shopping. Get you some new clothes, a costume, and uh . . . some bubble bath.'

'I like bubbles,' she said.

'You can take a bath without Mommy, right?' he asked, silently praying she knew how.

'Yes I can. I do it all the time, silly.'

Three

'We eat tonight,' Maureen said, lifting a forkful of lobster ravioli.

'We eat every night,' Shanahan replied, taking note of the restaurant's elegant, pleasantly stuffy dining room. The large fireplace was lit. The two of them didn't eat like this every night.

'I sold two houses . . . *two*. We can celebrate,' she said. She knew he was often uneasy at pricey places like this. But it helped that it was a renovated old industrial building and he was curious. 'So what do you say?'

'I like it when you're happy,' he said. He had scallops to finish, but he was nearly full after the smoked-duck-breast appetizer. He was trying to carry on a conversation, but his mind kept wandering back over the event earlier. It wasn't every day a man is shot at. Who? Why?

He had boarded up the window that afternoon after the police were done.

'I've been thinking,' Shanahan said.

'Oh oh,' Maureen said.

'Listen. Maybe it would be smart if we found you a place to stay for a little while.'

'The old two-targets, one-gun theory.' A grin hastily camouflaged by a sip of wine.

'That's part of it.'

'I have another solution,' she said, putting the glass down and looking him squarely in the eye.

'I'm waiting,' Shanahan said.

'Get another gun.'

Shanahan nodded. He'd tried thinking through all those who might have a motive. Most of them, maybe all of them, were still in prison. He'd check with Swann tomorrow. He'd have to try a little harder to find the guy who was after him. But the hunter had the advantage. He knew his prey.

'You want to talk about who is trying to kill you?' she asked.

'Nice dinner conversation.'

'No more baseball. The season is over. I'm tired of talking real estate. I think it'll be fun.'

'Where do you want to start?' Shanahan asked.

'Banana pie, I think.'

'You can do that?'

'I trained for this all day.'

Maureen was not a small or particularly slender woman, he thought, but despite her sinful habits, she stayed beautiful. Voluptuous. More voluptuous than he deserved, perhaps more than he could handle. But the two of them had handled it for a few years now and it was going well.

'What are you having?' she asked.

'Nothing. Believe me.' If the scallops weren't so good, he would have left the last one.

'Let's get this straight, buddy. The pie is mine. All mine,' she said in a tough-as-nails tone, one eyebrow arching. 'None of this "let me have a little taste" thing you do.'

'I don't do that. You do that,' Shanahan said.

'Oh, right. Well, let that be a lesson for you.'

Cross and Maya spent the afternoon and some of the evening picking up bubble bath, crayons, some children's books, various items of clothing, and last and longest, a Halloween outfit for young Miss Maya. Waiting this late wasn't a choice. After all, she just popped into his life. Even so, it didn't help the selection. No Cinderellas. No Tinkerbells. Nor anything dress-up. Just a few assorted monsters and characters from movies and TV that she recognized but Cross knew nothing about.

Maya was a trooper. Patient. Thorough. Deliberative. A true shopper.

By the time they got back, darkness and a heavy cold drizzle had settled in, little trick-or-treaters were already out on the streets, hurriedly herded house to house by parents with umbrellas. It was only Halloween eve; but there was a custom of starting a day early. Maybe get in a couple of neighborhoods before the holiday ended.

She chose a tiger costume, telling Cross that at night she could wear them for pajamas. Practical too. She was much like her mother. Almost porcelain skin, dishwater blond, quietly flirtatious. He ushered her out of the front door, the two of them under an old raincoat that Cross turned into a makeshift umbrella.

They would only go to a few homes. He was embarrassed enough. On Halloweens past, he'd turned off the lights in the house and waited it out. Few would go up the irregular stone steps, through the trees, then through another gate to knock on an old wooden door. Those few brave souls who did were met with stony silence. He felt guilty now, taking Maya around for Snickers bars and candied apples, if they still did that sort of thing.

At one doorway, when they were met by a particularly wary look, he told the woman, 'I live in that little house way off the street. Maya's my niece, I'm taking care of her while her mother works.'

'I'm not your niece,' Maya said quite clearly.

The woman looked even warier.

'Of course not,' Cross said, swallowing his momentary panic. 'You're my little tiger.'

That seemed to satisfy the woman and the little tiger.

There were no candied or toffee apples in Maya's take. Everything was branded and wrapped.

Fortunately it was cold and the rain was cold and the wind whipped the air into an unpleasant refrigerated soup. Even Maya was content to do just the one block. They were back inside in twenty minutes. She sat on the floor, matching her M&Ms with her crayons.

He sat at his small computer desk, trying to make sense of Booky Man. He was still torn about what to do. Call the police. Try to find her. Just wait. If Margot had wanted the police involved, she would have dropped Maya off at the police station. The fact that she drove off so quickly meant someone was following her and she didn't want the police involved. Why would that be? Because she was involved in something that the police wouldn't appreciate. Or because she thought the police couldn't protect her, or more important, Maya.

Whatever it was, Cross was sure now that it was an act of desperation, not selfishness.

Margot was independent. Having Cross watch over Maya was a last resort. She must have had to swallow her pride.

He should try to find her. Help her. But where would he start?

Booky Man. Boogie Man. Bookie. Gambling? Could be. She owed somebody. Maybe. Couldn't pay. But they lived together, Maya said. Books, maybe. An accountant. Accountants wore suits. Maybe there was embezzlement involved. Cooking books. Cook books. Where was this little exercise going? He needed more information. And there was an obvious question he hadn't asked.

It was getting late. Probably too late for a little girl to be up.

'Maya,' he said, stepping down into the living room. 'Did your mom say where she was going?'

She looked up brightly. 'No. She said she would call me.'

'I see.' Margot did have the number. 'Maya, if I get you a piece of paper, could you draw Mr Booky Man?'

'Could I draw him in the morning? I'm getting tired.'

'Sure,' Howie said, thinking that his thoughts might be a little more coherent after a night's sleep as well. He felt scrambled. How did that happen? He hadn't touched a drop of tequila. He'd change that once he tucked her in.

'Get ready for bed. Tomorrow you have to take a bath and you have to draw Mr Booky Man. Big day.'

She giggled. 'You're silly.'

'Yeah, you said that.'

Once she was in bed, Cross went to his desk in the small room where his computer was, and sat in the high-backed chair. He wasn't sure what else he could do but wait for a phone call. He was used to waiting for calls. Usually, he waited for a job, a repo job or a bail skip. Yes, he admitted to himself, he had often waited for a call from some woman. Sometimes that woman was Margot.

More often than not at times like this, he'd have a couple

of drinks to take the edge off the day even though most days didn't really have an edge.

'When am I going to get my gun?' Maureen said, looking up from her book and sitting up in bed.

'I'll call Cross tomorrow. He probably has an extra.' His eyes were closed. He was trying to picture what was outside the window before it exploded.

'Meanwhile?'

'Swann told me he's going to have officers cruise by here.'

'And if the murderer comes by between runs and shoots us in our sleep?'

'I guess that means we won't have to worry about making house payments,' Shanahan said.

'You're pretty nonchalant.'

'It was a cowardly attempt this morning. The guy wants to make sure he is in control. He wouldn't have control of a dark house, especially now that people know about him.'

'Grenade,' she said matter-of-factly. 'Boom. That's what I'd do.'

'Well, don't tell him. That's a damn good idea.'

'Thank you. I'd be a damned good killer.'

'I think he wants to see me die,' Shanahan said. 'It's something I've done or something he thinks I've done to him.'

'Or something you did to someone he loves,' Maureen added.

'Yep. It's not money. I have no money.'

'Jealousy,' she said. 'Have you scorned a woman lately?'

'Only you. Where were you this morning at dawn?'

'Sleeping. Sleeping until you and your playmate woke me up with your horseplay.'

'What about you?' Shanahan asked. 'You have somebody who wants me out of the way?'

'I have my share of admirers.'

'They wouldn't risk shooting me, they'd just wait me out. Are you scared?'

'I am. If it's revenge, he's coming back.' She clicked off the light. 'You have your gun nearby?'

'Under my pillow.'

'You know, if he's crazy, I mean really crazy, he's not

going to think all this through logically like you think he is.'

'Yeah. But the first attempt was very logical. Here before the neighbors are up. Outside in the yard at precisely the time I turned on the light and went to the sink in front of the window. He checked the place out. He knew my habits. He's a planner. That's why I don't think he'll be back tonight.'

'I hope you're right.'

'Does he think he got me? He might not even know I'm still alive.'

Shanahan felt his shoulders being shook and a voice.

'Wake up, Shanahan. Don't shoot me. Just wake up a minute.'

'Wake up a minute?' he asked, voice full of sleep.

'You awake?' Maureen asked.

'What time is it?'

'Three,' she said.

'And why are we up at three?'

'I couldn't sleep.'

'And misery loves company?'

'There was something gnawing at me,' she said.

'Probably Einstein. He's always hungry.'

'Then I remembered.'

'OK,' Shanahan said.

'Do you know who lived here before we moved in?'

'No, but since you were the real-estate agent who sold the house, I suspect you'll tell me.'

'Judge Bradshaw Ghery.'

'Oh,' Shanahan said. 'That is interesting. Did he go into hiding and just not tell us?'

'No, his wife died. He wanted a condo.'

Shanahan sat up in bed. 'Somebody gets out of prison, wants to get even. Looks up the judge in the phonebook or whatever.'

'He thought you were the judge who did him wrong,' Maureen said.

'Or did him right and he was just pissed anyway.'

'What do you think?'

'We tell the guy that I'm not the guy and he'll go shoot someone else. Good night,' Shanahan said. 'Problem solved.'

'You wouldn't do that.'

'No. But the judge would get real police protection. And he ought to know if someone is stalking him because he might follow him home from work. I'll call Swann in the morning . . . which is only a few hours away.'

'Go back to sleep,' she said.

'Yeah, right?'

Those were the last words he remembered until a slice of light squeezed through the blinds and woke him up.

Four

'Let's see what you have here,' Cross said, dropping down to his knees in front of the little girl in her tiger outfit. He'd been up long enough to start the coffee. She had been up long enough to fix her own breakfast and produce several drawings, at least one of which, Cross hoped, would provide a little more information on the mysterious Mr Booky Man.

'Do you have a broom?' she asked. 'I spilled some sugar on the floor.'

'Yes.'

She followed him to the space between the middle room and before the step down into the living room. Cross pressed on the wall and it opened into a narrow storage space in the area that was behind the fireplace. He kept a vacuum cleaner, mop, bucket, and broom in there.

'A secret place?' Maya asked. Her eyes were wide.

Cross had to think about it. 'I guess. Not intentionally, but yes.' He'd had a rough night. Awake, feeling guilty. He wasn't doing enough. Margot was in danger. Asleep, he dreamt about not being able to save a little puppy. He wasn't going to have to sift through dense symbolism here. Though she wasn't a puppy. She was the real tiger.

After she swept up, he followed her back into the living room. Maya handed him a piece of paper.

He examined it.

'Maya, this is a teddy bear.'

She nodded enthusiastically, happy no doubt that he figured it out.

'Where's Mr Booky Man? Let me see Mr Booky Man,' Cross said with surprising desperation. He looked at the other drawings scattered about her work area.

'Here,' she said.

It was another drawing of the same teddy bear. It was then that Cross noticed the teddy bear had glasses and wore a man's suit.

'You said . . . yeah . . . he looks like a nice . . . bear. Keep up the good work.'

One tiny bit of information and it's useless.

'Maya, why don't you go take a bath, have some bubbles.'

'OK.' She got up. 'Why don't you draw your friend while I'm gone?' She headed toward the bathroom.

'That's an idea,' he said. 'Maya?'

She stopped.

'Take some of your new clothes in with you and throw your old clothes outside the door. OK?'

'You'll come in and dry me off?' she asked.

'No. You're a big girl now. Use the big green towel. It's clean.'

He heard her run the bathwater.

'Make sure it's not too hot before you step in.'

'I know how to do it,' she said. She opened the door and tossed her clothing out. She wasn't bashful. She hadn't been told to hide her body. In a way it would have been odd if her mother had taught her to be ashamed of her natural state. And he hadn't meant to look, but the unexpected, momentary glance at her small body was unavoidable. She had a tan, something he wouldn't have noticed with her fully clothed. She had tan lines where a bathing suit had been.

Cross picked up her clothing. He examined the labels in her dress and panties – he felt a little creepy. Then again, some people would find what he did for a living a little creepy. The underwear was a common brand. The dress label was a designer name. Could be bought in stores in any city with a population more than 10,000. But his little investigation was fruitful. He found something in one of her shoes.

'Swann, please.' While Shanahan stood by the wall phone in the kitchen, Maureen was poaching eggs. She had a new love. English muffins, a slice of ham or turkey, and poached eggs. She went through breakfast-food fads. Scones were in for a while. Then came some Scandinavian cereal. Right before the poached eggs, she spent a month eating a special brand of yogurt and blueberries.

'This is Shanahan. There may be a twist here. Seems as if a Bradshaw Ghery lived here before we moved in a few months ago.'

'And?' Swann asked.

'Judge Ghery.'

'Oh. Got it.'

'You going to tell him?'

'Yeah,' Swann said. 'Have to. That makes this messy. Is the perp after you or him? You need to put a big sign in your yard. "Judge Ghery doesn't live here anymore."'

'You have anything?'

'The slugs we found are .223 Rem. Common with hunting rifles. Usually for smaller game. A little small for elk maybe, but some use it for deer. Basically it's a high-powered .22. Could have a scope. Probably not a single shot, since two rounds got off so quick.'

'I'm lucky. Footprints?'

'Checked your yard. It was wet, you'd think we would,' Swann said. 'We checked down by the creek. With all the leaves, we didn't get much. A couple of partials in the grass by the road. Kind of a public place.'

'You think he shot from there?'

'Since there was nothing in your yard, I'd say it was likely. With a scope he could have been pretty far away. If he was there, he left nothing behind.'

'Sniper.'

'And your enemies list?' Swann asked.

'I'm working on it.' It wasn't a lie. Mentally, he was going over the cases of the last few years.

What Cross found was a label inside the right shoe. It wasn't the manufacturer's label, but a store label, intended, Cross guessed, to help keep track of the inventory. The shoe was relatively new, but the label was worn. He used a flashlight and a magnifying glass to read the numbers.

'Maya,' he said through the bathroom door. 'Where did you get your shoes?'

'Mommy got them.'

'Where?'

She gave the name of a big national chain. They were everywhere, Cross thought.

He went to the small, middle room, to his desk. He pulled out the phonebook and dialed.

'I need some help,' Cross said. 'I'm investigating a missing little girl and I have a clue. She apparently had a shoe from one of your stores. I'm trying to find out which one.'

'I don't know how I can help you do that,' the woman said. 'Do you have any idea how many stores we have right here in Indiana?'

'But your stores have store codes, right?'

'I'm not the one . . .'

After several transfers, he was connected with somebody in security. In five minutes, he learned the location of the store.

'Kehei.'

'Kehei?' Cross asked. 'Where's that?'

'Kehei, Maui.'

'Oh, that makes sense,' Cross said, having just discovered Maya's tan lines. 'Thank you.'

'I hope that helps you find the missing girl.'

'I'm sure it will,' Cross said, feeling slightly guilty about his lie. But it was just as important, wasn't it? He just figured he'd get more cooperation for a missing little girl than for an older one. Now he knew what? Doesn't mean they live in Hawaii. Doesn't mean Margot went back to Hawaii. Maybe no more ties to the island than two leisurely weeks in a condo by the Pacific.

Cross was frustrated. The Maui lead was no lead at all. And for all the time he spent asking questions all he ended up with was a silly teddy bear. Mr Booky Man, my ass, he thought.

'Someone's trying to kill me, Harry,' Shanahan told his old war buddy and current bartender.

'I've thought about it more than once, myself,' Harry said, setting up the long-necked Miller Highlife and a jigger of J. W. Dant bourbon.

Before meeting Maureen, Shanahan spent most afternoons and many evenings sitting at this small, dingy little neighborhood bar on 10th Street. Occasionally, they'd play dirty clubs in the back booth. If not, then Shanahan would have his usual perch at the bar. If Harry were the sentimental type, Shanahan would have a plaque on the stool next to the cash register. But there were others, a couple of them sitting there now sipping their beers, who had more seniority than Shanahan.

'What do you want me to do about it?' Harry asked as he returned to the register to ring up a Budweiser.

'I'll invite him here, and you feed him your stew.'

'Dammit, Deets.'

Harry shortened Dietrich to Deets and was the only one to use the nickname. Shanahan was Shanahan. Not Dietrich, not Deets. Even to himself. But if he told Harry to stop, Harry would use it in every sentence.

'How many years am I going to suffer for not fixing the stew as good as Delaney? I fixed the stew. The stew is . . .'

'Edible is the word you're searching for. Only because it comes out of a can.'

'See, this is why people want to kill you.'

'I'd think it was you, but you can't hit the broad side of a barn with a shotgun.'

'This is the truth you're tellin'.'

Shanahan told him the story.

'Where's Maureen? You sent her away, right?'

'Yes, she's an obedient wife.'

'Where's she now?'

'At her office. The guy wants me or he wants the judge. He doesn't want Maureen.'

'Unless he figures he can get to you through her.'

'We can't stop living.'

'Oh yes you can. All of a sudden.'

'She'll call me before she goes home. I'll be there. Swann has some cruisers driving by. I don't think the guy is that stupid. To come back again. So soon.'

'Sounds like you know who it is. You don't, though, do you?'

'Nope. It's just that he's a planner. And he might think he got me.'

'Nothing in the papers?' Harry asked.

'Nope.'

'That means he knows you're not dead. Neither you or the judge.'

Harry was wrong as much as he was right. And Shanahan hated to admit when Harry was right. He could gloat for days, so he just nodded, downed the bourbon, took a sip of beer.

He reached for the bar phone next to the cash register.

'Another shot, Harry.'

'This is Maureen,' the voice said after a few rings.

'Why don't you stop by Harry's when you're done? Have a drink with me and we'll go find some food.'

'You're worried about me?'

'No,' Shanahan said. 'Harry is.'

'Harry is what?' Harry said, setting down the shot glass.

'A helluva guy,' Shanahan said.

'And you always do what Harry wants, right?' she said sarcastically.

'You're full of it,' Harry said. 'Tell Maureen when she's tired of you . . .'

'I know,' Shanahan said. 'But she'd only leave me for a cook. And you can't cook.'

Maya had found a wooden wine crate and was standing on it, doing dishes. She had tied a towel around her waist and was deep in her work. When she was done, she stepped down, removed her makeshift apron, and approached Cross, who stood by the window, looking at her, befuddled by her mix of childhood and maturity.

'You were in Hawaii, right?'

Maya nodded. 'Do you have a hair dryer?'

'No, I'm sorry. Never owned one.'

She shook her head as if to say, 'Men, what can I say.' She was now pretty relaxed and settled in.

She had on a T-shirt, sweater, and blue jeans that were just a little large. She had to roll up the cuffs.

'Were you on vacation?'

She shook her head.

'You live in Hawaii? Maui, right?'

She nodded.

'You and your mom, did you live by yourselves?'

'No.'

'I mean besides Mr Booky Man, was there anybody else living there? Human, I mean.'

Grinning, she shook her head.

'Did your mom have any special friends? People who came over a lot? Was Mr Booky Man her boyfriend?'

'No,' she said, losing interest in the conversation.

'Did she have a boyfriend?'

The little girl was beginning to fidget. She didn't want to play this game anymore. It wasn't fun. Or she didn't want to think about it.

'Your mommy worked, didn't she? She was away a lot, wasn't she?'

Maya nodded, but her eyes were traveling everywhere but toward Cross. He didn't have much time left in this little interview.

'Who took care of you when your mommy was away?'

'Auntie.'

'Was she your mother's sister?'

'No. We call her Auntie 'cause her name is too hard to say.'

He was about to give up. 'Where did she live?'

'Next door.'

'Bingo,' Cross said out loud, though he wasn't entirely sure that helped. If he could find out where Margot lived, he could find Auntie. Maybe Auntie knew something.

But there was a problem. He didn't know Margot's last name. He knew her only as Margot. That's how she was billed at the club, simply Margot. He wasn't even sure it was her real name. Fortunately, as it turned out, it was. But in the years they had their off-and-on relationship, he wasn't sure he ever knew her last name, let alone that she had a child. It was all in the now. No history. And, as he came to find out, not much of a future.

'One more thing, Maya. Could you sign your portraits?'

She looked confused. He led her back down to the living room. He picked up one of the drawings of Booky Man.

'All the famous artists signed their work. Pablo Picasso . . . and uh . . . all of them.'

He handed her a pencil and watched her patiently, all too patiently, make each letter of her first name.

'Mayaaaaaah.' Cross was trying to drag her from the final 'A' in Maya to the last name. Mentally, he prayed. 'Please give me more than Maya, please.'

Five

Dinner at Amici's, an informal Italian restaurant. They both liked the place. Some pasta, some wine for her. Some pasta and a beer for him. The place was dimly lit, all the better for dating couples and those engaged in illicit affairs. Not bad for Shanahan either. When he was in public places, he liked to find the dark corners. It seemed even wiser now, given the circumstances.

'You talk to the judge?'

Shanahan shook his head. 'Swann will. Probably has.'

'Someone with a hunting background?' Maureen asked.

'Or a hit man.'

He could see her eyes widen even in the shadowy light.

'It occurred to me that judges sometimes make some pretty powerful enemies. May not have been a past case. Could be a future one and they don't like the way he judges. Maybe they couldn't get to him any other way. Who knows? But it could be a paid hit. That might explain them shooting at me. They assumed I was the judge because our place was his last known address.'

'I don't know if that's comforting or not,' she said, spearing a piece of sausage.

'We keep the curtains closed.'

She put the piece of the sausage in a paper towel she had in her bag.

'What are you doing?' Shanahan asked.

'Taking this to Einstein.'

'Why?'

'He likes sausage.'

'It's a bribe, right?'

'Your dog loves me. Your cat, on the other hand, still hasn't adjusted to having me around. And now with the new house. He's not a happy camper.'

'Here in this US of A, we are only guaranteed the right to pursue happiness,' Shanahan said.

'This will give him a moment or two of bliss.'

'Hudson,' Cross read out loud. 'Maya Hudson. Margot Hudson.'

'You want me to sign the others?'

'Yes, Maya, please do. Some day you will be famous and these will be worth millions.'

She smiled.

He remembered the name now, from somewhere; but he would never have been able to dredge it up from the sludge of his gray matter without help.

Even though he had known Margot off and on for years, he and Margot were never really together in any conventional sense. Just when she was in town and for odd stretches of time. Sometimes a couple of days. More often, the early morning after she got off work until noon when she was ready to go about her life.

Now, with her name, he could find her address. With her address and the help of the Kehei police, he could find the lady next door and perhaps enough information to kick start his search.

'Can we go trick-or-treating?' Maya asked.

'It's raining, sweetheart. You've got plenty of candy. We'll have our own Halloween party, just the two of us.'

'OK.'

'Should we have a funny party or a scary party?'

'Fun,' Maya said. 'I don't like to be scared.' She was seeing something in her head. He could see it in her eyes.

'Anybody or anything scare you lately?'

She didn't answer, another characteristic in her DNA. Her mother chose to answer some questions, and not others. That seemed, in Cross's mind, to be completely random.

The phone was ringing when they got home. Shanahan got it as Maureen closed the curtains before switching on any lights.

'You're late,' the male voice said.

'For what?'

'I've been calling all evening. You're usually home by now.'

'You were worrying about me?'

'In a way. I have your dog.'

'What?'

Maureen came in the room. Shanahan put his hand on the receiver. 'Find Casey,' Shanahan said.

'I have your dog. And he doesn't like me. So I can either give him back to you or I can shoot him.'

'The first option works, doesn't it?' Shanahan said.

'It can.'

Maureen came in, shaking her head, eyes questioning.

'What do you want me to do?'

'Come get him.'

'Sure. Where are you?'

'In due time. You're not even a little bit curious about all this?'

'Sure. Tell me what's going on,' Shanahan said.

'No.'

'You just want to get me out of the house to shoot me, right?'

'Maybe you could talk me out of it,' the voice said.

'I'm not much of a talker.'

'The usual applies. No cops. No friends. Nobody. Corner of Highway 37 and West County Line Road. I know how long it takes to get from your house to this location. If you're late, I kill the dog. Leave now.'

Shanahan heard the click.

'Maureen, you need to leave when I do, get in your car, and drive over to Howie's place.'

'What?'

'Stay there until I call you.'

'What's going on?'

'We don't have much time,' Shanahan said. 'It's the guy. He's got Casey and he wants to talk.'

'He doesn't want to talk. He wants to kill you.'

'I know. I'm meeting this guy on 37 and West County Line Road.' Shanahan went to the bedroom, retrieved his .45.

'The police?'

Shanahan shook his head, got his coat. 'We don't have time to finesse it with them.'

'This may be the dumbest thing you've ever done,' Maureen said.

'I know. I don't want you here, because there's a chance to lure me out of here in order to get to you.'

'Why can't Howie go with you? He's a former cop.'

'Time. I have to leave now. Tell him the situation.'

It wouldn't take Shanahan that long to get there. He could get to the interstate loop that circled the city, take it south and then west, around to the 37 exit. It would be only minutes after that. Thirty minutes this time of night, maybe.

Cross wasn't answering the door. Trick-or-treaters. He hadn't expected them. He had nothing for them. It wasn't until he saw Maureen's face pressed against the wet glass in the living room that he responded.

'Good grief,' he said, letting the shivering woman inside. 'Aren't you a little old to be out looking for candy?'

'Looking for a drink, OK.'

'This is Maya,' Cross said, nodding toward the little girl asleep on the sofa in her tiger outfit, heading toward the bathroom, coming back with a towel.

'Those showgirls, they just keep getting younger, don't they?' she said.

'You don't know how close you are to the truth.'

She dried her face, followed him to the kitchen, told him the story. She sipped her rum and tonic without the lemon. It was obvious she was trying to look calm. But her hand shook so much the ice rattled in the glass.

'Why didn't he call me? Why didn't you? I can't possibly catch up with him.'

'It all happened so suddenly. He got a call. The guy said "now." He didn't want the police screwing it up with sirens and lights. Didn't have time to work out a plan with you.' She held back something she really wanted to say. She also held back an obvious but smothered anger. 'He just went. He gets that way sometimes.'

'I should go,' Cross said. 'Late may be better than not at all. I'll be discreet. Call me on the cell if you need me.

Answer here if the phone rings.' He went to the desk drawer
in the small room between the living room and bedroom,
selected a small 9mm for Maureen.

'In case he followed you. Food in the fridge if you get
hungry.'

'I'm sorry. The little girl. I shouldn't have come here.'

'Just in case.' Cross went into the bedroom, came out
putting a snub-nosed .38 in the back of his jeans.

'How many of these things do you have?'

He smiled.

'What if she wakes up?' Maureen asked.

'Tell her you're the good witch.'

'And she is?'

'A little tiger.'

'You're not going to tell me who she is?' Maureen asked
as Howie slipped on a rainproof jacket and looked for his
car keys.

'Left on the doorstep,' Cross said. 'If you can find out
anything about where her mother might be, that would be a
big help.'

She shook her head as if to say, 'What a strange and sad
night.'

Despite the hour, the interstate was busy. Big trucks domin-
ated. Their tires on the wet pavement made the highway hiss.
The windshield wipers of Shanahan's car were obstinate, the
rhythm either too slow or too fast for the rain and the speed
of the automobile.

The radio was off. Just the hiss and the sound of the wipers.

Shanahan hated interstates. They were all alike. Not like
the early two-lane highways with diners, small motels, and
root-beer stands. At night on these mega-highways, you might
as well be traveling in a vacuum. Nothing told you where
you were except for signs that popped up suddenly in the
headlights. This was cold, lonely transportation.

His mind ran through those he'd helped send to prison.
One would be the type to hire a hit man. But time had passed.
Why now? The rest of them would have most likely done it
themselves. But as far as he knew they were all still in prison.
A couple of them forever.

He noticed the word 'EAT' high in the sky ahead of him. The red neon pierced the wet sky with its simple message. It also meant Shanahan was coming to the Highway 37 exit – more quickly than he thought. No sooner had he gotten off the interstate and made the turn on to 37 than he noticed the difference. Real darkness. Flat empty land on one side. Scattered house lights well off the road on the other. Just as the single-lane highways of the fifties gave way to dual-lane highways in the seventies, the interstates had made the dual-lane version nearly obsolete. Highway 37 didn't lead to any significant population centers. Other than a few lit billboards, the road was quiet, nearly desolate. It was a dramatic change. He felt for his .45. It was there.

The rain had stopped. The sky was clearing up. He could even see the Halloween moon.

An occasional oncoming car sped by. A hill rose on the left. He could see a few fuzzy lights hidden back in and up the hill. On the right, he could see nothing.

He didn't have time to react to what might have been a gunshot because his car suddenly lurched out of control. For a second, he relaxed. It was a flat tire, not a shot. The next second he realized that this would delay his arrival.

He slowed the car gradually and wrestled it on to the shoulder of the highway. He pulled it to a stop, reached down, pressed the trunk release by the seat. If he remembered correctly, he had one of those little temporary tires, not quite full size. He hated that. But he didn't have much choice in the matter. On the positive side, he was smart enough to carry a lantern.

He looked in the side mirror. No cars were coming. He got out of the car, shut the door, and headed toward the rear when he felt something hit his head. It had barely registered when he felt himself falling. He was down. He wasn't sure how long he was down when he heard the car. He heard a door open and then close. He heard soft footsteps. They weren't in a hurry. He saw that as bad news.

Six

Cross went north up Meridian Street to catch Interstate 465 to head west, then south to 37. He drove an old Isuzu Trooper, on temporary loan from the company that sent him out on repossessions. He was never quite sure how fast he could take turns inside this tall, narrow box without rolling it. The rain let up, but the roads were wet and slippery. All in all, Cross preferred cars built lower to the ground.

But beggars couldn't be choosers, could they?

Thoughts zipped randomly through his brain. Speed. Time. Maya and Margot. Shanahan as target. There was the matter of Cross's life, future. What was he to do generally? What was he to do specifically? Now. With the little girl and the old man?

He and his Trooper passed the airport. He was on the Southside now. That meant he was closing in.

He didn't know what he could do. Chances were that whatever business was to be transacted would have been transacted by the time he got there. He debated about calling the police. It was something he always advised his clients to do first. But it was also something he wasn't doing with Maya either. And clearly, that was something Shanahan wanted to avoid. He'd have to go with Shanahan.

Then again, unless they had a little time to plan, the police could be ham-fisted. But was Shanahan a match for someone he didn't know, but knew him? Someone with a rifle capable of shooting long range. And it was this stranger who was calling the shots. The odds were against the old man.

As the cold puddle in the asphalt highway settled from the impact his face had on it, Shanahan could make out the moon's reflection. He could only see straight forward. He couldn't move. He didn't feel pain. He wondered if he was dead.

Padded steps were coming closer. A Samaritan? Before the man's boots disturbed the mirror-like surface of the water, he got a glimpse of a face – a reflection of a face.

He heard the bolt of a rifle and a bullet being inserted into the chamber. He heard the bolt close. Heavy metal on metal. He knew the sounds well. And he knew what it meant. He had been shot and the man who did it was there to make sure he was dead.

The man said something Shanahan couldn't make sense of. Then, he heard the click of the trigger, but there was silence, broken only by the man's voice, 'Fuck, Goddammit, shit.'

Shanahan heard hurried steps in retreat and then in moments a car stopped. A door opened. A woman came to him.

'Oh my God,' she said. 'Are you all right?'

'No, I'm just napping,' he said, but nothing came out. His mouth didn't move. It was then he realized he wasn't blinking either. He saw her legs, her high heels. Something metal clicked and he heard electronic sounds.

'Yes, I'm on Highway 37, south of 456. There's a man on the highway. He's had an accident.'

'Yes, I walked in the way of a speeding bullet,' he said. But there was no sound.

'Belmont Road.'

There was a pause. He saw headlights. Others were stopping.

'I don't know if he's breathing or not. Yes, I'll stay here until the ambulance gets here.'

He didn't know if he had remained conscious or not, but he heard sirens and the audible but unintelligible sound of chatter. People had gathered. Lights were flashing – blue ones, red ones.

He was blinded by white light. Was this death? The light lingered then with suddenness disappeared. It was a flashlight, not death, he saw. He was alive.

He felt something pressing against his neck in the back of the jaw.

'Is he alive, Sheriff?' asked the woman.

'He may have bought the farm,' a male voice said. 'No, I'm getting something here.'

'Don't park there. We need room to get emergency in here,' Shanahan heard someone shout at a distance. 'No, shut down the road, get Traffic out here and close off the road.'

'Gunshot. Damn.'

Shanahan felt a hand move across his forehead.

'Hey, Doug, flat tire.' The voice was coming from somewhere else, moving closer. 'What happens is, I think, guy gets out of his car, bang! Somebody shoots him.'

The man whose hand felt Shanahan's head told the guy to call the city. 'Tell 'em to get Homicide out here.'

'Hunting accident?' said the woman.

'Only things hunting this late are bats and owls. Davis, you and Barclay find some witnesses. Maybe someone back up in those houses.'

No one from those houses could see through the trees and down the hill to this unlit highway, Shanahan thought. Maybe I'm paralyzed. Maybe I can't move. Maybe I'll never move. Poor Maureen. This will screw up her life. What an idiot I am. I knew better. The clever bastard. No, I'm not all that smart, Shanahan thought. He knew who the stupid one was – the one face down in a cold puddle.

He felt someone reaching for his wallet. That was good, wasn't it? Good. Hell, if it weren't for Maureen, he'd just let go. That's what he would have done before she came along.

So who is this bastard? Set me up for down the road and hit me on the way. How could I have done this to Maureen? Why can't I feel pain? I could have told her I loved her sometimes. She knew. She knows. That's the way we are together. Don't have to say things like that. We both know. What will happen to her now? Will the guy go after her? Who will protect her?

The ambulance that passed Cross on Interstate 365 was now ahead of him on Highway 37. He could see where the vehicle was headed, toward the flashing lights. His stomach dipped. He knew what that was about. He hoped it was the other guy.

The highway ahead looked like a parking lot. Some cars made U-turns and came back toward him. Not much farther ahead Cross was flagged down by a deputy sheriff and told to turn his car around or get on Belmont and cut back to the highway farther up the road.

'I think I know the guy,' Cross said.

'What guy?' the cop said, irritated.

'The guy involved in the accident.'

'Who are you a reporter?' the sheriff asked, cocking his head warily.

'No. A friend.'

'And you know that's him up there because?'

'Look,' Cross said, but stopped himself. His tone wouldn't get him anywhere. 'Please. Call up there. See if whatever that is involves a man named Shanahan.'

The deputy turned away, touched a button on his collar, and mumbled something. All Cross could hear was 'Shanahan.' He took a deep breath.

The deputy turned back, still talking, but looking at Cross with the cop stare.

'I have information,' Cross said.

'He has information,' the deputy said.

'I'm a former cop.'

'Park your car over there, walk on down. Find O'Herlihy. Talk to him.'

'Where's the bus?' a voice said. 'This guy needs help.'

Shanahan's eyes closed. Was this it? He couldn't open them. The voices and other commotion around him became less distinct. It was as if he were under water and the sounds were coming from land. Was he slipping away?

He knew death was coming. He was old and it was inevitable. But the timing was for shit. He wanted to spend more time with Maureen. It seemed as if he had just met her and she was the one in his life. Why did their time together have to be so short? And he wanted to find the bastard who took his dog.

'Hey!' the voice was familiar. It was Cross's voice. 'We're going to get you to the hospital. We're going to find this asshole. I promise.'

How did Cross know he was there? Oh.

'I'll be back,' Cross said.

He heard faintly Cross's voice and that of another man. He was explaining what had happened earlier – that he'd been shot at earlier. He explained about the judge. Suggested that they talk to Lieutenant Swann at IPD Homicide.

Maureen answered.

'I'm sorry, Maureen,' Cross said. 'He's seriously injured. He had a card in his wallet saying to take him to Methodist Hospital, so that's where they're going. We'll meet there. Bring Maya along.'

'Do they think . . . ?' Maureen asked.

'He's unconscious. A bullet to the head.'

There was a long silence.

'You OK to drive?' Cross asked.

'Yes,' she said.

He liked it that her voice was strong. She was a tough lady.

Cross watched as Shanahan was moved to a stretcher and lifted into the van with the flashing lights.

'He's on his way, Maureen.'

Shanahan was in a warm, comfortable place. He wondered where or what it was. It was as if he were suspended without wires. He found that his mind could go toward the sounds of voices, and through the thickness of the atmosphere that softened them. He could make out words, sentences. He had to concentrate; but he could do that.

He also found that if he did nothing, his mind would drift. It went to various places, various times. These events – talking with his friends at school, or fellow soldiers in a barracks – didn't follow in any order. A change in place or time could be prompted by a word, a scent, the way the light fell. These moments were more vivid than the tenuous hold he had in the other world.

He would gladly give in to the world that tempted him away; but his work wasn't done. His life wasn't complete. He tried to find the soft voices that were sure to be somewhere around.

Seven

'We don't know anything about this guy,' Cross said.

'We know what he shoots,' Swann said. 'Rem. 223. Lots of the rifles that use it are hunting rifles, small to midsize game. Military and the police use it. Many of the weapons accommodate a scope.'

'Hit man?' Cross asked.

'Maybe. I'm thinking hunter. Deer, don't know what else around these parts. Rabbit.'

'If he were hunting deer, he'd use a 30/30, wouldn't he?'

'Most would. But not all. Look at it this way. He tried twice and failed. I think that eliminates a pro. Maybe even a professional hunter.' Swann had a flat-top, had since they were fashionable and was not inclined to change just because the world did. His suits were old and worn and fit a tad tight. He didn't have a cop face, hardened by what he'd seen or been forced to do. He looked approachable. 'He could have been paid to do it, I suppose, but I'm thinking this isn't his regular line of work.'

Cross turned to look at Shanahan. Unmoving. Tubes ran from various plastic bags to various places on his anatomy. Could he hear them talk? Cross wondered. Was he in pain? The doctor had told Maureen he wasn't; but how would he know?

'He was professional enough,' Maureen said. She sat in the chair next to the bed. Maya, sitting on the floor beside her, thumbed through a children's book the nurse brought.

'I'll take Maya back to my place. She needs to get some sleep,' Cross said.

'I'll be here tonight,' Maureen said.

'You can't go back there anyway. We don't know what this maniac is after. He may have had more on his mind than

Shanahan.' Cross glanced at Swann, who looked tired. It was good of him to come, Cross thought. He was off duty. He was a decent cop who tried to stay out of politics and tried to do the right thing. He and Shanahan had a history.

'We're going through his cases . . . to the extent we know them,' Swann said. 'Both of you were involved in some of them. So let me know who we should take a look at. And I'll let you know what we find out. When he wakes up, give me a call.'

Cross liked the fact that Swann used the word 'when' rather than 'if.' Cops tend to be cynical about most things. It comes with the job. You can't afford not to be. Optimism is dangerous.

Swann took a last look at Shanahan, nodded toward Maureen, and put his hand ever so briefly on Cross's shoulder as he left.

'Listen, Cross, I know you're going to go after him your own way. Keep me up to date. Be careful.'

'In what way, be careful?'

'You know. Both ways. Don't get hurt. Don't go running around outside the law.'

'You can't go back to your house until this guy is caught,' Cross said to Maureen, not so much as an order, but as a thought bordering on a question. Maureen was not someone who needed or welcomed others telling her what was in her best interest.

'I'll think about that tomorrow,' she said. 'You want to tell me about your friend?' She smiled, but lacked the usual spark.

Cross looked at the little girl.

'I'm looking after her until her mother gets back?' Maya responded to the question with curiosity. Once answered, her curiosity was taken care of, and she returned to her book. Cross shook his head. 'I'll tell you more later,' he whispered. These last few days weren't happy ones, he thought. It occurred to him, he had his hands full now – finding a wayward mother and some guy who was determined to kill his friend Shanahan.

'She's pretty.'

'Just like her mother,' Cross said. 'You have any ideas about the shooter?'

She shook her head.

'Don't know where to begin.'

'I know the feeling.'

He knew Maureen was close by. He hadn't heard anyone talking in a while, though he didn't know exactly what 'a while' was – hours, days, months, years. He had just returned from Paris, where he was stationed as a noncommissioned officer in US Army Intelligence, also where he lived briefly and intensely with a ballet dancer born in London.

He had dinner with her at a small restaurant down the street from Café Flore. Outside. He had a second beer and she a second glass of wine as the waiter removed the plates. A damp chill was settling.

'You're going back to your wife, aren't you?' she said.

Shanahan didn't answer right away. He had to tell the truth, but how was he to say it?

'I'm sorry,' he finally said, not finding any words to describe how he felt.

There was another long silence. She looked around, at the trees, the passersby, the small cars darting about on the street a few feet away.

'Duty before passion?'

'Duty before love,' Shanahan said. He meant it.

'If that's the case, it's the wrong decision.'

'If it had been passion?'

'In that case, you would be making the right decision. Are you sure you know how you feel?'

He didn't. He was rarely sure of his feelings. Of his opinions? Yes. But feelings? They seemed complicated. He was confused. It was true. These were areas in which he had a limited vocabulary.

'I have a child on the way.'

'I see,' she said.

'I don't know if I do.'

'But you don't love her?' She sipped her wine.

'We're strangers,' Shanahan said.

'How did that happen?'

'Time. Distance. I guess. I can only guess.'

'And you and me? It would be the same. I don't know

where my work will take me. You don't know where the army will put you. This moment was inevitable.'

Her eyes were wet, but she wasn't crying.

'Things come and go,' she continued, speaking slowly to keep emotion from dragging the words away. 'People in our lives. Ourselves. There will be a day we leave everything.'

It began to drizzle.

'Shall we go?'

He looked at her.

'Go where?'

'My place. You remember my place. The small fireplace, the big, soft feather bed, the refrigerator that hums a little too loud. My place. Let's make a night of it.'

'OK,' he said, leaving his beer.

'And,' she said, grabbing his hand, 'let's pretend this was all about passion and passion only.'

He left in the middle of the night and never saw her again.

'Here's your bed,' a strange voice said.

Paris vanished. Shanahan was in darkness.

'It's not the most comfortable in the world. Maybe we can work out something better later,' came a woman's voice.

'Thank you. This will do fine,' Maureen said.

He tried to open his eyes. It didn't work. He tried to imagine her, create her as he had apparently created Paris.

A few moments passed.

'OK, Shanahan, you better not be dreaming of other women,' she said.

He felt the lightest of pressure on his lips.

'I don't want to be this far away from you,' Maureen said. 'I want to be where you are.'

There was a long period of quiet. Shanahan felt relaxed. He heard her voice again.

'When you were young, did you play the under-the-sheets game?'

What a strange question, he thought.

'In a diner somewhere. You know. There used to be these small wall-hanging jukeboxes in each booth with pages of popular songs. We were in junior high maybe and it was a little game we played. We'd read the names of the songs and then add "under the sheets." We laughed.

'The song "You Make Me Feel Brand New" under the sheets. "Fifty Ways to Leave Your Lover" under the sheets. Never mind. It was funny at the time. I'll be quiet now. I'll be here, but I'll be quiet. I wish I knew what you wanted . . .'

After a long quiet, he tried to get back to Paris, but he couldn't.

It was late, but not all that late in Hawaii. Perhaps he could catch someone at the Maui police department. Was there a Maui police department? He wasn't sure how all of that worked where islands were counties.

After getting Maya back to the sofa and tucked in – she was tired and fortunately not at all talkative – he went to the computer. He searched for Margot Hudson. Found her. An address in Kihei. He called information, found a listing for the Police Department of Maui.

'I need your help,' Cross said once he was transferred from the station operator to an officer. 'I'm a former cop here in Indianapolis. A little girl has been left on my doorstep. I know her mother, Margot Hudson. She is a resident of Maui and I'm trying to locate her whereabouts.'

'I'm not sure . . .' the officer said.

'The thing is, the woman who lived next door to her at her house in Kihei took care of the little girl quite often. I'm hoping you can give me the phone number of the houses on either side of Margot's residence.'

Unsure, but seeing no real harm in it, the Hawaiian cop used a reverse directory to give Cross two addresses, homes on either side of Margot's.

'Thanks,' Cross said. 'How's the weather?'

'The weather's always fine in paradise,' the cop said, a little bit of an edge in his voice.

The chances of getting the right person on the first call were 50–50. He lost. The gentleman who answered was an elderly man, Cross guessed. His speech was halting, but soft, and he wanted to help.

'You want Mrs Handlehauser,' he said. 'She lives on the other side of Margot. She takes care of her little girl.'

'You a friend of Margot?' Cross asked. It didn't hurt to get as much information as possible.

'To talk to. She's a very nice woman, but not around a lot.'

'Sure. She have many visitors?'

'No, can't say that she does. You're calling from Indianapolis, you say?'

'Right. I'm trying to find out where she is.' Cross weighed his options. 'She might be in trouble.'

'I'm sorry, but I wouldn't know.'

'Have you seen anyone coming and going from her house?'

'No. I've got a lot of time on my hands, but I try not to use it trying to figure out my neighbor's business.'

'You're a good man,' Cross said. 'But this time it might help.'

'I'm not sure what I should say or shouldn't say,' the man said.

'Any observation would help.'

'There's a guy who drives up in some little sports car. I've seen him a few times. He's got a sports car and all that, expensive I think, but he doesn't seem to be all that happy when I see him.'

'You ever hear anything next door?'

'No, I don't.'

'You wouldn't happen to know the guy's name?'

'No.'

'What he looks like?'

'Blond. In his late thirties, early forties. Skinny. A smart-aleck. I can see that,' the man said.

'You can see a smart-aleck from a distance?'

'Yeah. It's the way he walks. He thinks he's a big-shot.'

'They go out together? This guy and Margot.'

'Yeah. Sometimes. I think to dinner. It's usually around that time. Around sunset.'

Mrs Handlehauser wasn't particularly helpful, though it wasn't for the lack of trying. She was willing to tell too much to a complete stranger, her complete life story if he'd let her – a natural mark for telemarketers selling aluminum siding or plastic windows. She didn't pry into Miss Hudson's affairs, she said. On the occasions of Margot's many and long-lasting 'business trips', Mrs Handlehauser took care of Maya. The woman didn't know who Margot worked for, or anything about her private affairs or her boyfriends, though she corroborated the gentleman's account of a blond man in Margot's life.

'Do you know when Margot gets back?'

'I didn't know she was gone,' she said. 'Where's Maya? She's not with me.'

At the end of the calls, Cross didn't know much more than he knew before. In the morning he'd ask Maya about the blond man and the little convertible. Surely she knew something.

This problem was much like the problem with the man who was trying to kill Shanahan. There wasn't a trail to follow. Margot could be anywhere in the world for just about any reason at all. And Shanahan's dangerous stalker? For all practical purposes, he was invisible. And motive? Couldn't be sure he even wanted Shanahan. Maybe there was a little more there.

Cross was feeling restless. Usually, when he felt this way he'd slip off to a dance bar and have a few drinks. But he couldn't. There was Maya keeping him entirely too respectable. How long would this go on?

There was a little chill in the room. Would be colder where Maya slept. He turned up the thermostat, gently tossed another blanket over the sleeping child, went to the kitchen, and poured himself a glass of spiced rum.

It was very quiet. Shanahan thought he was suddenly aware of his existence. It was as if he had been somewhere else and had just returned. He didn't know where exactly. But he was here now, wherever that was. Still dark.

His face was cold. He could see the moon in the reflection of the puddle in the black asphalt. He remembered now that he'd been shot, that a foot stepped in the puddle, disturbing the mirror-like surface. He could see the boot. With the dim light of the moon, he could see that there was a little tab. It said 'Cat'. The cuff of the trousers slipped up. The man was kneeling. Was this the killer? Shanahan could read the word 'Caterpillar' on the top of the boot. He could read the words 'steel toe' branded in the leather at the rear of the boot near the heel.

Shortly after, he heard a click. A bullet meant for him refused to leave the chamber.

The man went away. The puddle smoothed into a sheet, the smallest of ripples caused by his shallow breathing. He could see the reflection of the moon again, a mere reflection itself. It reminded him how small and lonely he was in the universe.

His brother dove into the slick surface of the night water. The gangly thirteen-year-old screamed with happiness until he penetrated the glass-like sheet of water. Shanahan waited on the dirt ridge that surrounded the pond. He waited to see if it was all right, whether or not some monster resided there, gobbling up little boys who swam at night. Given his druthers, Shanahan would prefer to poke around the water with a stick before getting in.

The air was sweltering hot as it can be only on a few midsummer evenings in Wisconsin.

His brother, in the moonlight, was pale as the porcelain of the bathroom sink as he climbed from the water, up the dirt mound toward Shanahan.

'C'mon, Dietrich. You gotta do more than look in this life,' Fritz said, shaking off the water. 'You got to live.' He laughed. 'There are no sharks in there. Anyway that's why I'm here. To protect you. And you to protect me. OK?'

Shanahan said nothing.

'We gotta protect each other,' Fritz said.

Shanahan watched as the water went slowly still and became a perfect mirror. Shanahan could see his own face.

'Take your clothes off, you prude,' Fritz said. 'No one's here but you and me.'

The picture went away. Shanahan was alone, suspended in the darkness.

Eight

'I talked with the judge,' Swann said.
'And?' Cross said.
'And he's a civil judge. Could easily have pissed someone off.'
'So what we have, if we have anything at all, is two sets of suspects, one from Shanahan's past and one from the judge's?'
'Yep,' Swann said.
'You trace the call to Shanahan?'
'Public phone. Downtown. Union Station.'
'Do we know anything new?' Cross asked.
Maya wandered through the little middle room to the bathroom.
'No. How's Shanahan.'
'Quiet as a church mouse,' Cross said.
'And Maureen.'
'With him, when I left.'
'She's quite a woman,' Swann said. 'You find anything?'
'Not looking yet. Don't know where to begin.'
'The cases, Cross. The cases. If they were really after Shanahan, it would have to be someone he investigated, probably sent up. See you around.'
Maya wandered back through the room. Cross followed her into the living room, where she had already folded up her sheet and blanket, placed them neatly at the end of the sofa.
'You know a blond guy drives a little convertible?' Cross asked her.
'Eddie,' she said.
'Eddie. Eddie who?'
She shrugged. The light, filtered through the pines, came

in through the sliding glass windows, warming up the cool room.

'You ride in his car?'

She nodded.

He decided to ask a foolish question.

'What kind of car is it?'

'Blue.'

'Ah . . .'

'Maserati.'

'What did you say?' Cross asked.

'Maserati.'

'Bingo,' Cross said.

'You are silly,' Maya said.

'And you are quite lovely, Maya.'

'I know,' she said.

'But how did you know he drove a Maserati?' She hardly knew her last name or where she lived. How did she know Maserati?

'He kept telling me,' Maya said. 'He said it was his favorite toy. He said he would get me one when I grew up.'

'I'll bet.' Cross checked his watch. He could call Hawaii. He'd already checked in with Maureen at the hospital. No change. He'd promised to go back with her to the house. Feed Einstein. 'Have you had your lunch?'

'Yes.'

'You OK for a little while, so I can make some phone calls?'

'Of course,' she said.

'I know. I'm silly.'

She smiled knowingly.

He called the officer he'd talked to in Hawaii. The blessing was that this wasn't your ordinary convertible. On an island of less than 100,000 permanent residents, there weren't that many Maseratis. And one just didn't drive to Maui. So the car was probably still in Hawaii. It was either a high-class rental, which meant the owner could be traced easily, or a permanent resident, which meant the owner could be traced easily. And he had the name 'Eddie.'

'Lonala Kielinei,' came the voice.

Cross had written down the name as best he could – too

many vowels – from the earlier call and asked for him by name. The guy was cooperative. He didn't want to gamble with someone else.

'This is Cross again . . . from Indianapolis.'

'How can I help you?'

'I'm looking for a guy named Eddie.'

There was a laugh. 'You're putting me on.'

'He drives a Maserati.'

'A blue GranSport Spyder?'

'Could be.'

'Why do you want Eddie?'

'Somehow connected to Margot Hudson. So you know Eddie? Just like that, you know Eddie.'

'It's a small island. Eddie lives large.'

'Is he a good guy or a bad guy?' Cross asked.

'Far as I know, just a guy. You think he's involved with Miss Hudson's disappearance?'

'Don't know. But he may know something that would help me locate her whether he was involved or not. What else do you know about him?'

'Owns a couple of restaurants, some land. You want me to call on him?'

'Could you just give me his name and number?'

'Sure, give me a second,' Kielinei said.

'What have we got here?' Harry asked as Cross lifted Maya up on the barstool.

'A lovely young woman.' The bar had its usual early afternoon regulars, quiet folks, looking at their beers or watching the big-screen TV attached to the ceiling, slanting down to entertain most every seat in the bar.

'And you'd be the man breaking the law,' Harry said.

'I've got to do a little work,' Cross said. 'She needs a place to hang out.'

'I need to keep my license,' Harry said. But he didn't say it with any force. He knew this was about Shanahan. 'No other place?'

'No, Harry.'

'I'll take an orange juice and a bag of pretzels,' Maya said, giving Harry a big grin.

'Comin' right up,' Harry said. He looked back at Cross.

Cross knew the law. He had been in vice. Nobody under twenty-one was allowed in a bar, accompanied by an adult or not. Indiana was always a little uptight about moral matters. It wasn't that long ago that a woman no matter what her age wasn't allowed to sit at the bar at all.

'Couple of hours,' Cross said. 'I promise.'

'Listen.' Harry leaned across the bar. 'I can help. Shut down the bar for a while and get this . . .' He looked at Maya. 'Son of a gun.'

'Maybe. Let's get something to go on, first.' Cross looked at Maya. She seemed very much at home at the bar. That struck him as both funny and sad. 'If she says you're silly, don't take offense.'

'She wouldn't be the first,' Harry said, turning to Maya. 'And would you like to hear something on the jukebox, m'lady?'

'"Itsy Bitsy Spider."'

'No, sweetheart, we don't have that one yet.'

'Do you have "Cry Me A River?"'

Maureen hated to leave; but needed to get back to the house to change, feed Einstein, check email and phone messages. She had a job and clients to answer to. Cross was happy to be free of Maya and have a moment of adult company but he couldn't leave the child at the bar indefinitely.

Shanahan hadn't moved. Cross thought he not only looked pale, he looked dead.

It was a short trip from the near Northside hospital to the Pleasant Run Parkway where Maureen and the detective lived. There was a surprise waiting for them as they pulled up the drive.

Casey was relaxing on the porch in front of the door. He stood as Maureen and Cross approached.

'Where have you been?' Maureen asked. Casey wagged his tail, obviously happy to see someone he knew. 'How long have you been here?'

She looked at Cross for a moment, obviously confused. She put the key in the door.

'What's going on?' she asked.

Cross pulled the pistol from the back of his pants and moved in front of Maureen. 'Wait a minute,' he said. He went in, moved quietly and carefully from room to room. Casey followed.

'He brought you back?' Cross whispered to Casey.

Maureen came in, went to the kitchen. Einstein appeared from some hidden spot and Casey waited to be fed.

'Too weird,' Cross said. 'He lets the dog go?'

Maureen didn't answer. She seemed emotionless. She didn't talk at all on the way over. She put Einstein's food on the counter and the dog's on the floor.

'Did you get any sleep?' Cross asked.

'I think so.'

'Anything come to mind? Something that might give us a start on this?'

'No,' Maureen said. 'Just the shot in the morning. Then the phone call. Shanahan will be happy Casey's back.'

'We need to talk.'

She nodded. 'I've been mulling over the cases, the ones since we met. They're all still in prison. So if it's one of them, they've hired someone on the outside. But then, why now? I don't see it. It's got to be the judge he's after. Has to be.'

'I still want him,' Cross said.

She nodded.

'Any news from the doctors?'

'Same. Wait. We wait.'

Cross didn't know what to say.

'Thanks, Howie,' she said.

He didn't mind when she called him Howie. It sounded nice.

'You're not planning to stay here?' He was pretty sure she was.

'I'll be at the hospital most of the time. But I've got some calls to make, some business to take care of. And there's Casey and Einstein.'

'The guy's still out there,' Cross said. 'Maybe I should stay with you.'

'You've got the little girl,' Maureen said. 'You can't put her in jeopardy.'

'Don't want you in jeopardy.'

'I've got a gun and a dog,' she said, her smile tired but teasing. 'What more could I want?'

'A missile with a nuclear warhead. Hungry?'

'No,' she said.

Cross shook his head, more at the thought that she was going to stay there, inviting catastrophe, than denying hunger.

'You can't just stay here alone.'

Shanahan stopped, looked through the window. Elaine fussed with the irises, thinning them again. Purple iris. The flower bed now extended the full length of the fence. It was the only nurturing she did. She was all business even with the kid. As for Shanahan, she was disinterested. He could have been a boarder, not a husband. Not that he blamed her. They had been heading in that direction. The birth of their son – while he was away on a long tour of duty – had been a burden, not a blessing.

He watched as she stood, threw down the small shovel. He saw her shoulders shake. She was crying.

He went outside. He felt the soft late-June heat on his back.

'Elaine?'

She turned. He reached for her. She shrugged him off.

'I'm leaving you, Dietrich,' she said. Just like that. As distant as they were, and had been for some time, he hadn't expected it.

'Elaine . . .'

'I'm leaving with Tom and I'm taking Ty with me,' she said. She had stopped crying. She talked firmly and in a way that sounded as if she had said this dozens of times before.

'You can fight it if you like,' she said, 'but it would be foolish. You can't take care of a child while you are in the army and you can't keep me here against my will.'

'Elaine . . .'

'Don't try to stop me,' she said angrily.

'I'm not,' he said. He turned to go back into the house. The sun now on his face, he felt a sad relief. He also felt lost. His life was tied up with duty. That's what he had at the end of the day to explain what he would do the next day.

He went to Delaney's bar on 10th Street. Had a Miller's High Life Beer and a shot of his usual bourbon. He repeated the process until night fell. When he walked into the house, there was a vase full of irises on the coffee table. She was gone. So was his son. No note. No forwarding address. He turned off the lights.

Darkness again. Shanahan didn't know what was going on. He sensed movement, heard muffled sounds. Where was he? Slowly light and images crept back in. Different time. Different place.

One side of his face was in a puddle of water. In the moon's reflection Shanahan caught sight of the man's arm. Something shiny around his wrist – a watch that looked like one of those pressure gauges on a submarine. The hand came close to his face and he was suddenly engulfed in darkness.

Cross picked up Maya at the bar. Harry didn't want to give her up. He was enchanted.

'Some guy came in and ordered a royal gin fizz,' Harry said, as Cross lifted the little girl from the stool. 'Well, nobody comes in here orders anything that high-falutin'. So, embarrassed, I'm stammerin' about the ingredients when little Shirley Temple here tells me how to make the damn thing.'

Because her sleep was interrupted the night before, Cross was able to convince Maya to nap in the afternoon. This allowed him some time to make some calls.

'Hey, Eddie,' Cross said, hearing the businesslike tone of Eddie Creek's voice over the clear drone of a high-performance engine. A sensitive cellphone.

'Yeah?'

'Name is Cross.'

'Calling from Indianapolis. Didn't know I knew anybody there?'

'That's pretty good. You memorize all the area codes in the country?'

'I did. I got a thing with numbers,' Eddie said. 'So now I've got your phone number in my head permanently. It's been hell since caller ID. But you didn't call me about my special talents, did you?'

'Depends. What other talents do you have?'

'Is this a talk-dirty phone call? 'Cause if it is you really have the wrong guy. About as wrong as it can get.'

'No, I called about Margot.'

'Margot Hudson?'

'You know a lot of Margots?'

'No,' he said, with a little laughter in his voice. 'She all right?'

'Don't know. Can't find her,' Cross said. For all he knew Eddie was involved in whatever the hell was going on, but he didn't have another approach.

'Why are you trying to find her?' Eddie asked.

A good question, Cross thought. And he wasn't sure he wanted to explain about the kid.

'I'm a private investigator.'

There was a long silence.

'Who are you working for?' Eddie asked.

'I want to make sure she's all right. When was the last time you saw her?'

'Before she left for Louisville.'

'What was she doing in Louisville?'

'You're the detective. Don't you know?'

'It's early in the investigation. You wouldn't happen to know what she does for a living, would you?' He tried to sound as casual as he could.

'You know, frankly, fella, I don't know who the hell you really are. But I've got your number.'

The phone went dead.

If Eddie was the person Margot was running from – and it could make sense because she took the kid off the island – then Cross had revealed too much. The problem was Cross didn't know who or what Margot was running from. If he knew that he might be able to figure where she was going. The reverse was true. If he knew where Margot was going, perhaps he could figure out who or what she was running from. Thing was, he came in in the middle of the movie.

Nine

Call number two got Cross an appointment with Judge Bradshaw Ghery. The judge wasn't about to talk to a private investigator, he said at first. Law professionals looked at PIs the same way physicians looked at chiropractors and cops looked at security guards – pretenders to their professions.

'Look,' Cross said, 'a friend of mine may have taken a bullet intended for you. And I want to find out who did it. The worst that can happen is that I keep you from spending the rest of your life in a coma.'

'Let me call you back,' the judge said.

'Brush off?' Cross said.

'No. I'll call you back.'

Cross wasn't sure he was sincere, but he had said it firmly. There was no negotiation.

Cross called the hospital to check on Shanahan's condition. No change. At the moment, Cross's small world was a mess. His friend Shanahan might not survive. Maureen's life might be in jeopardy. Margot, the impossible love of his life, was back in it, yet she wasn't. And what in the hell was he going to do with the kid if he couldn't find her?

He wanted the simpler days. Repossessing a car. Finding a bail jump. Tailing a wayward husband or wife. And having a quiet evening at home.

The phone rang. It was the judge. Come to my home, he said. Tonight at eight.

Cross wrote down the address. The good judge lived on the city's revitalized Canal.

'Casey's home,' came the voice Shanahan recognized as Maureen's. He heard this the way he heard this world, through a wall or from underwater. Vague in some way. Distant certainly. Shanahan wasn't sure what it meant. Of course Casey was home. Where else would he be? Yet it was reassuring.

'We need you home too,' Maureen said without emotion. 'It's too early for you to go.'

Was that true? This world, the one he could hear, was separated from him by something. He didn't know what it was. The other world, the one he drifted in and out of more frequently, was more immediate. Which was real? Should he try to knock down this wall and get back to Maureen? Was that the real world? Would he regret it? Could he even make the decision?

'We're trying to find out who shot you,' Maureen said.

Shot me? A shock first, then a memory. He could feel the coldness on his cheek.

'Fuck, Goddammit, shit,' the man said. Shanahan recognized the voice. Not who spoke it exactly, but its familiarity. He knew or had met the man who shot him.

'I know him,' Shanahan said. But he was sure the words merely rattled around in his head. He couldn't hear his own voice. He knew he hadn't really spoken.

He felt Maureen's presence. It was soothing. It made the moment right and comfortable despite the memory. She was the only thing he would go back for. If he could.

'I'm here if you need me,' Maureen said. 'I'm going to read awhile. But I'm here.'

Shanahan found himself staring down at the asparagus. What was he supposed to do with them? Boil them? Steam them? He opened his refrigerator and looked into the freezer compartment. Buried in the glaciers was a package of frozen peas. His insurance policy in the event he wrecked the asparagus.

Maureen was due at eight. He was nervous. If he didn't count the affair he had with the ballet dancer, he hadn't really dated in nearly fifty years. And Maureen was younger, beautiful, smart, spirited.

She was a nice person. What in the hell did he know? He had known her for precisely one hour last week. He had been nervous then, as he always was when he went to these places. So he was nervous now. So what. He'd get over it or he wouldn't. She'd liked him or she wouldn't have agreed to dinner. He took a deep breath, let it out. He convinced himself that he felt better.

It was all by accident. He went to the place where he'd gone before. A massage. Good for his bones, a break in the monotony of his life.

The woman at the desk lined up Shanahan with Maureen and they hit it off. Dogs. Cats. The Cubs. Food and drink. Well, she for food. He was the drink part of the equation. He invites her to dinner. She accepts. That's all there was to it. Why should he be nervous? A half a glass of J. W. Dant with two ice cubes settled him down the rest of the way.

Maureen arrived after the third sip, carrying two bottles of wine. One red. One white.

'Didn't know what you were cooking,' she said. Crossing the room, she kissed him quickly on the cheek and headed toward the kitchen as if she'd lived there all her life. He heard the refrigerator open and close and she was back, sighed, looked squarely in his eyes. 'Smells good.'

'Me or the kitchen?'

'Do I look all right?' She knew she did.

A loose white blouse, a couple of buttons open, and high-waisted khaki slacks that fell loosely after the fabric passed her hips.

'Fine.' Shanahan was nervous again. She was even prettier than he remembered. Auburn hair, green eyes. She looked younger too, but anyone would look younger out of the harsh light of the stark white room and the green-tinted fluorescence of the massage parlor.

'Would you mind fixing me a drink?' She smiled, forward, playful. 'What do I call you, anyway? Shanahan? That's what you wrote down. Just Shanahan.'

Shanahan nodded. He was pretty much speechless.

'My last name is Smith,' she said, grinning ever so slightly.

'Right.'

'No, it is. For God's sake, there are a million Smiths in the world, real ones, somebody has to have that last name. Actually, it's my husband's name. We're divorced. And what are you? Like Liberace, only have one name?'

'It's Dietrich. Some people call me Deets.'

'What do most people call you?'

'Shanahan.'

'All right, Shanahan it is. I like that best.'

From there, over wine, over dinner, the two talked. Shanahan told her things he'd told no one else – about his wife and child and his failure as a husband and father. They drank more wine. She told him about her marriage, so perfect at first. Her son died. Her life and her husband's plummeted. He turned first to depression, followed by violent grief. Finally he found the Lord. As he became more righteous, she turned more and more to self-destruction. Years of drugs, halfway houses, and false starts.

Shanahan told her he understood her husband's anger at losing a child. He didn't tell her how long he kept his rage – that, in fact, he still had it.

'I feel as if my life is taking another good turn,' she told him that first night.

He told her he was coasting, just paying the bills until the end.

'I won't allow it,' she said, smiling.

Shanahan slipped into darkness. He searched for some light, for some sound, or smell. Emptiness was all there was. Was this it?

Cross stood at the entrance, a directory of numbers and names. He pressed the one for Judge Ghery and heard static then the electronic sound of digital dialing.

'Yes?'

'Cross and company,' he said, looking down at little Maya.

A harsh, hellish buzz indicated entry was granted.

The two of them found the small elevator that went only four floors and punched in four. The elevator was quiet. They could make out distorted discolored images of themselves reflected dimly from the brass walls. The elevator came to a barely noticeable stop. The doors opened.

As they stepped into the hallway, they were surrounded by police officers, weapons drawn.

'Get down on the floor, hands out,' a voice called out.

Both began the process. A voice said, 'Not you, little girl. Come over to me.'

'You'd better be careful, she's tougher than she looks,' Cross said.

'Shut up.'

He was frisked, de-phoned and de-keyed.

'Call Lieutenant Swann in homicide,' Cross said, using Swann's name again to gain a little credibility.

'Shut up,' the voice said.

'Cross, private cop,' another voice said after relieving Cross of his wallet.

'Get up,' the voice said. Cross got to his feet, straightened out his clothes. The man doing most of the talking was a tall black man in a suit. 'What are you doing here?'

'I have an appointment with Judge Ghery.'

'Why?'

'I'm working for Deets Shanahan. Someone has tried to kill him. Twice. We don't know whether it's somebody really pissed at him or someone who thinks he's Judge Ghery. I'm trying to sort that out by chatting with the good judge. All right?'

The cops, all five of them, Cross now counted, were quiet.

'Now, why are you here?' Cross asked.

'To protect Judge Ghery.'

'And you are?'

'Your worst nightmare if you cause me any problems.'

'So you thought I was the killer?' All this was for him. It was a setup.

'There was a good chance,' said the man doing all the talking.

'It would have been nice if you turned out this way for Shanahan. Can I see the judge?'

'He's not here. I suggest you leave the investigation to professionals, Mr Cross.'

'So when someone shoots Shanahan a third time, you'll take an interest in his welfare.'

'I wouldn't wise off if I were you.'

'You're not,' Cross said, taking Maya's hand and heading back to the elevator. 'Wasn't that fun?' he asked the little girl.

'It wasn't fair,' she said.

'No?'

'Five against one.'

Cross hoped the cops heard her. She was growing on him a little bit more each day.

Cross felt better once they were out on the Canal. They went for a walk, rented a paddleboat, and paddled in the cold night from one charming end of the canal to the other.

Shanahan heard Maureen speak. As was the case in the world, it seemed the voice was coming from a considerable distance.

'I have to tell you something.'

There was quiet. He felt sad for the sadness in her voice.

'I want you to do what you want or need to do,' she said. She was whispering. 'I'll understand and I'll be all right. But surely to God you know I want you back here with me.'

So much pain . . .

It was sudden. White light violently invaded his senses. He could not be sure what was happening. The only thing he knew was that he was being pulled away from Maureen, away from that life.

'No, that's not my decision,' he said to nothing or no one as he was swept or was it sucked through something that felt like a tube; but there were no walls. He experienced sensations he couldn't recognize, feelings he couldn't understand. His will was weakening. He was gaining speed, losing mass.

This was still another place. Not the quiet blackness, not the Technicolor snatches of his past, not the nether world of what had been day-to-day reality, sounds seeping through a wall of some sort. This was hot, white light, signifying . . .

Whoosh.

Ten

When Cross tried to enter the hospital room with Maya, he was blocked by an orderly. Cross could see the scurrying, heard the frantic voices. He noticed Maureen standing at the end of the hall, looking out of a window.

Maya took off to be with her. Cross followed slowly. Maureen had been crying, but she was over it.

'They're trying to revive him,' Maureen said. 'They sent me out.'

'He's tough.'

Nurses and doctors were leaving the room.

'What did they say?' Cross asked.

'The neurologist said that he received a concussion from the fall and a laceration from the bullet. They ran a CT scan or something. They're not sure. It didn't seem too serious. Not a lot of swelling at the moment. They've given him something for it. They thought he might improve, but . . .'

'What happened?'

'He stopped breathing. His heart stopped.'

The first thing Shanahan saw was the little girl, smiling at him.

'You woke up,' she said. 'It's about time.'

'OK,' Shanahan said. He couldn't speak. Something was buried in his throat.

'You look like a huge puppet,' Maya said.

That was when Shanahan noticed all the tubes. He had something clipped to his nose that provided a kind of chilly air. He was hooked up everywhere.

The second person he saw was Maureen. She looked tired, very tired. Her eyes were damp. But she was smiling. A big smile.

Shanahan pointed to the tube in his throat. She rummaged in her purse and found paper and pen.

'Who's the little girl?' Shanahan scribbled.

'Maya,' Maureen said.

'We have a child while I was gone?' he wrote.

'You weren't gone that long. Belongs to Cross,' Maureen said, as Cross entered the room.

'Don't you think she's a little young?' Shanahan scribbled.

'That's the pot calling the kettle black,' Cross said, smiling as he read the note over Maureen's shoulder.

'How long was I gone?' Shanahan wrote.

'A few days,' Maureen said. 'What do you remember?'

'A big "EAT" sign.'

'Nothing about being shot?' Cross asked.

'Have I got all my parts?' he wrote.

'A few brain cells might be missing,' Maureen said.

'I've been losing them all on my own. They get who shot me?'

'No,' Maureen said.

'Where are my clothes?' Shanahan asked.

'Oh dear,' Maureen said.

Cross was surprised that Shanahan went from a coma to pretty clear consciousness. The doctors were too. They had steadied his breathing and his heartbeat but he was still unconscious when they left the room and chatted with Maureen and Cross. They didn't want to remove the tube, but Shanahan insisted. A note with big print and a vulgarity he rarely used was handed to the doctor.

The doctors asked Shanahan questions. Who was President? How old was he? What city did he live in? He answered quickly, sharply.

He was able to walk, though only with help at first. He was frustrated at his weakness, and angry that he couldn't leave right away.

Cross was glad Shanahan would be in the hospital a few days longer. He was concerned about the 'third time is a charm' possibility. The assassin missed the first time, though very close, and got him the second time almost fatally. Cross had nothing to go on with the attempt on Shanahan's life.

He was nowhere with this case. Cross reminded himself
about Margot. He was nowhere with either of them. He was
hopelessly behind.

Cross, Shanahan, and Maureen, with Maya watching tele-
vision, went over Shanahan's cases – one by one. Occasionally
Shanahan would drift off, and Cross could see the fear on
Maureen's face. She said nothing for a while.

Finally, she said, 'I don't want him to sleep ever again.'

Late afternoon, they went over again the list of the people
who might hold such a powerful grudge. The next day both
Cross and Maureen would look into them, run them by the
police, check on their whereabouts.

'I'll stop by the house, take care of the animals,' Cross
said. 'Unless you want a break?'

'I'll stay here,' Maureen said.

'Nonsense,' Shanahan said. 'I'll be fine. Catch up on your
business. Get a good night's sleep. Don't forget I lived alone
for a few decades. I can handle a night away. I've been away,
anyway.'

'Where have you been?' Maureen asked.

'I don't know. I think some strange places.'

'Oh,' she said.

'Don't be jealous. I didn't go to any restaurants without
you,' Shanahan said. 'Or did I?'

'You better not have,' she said. 'Or see any women.'

'Well,' Shanahan said, his Paris girlfriend popping into his
head.

'Well what?' she said, grinning.

'I might have cheated on you recently. But it was before
I met you.'

'I like that,' Cross said. 'I never thought about using a
wormhole in time or maybe a parallel universe as an excuse.
Good one.'

'This from a man who's dating a four year old.'

'I'm five,' Maya said, looking up. 'And we're not dating.'

'You're lucky she didn't call you silly,' Cross said to
Shanahan.

As Cross in the battered old Trooper, with Maya safely
buckled in beside him, followed Maureen's Toyota back to

her house, he tried to figure out how he could keep everybody safe. Maureen. Maya. Margot. Shanahan. Himself.

He needn't have worried about protecting Maureen; she wasn't about to be protected.

'You have Maya to worry about. Go home,' she said, opening a can of cat food under the sober eye of Einstein. 'I don't mean right now. What I'm trying to say is that I can take care of myself. I hope he pays a visit.' She looked at Cross. Cross was convinced she meant it. 'You want a drink?'

'I do, I do, but no. Not right now.'

Casey came in the kitchen.

Cross dropped down on his haunches. 'Hey, old boy, how did you get away, anyway?' Then, noticing something, 'Maureen, was this tooth broken before?'

Maureen set the plate down for Einstein, who studied it first, as if he might send it back to the kitchen.

'No,' she said.

He looked closer. There was blood on the fur on one side of his lower jaw.

'I think Casey got a piece of the killer,' Cross said.

'Or a possum,' Maureen said. 'I love Casey, but he isn't Lassie. He's not going to lead us to the killer.'

'The blood might. And it looks almost fresh.' He went into the kitchen and called Swann.

'Cross, you've been watching too much television,' Lieutenant Swann said.

'Look, blood, DNA, matches the person trying to kill Shanahan or, if you don't give a shit about citizens of this fair city,' Cross said nastily, 'then just remember, you've got a judge who might be the target.'

'I'll send someone out. That it? How's Shanahan?'

'No, that's not it. Shanahan's awake, but doesn't remember anything. But the judge and some of your colleagues set me up. Had me down—'

'I heard. You know how it is here. Right-hand, left-hand problem. I talked to them. But let us handle the case on the judge's side. He's not gonna work with a private cop. We'll keep you informed.'

'Like you do each other, remember?'

'We done here?'

'Maureen's staying at the house.'

'Crap. Can't you talk her into staying with friends?'

'It doesn't work that way with her.' He looked at Maureen, shook his head, grinned.

'I'll talk to Shanahan tomorrow. Maybe his memory will improve.'

'By the way, who is the homicide cop I ran into?'

'Collins. He goes by Ace.'

'Ace?' Cross said mockingly.

'Well, it's better than Maurice. And I didn't tell you this, right?'

Cross started to leave. He grabbed Maya's hand and headed for the door.

Maureen moved into the hallway. Before Cross could leave.

'Howie?' she said. Her voice was faint, tentative. She sounded frightened.

He went toward the hall. She came out of the bedroom, bringing the door to near closing. She shook her head.

'What?' Cross asked.

She motioned toward the door, taking Maya's hand as he went inside.

The bed was unmade and in the center of the white sheets was a large pool of blood.

He looked around. Nothing else seemed to be disturbed. Blood. Whose blood was it? There was no body. He went back into the hallway where Maureen stood pale and silent. Her eyes stared ahead blankly.

Cross went to the kitchen, played the answering machine.

'Third time's going to be a charm,' the voice said. That was the only message. The voice sounded neither young nor old. There was a bit of playfulness in the tone, as if the caller were having fun.

'You have to get out of here,' Cross told Maureen.

'That bastard won't scare me out of my own home,' she said. Then she looked at Maya. 'I'm sorry, I shouldn't use such bad language.'

'I'm sure she's heard worse,' Cross said, going back to the kitchen to use the phone.

'Yes,' Maya said matter-of-factly. 'Bastard. Eddie says it all the time.'

'Swann, please,' Cross said and waited. A voice told him that Swann was unavailable. 'I just talked to him.'

'It happens that way sometimes.'

'Send a car over. It's the Judge Ghery case,' Cross said, knowing that this meant more than an old PI. 'The killer was here, left a pool of blood.' Cross gave the address and waited.

Cross went back in the bedroom, shut the door behind him. He didn't want Maya running in. There was an envelope on the bedside table. It was postmarked Healdsburg, California and addressed to Dietrich Shanahan and Maureen Smith. He opened it. It was a card from Shanahan's grandson. On the bureau was a photograph. It was a photograph of Shanahan and Maureen on the beach. Hawaii, probably. A good likeness of Shanahan. He opened the closets. Not a suit in sight. He checked the window.

Cross came back out in the hallway. He pulled out his cellphone.

'Maureen, I'm going to call you. Don't answer.'

He punched in the numbers. The phone rang four times. There was a click. Then Maureen's voice. 'Shanahan and Smith. We're not here at the moment. Leave a message and we'll get back to you as soon as we can.'

Cross clicked the phone off.

'Maureen, was the door shut or open when you went in?'

'Shut.'

'Do you usually leave it shut?'

'No. That's why I opened it.'

'And the window. Do you keep it locked?'

'Yes. Of course, after all this. Even more conscious of locking things up. Why?'

'It's unlocked. I don't think the killer is after the judge. He had time in the bedroom if he wanted it. He would have noticed things inconsistent with being a judge. The most obvious is that there was an envelope addressed to you and Shanahan. He would have known the judge's name if it were revenge. He would have known the judge's face if he was a hired gun.'

'Either that or he's stupid,' Maureen said.

'He can't be that stupid and live. He left word on your answering machine. Your message tells the caller that you and Shanahan live here. By name. Not Judge Ghery. Another thing. I'm betting the blood on Casey's snout and the chipped tooth came from today, not the day he was dog-napped. Otherwise, it would be gone by now. The blood could be the same as the blood on the bed, but I doubt it. I think the killer came in, ran into Casey, hid in the bedroom, did his dirty deed, and left by the window.'

The real puzzle was why the killer didn't kill the dog. He'd had two run-ins with Casey. Why was the dog still alive?

A patrol car showed. The cop parked on the street, down the grade of the front lawn. He waited. A van pulled in behind the patrol car. A man and a woman got out. They each carried bags, moving businesslike up the drive. They were going to investigate the crime scene.

Maureen took Casey to the other bedroom and shut the door. The dog howled. She would have put Maya in to entertain him, but Casey was not always fond of children. And, in fact, had been giving her dirty looks since she arrived.

Cross took them to the room. When he came back out, Lieutenant Collins stood in the living room. Beside him in a stereotypical trench coat was his partner, who looked around and was apparently bored with what he saw.

'Where's Swann?' Cross asked.

Collins didn't answer. Instead he had questions of his own.

'What are you doing here? I told you to stay out of it.'

'I wasn't in it. I came home with Maureen. She found the blood. I called the police and they sent in the bench.'

'Oh, don't do that,' Collins said.

'This guy seems to not only have the run of the city, but can come back to the scene of the crime twice, and you? What do you know about this? Any progress in the case at all?'

The woman, dressed in white and wearing plastic gloves, came out. She headed for the door.

'Ma'am?' Cross called out to her.

She stopped.

'The dog has some blood on his muzzle. He may have bit the intruder.'

She nodded. 'I'll be back. Thanks.'

'Somebody is a professional on the force,' Cross said.

'We did a check on you,' said Collins' partner. 'You were a cop. Didn't cut it. So what makes you think you can second-guess the professionals?'

'Because some of the professionals don't have a clue, apparently.'

'So why are you off the force, Howie?' Collins asked, with a grin.

'I don't look good in blue, Maurice.'

Collins' face froze without expression. But the eyes told a different story. He took a breath, relaxed.

'You're the victim's friend and you want to help. That's good. I admire it. And I don't hate PIs. But I want them to stay out of the way.'

'Don't worry about me. I'm trying to find out who tried to kill Shanahan, so it's not likely that our paths will cross.'

'I'm trying to be nice. You and the missus and the little girl and all of God's little animals have to get out of here.' He looked around. 'This is a crime scene.' He said this without malice, but firmly. It was a statement not to be questioned.

'How about that?' Cross said to Maureen. 'He's figured out that this is a crime scene. Things are really coming along, don't you think?'

She gave Cross the 'be careful' look.

'I'm sure they're doing all they can,' she said, but the words had a hard time coming out.

'As soon as the officer checks Casey,' Cross said to Collins, 'we'll be on our way.'

'And you'll be where?' Collins' partner asked.

'My place. Check with Swann.'

Eleven

S hanahan sat in a chair by the window reading the newspaper. He didn't notice Lieutenant Swann standing in the
doorway until he heard him.

'You can't take a hint, can you, Shanahan?' Swann said.
'Any reasonable guy would be dead.'

'You have any news?'

'You're reading it,' Swann said, stepping in but not too
close.

'All it says here,' Shanahan said, tossing the newspaper
on the bed, 'is that Judge Ghery has a stalker. What am I?
I guess I'm still a hunting accident.'

'What do you remember?'

'I've got nothing. You trace calls to my phone? You find
anything at the scene? Either of the scenes?'

'All calls were on a public phone in different places in
the city. We're trying to find patterns.'

'That's it?'

Swann looked uncomfortable. 'Listen, Maureen's all right,'
he said, slow to follow up.

'What are you talking about?'

'He stopped by your house again. It was before she got
home,' Swann reassured him. 'I got the call just before I got
here. Cross is with her.'

'My guess is that the good judge, who hasn't really been
touched by this, had round-the-clock security and this asshole
has unlimited entry to my house.'

'I know how you're feeling. It's the way it is. The good
news is she's going to have to get out of there. I suspect
Collins has already booted her out. It's a crime scene.'

'Who's Collins?'

'A colleague.'

'A colleague? The police department has suddenly turned into Yale?'

'He's a homicide detective just like me. OK? He's supposed to be good.'

'Supposed to be.'

'He transferred in. Came from Detroit. Listen, Shanahan, I don't have first-hand knowledge. But he's supposed to be really sharp. And I'm looking into this too,' Swann looked away, 'but less officially. No matter what, you've got to help. You've got to probe that gray matter and pull out something useful. The make of a vehicle, maybe.'

He turned back, his face saying he wanted agreement.

'We made a cast list of characters in my cases,' Shanahan said. 'I don't see anything, but maybe you could check a few of them out. Cross can, but you can do it quicker and with a little more authority.'

'I've done a little checking already,' Swann said. 'I don't see anything. One guy's dead. Some are still in jail . . . and hey, there aren't many who'd have the money or the connections to hire somebody. The ones that are out, why would they want to risk another stint? They'd have to really be pissed. Then again, you've pissed off more than a few cops and prosecuting attorneys. You never know, right?'

'You don't, do you?' Shanahan said as he reached down to pick up the newspaper.

The dog sat in the small middle room that also served as Cross's office. The cat wandered off to inspect the place. Maya went into the living room, no doubt attracted to the notion of being alone and having a television she could control. Maureen set her bags down.

'I'll bet this scares the hell out of you,' she said to Cross.

'Instant family.' He shook his head and grinned. 'We can work it out.'

'You're overwhelmed,' she said, laughing. There was sympathy on her face. 'I appreciate your help. I don't have family here – pretty much anywhere – except for Shanahan.'

'You and Maya take the bedroom after I get the sheets washed,' he said, wondering how he was going to cram all this in and still make progress with his two cases. 'And I'll take the living room. The sofa's great. Really. I sleep out there half the time anyway.'

'This is temporary. Just tonight so I can sort things out. Tomorrow a hotel maybe,' she said.

'Sure, with a grumpy dog and an ancient cat. I don't think the Westin will welcome you with open arms.'

'How long do you think the house is off-limits?'

'Until we find the killer is the right answer.'

'I'm talking about what time tomorrow. Morning or afternoon. After they've finished with the house,' she said. 'But for tonight? How about I make dinner? A place to shop near here?'

'A few blocks. Walkable. I'll get the sheets and towels to the Laundromat,' Cross said. 'That should take me an hour and a half.'

Maureen looked at her watch, nodded. 'I'll take Maya.'

'Yes,' Shanahan said into the phone. 'No need to come.'

The call was from his son, Ty, in Sonoma County, north of San Francisco.

Shanahan had already hosted a string of surprise visitors – anti-authority defense attorney James Fennimore Kowalski, who brought him a bottle of J. W. Dant, the state attorney-general, Jennifer Bailey, for whom he'd done some investigations, and his best friend, Harry, who left his bar in the hands of the soberest of his customers.

Kowalski asked who'd done that to him.

'Some man wants to kill me. Can't figure out who,' Shanahan said.

Kowalski laughed, shook his head. He had that look about him that suggested that the guy who did this was in trouble. Shanahan had no idea what Kowalski could do in this case, but he knew that the attorney was not only fearless, but also engendered fear all on his own. He was a big bearded Harley-riding attorney with long hair. In his suit, he looked like a cross between the stereotypical biker and a Wall Street analyst. In a way, that's what he was, Shanahan thought, a renegade, someone who saw through the various shams of the established powers and passionately wanted to bring them down.

'I'll look into it,' Kowalski said in his man-of-few-words way before leaving. Whatever he did, he wouldn't be asking permission to do it.

The Sonoma call was something different.

'I can be there by late evening or in the morning at the latest,' Ty told his father.

Shanahan didn't know what to say. While he was no longer estranged from his son, he wasn't used to the intimacy that some families knew. What in the world would he do, infirmed as he was? Dependent as he was?

'Thank you. But you have things to do. And I'm going to be out of here in a day or so. So let's save it for a time when I'm feeling better.'

'Or you could come out here to recuperate,' Ty said. 'Qin Qin and Jason would like to have you come out and stay awhile. You and Maureen.'

'A few loose ends to tie up. Then we'll see.'

He could picture Ty's lovely wife, Qin Qin, and the handsome young man who was his grandson. The boy, in his late teens, had a crush on Maureen. But then, who didn't?

'Are you getting any closer to finding the guy?'

'She told you?' Shanahan asked.

'Yes, but only after you were out of the woods. I really want to come . . .'

'At the moment,' Shanahan said, trying but failing to phrase his sentence in a less awkward way than he usually did, 'it would just make things harder.'

'Yeah.' Ty's voice struggled to be upbeat.

'No, I mean more people to protect. Let's keep the targets to a minimum.'

'I understand.'

'I hope so. We want to come out to see you. We do.' He did. The afternoon he spent at Ty's winery was as pleasant as they come.

'Next time for more than dinner,' Ty said.

'We promise. It won't be business.'

After saying goodbye to his son, Shanahan realized how strange it was, how foreign to him, to have people in his life who cared for him. Stranger still, there were people in his life that meant something to him.

He didn't have long to feel strange. He sensed someone in the room. It was a tall, athletic-looking man in a gray suit, starched blue shirt, and bluer tie.

'You are a tough, stubborn old bird,' the man said to Shanahan. 'That's what they told me about you.'

'I don't know about tough, and stubbornness hasn't always worked in my favor,' Shanahan replied. 'Who are you?'

'Collins. My friends and enemies call me Ace. I'm homicide.'

'I've talked with Swann.'

'Swann's a nice guy, but this is my case.'

'And we're just now talking? You see, this isn't very encouraging,' Shanahan said. 'The judge took up all of your time, right?'

Collins smiled. His eyes were lively, mischievously lively.

'Everybody is equal under the law, except that some are more equal than others,' Shanahan continued. 'I know most everybody in homicide. Never heard of you.'

Collins came farther into the room.

'I heard about you,' Collins said, sitting down on the edge of the bed. He pulled up the legs of his suit pants just a bit to protect the crease as he sat.

'You said that,' Shanahan reminded him.

'I'm from Detroit. Moved here a few weeks ago.'

'Why?'

'They wanted me.'

'Why?'

'Detroit's murder rate is high, but it's going down. Here the murder rate is low, but going up. They thought I might help reverse the trend.'

'Why did you want to come?'

'Career move. Maybe I wanted a quieter life. Compared to Detroit, this is Mayberry.'

'C'mon, Ace,' Shanahan said, 'you believe Mayberry exists?'

Collins smiled again.

'You calling me Ace because I'm a friend or enemy?'

'Don't know yet, but it's probably one or the other,' Shanahan said. 'Coming in from out of town and right into homicide, I'm guessing the rest of IPD isn't too happy with you.'

'If I wanted to be popular, I wouldn't be a cop. Talk to me,' Collins said.

Shanahan told him all he remembered.

'I've got to ask it,' Collins said. 'Why did you go after your dog by yourself?'

'I wanted my dog back.'

Collins grinned. 'Chicken crossing the road, OK.' He stood. 'Look, I don't think it's the judge he's after. I thought so. I mean, why in the hell would anybody be that pissed at some old private eye?'

'Now you know better, right?' Shanahan asked.

'You bet.'

'Also, by now the killer would have to have figured out I wasn't the judge and would have changed his target. I wouldn't have gotten shot at twice.'

'Right,' Collins said. 'I'm posting someone to guard you.'

'That's expensive.'

'I hope you're worth it.' Collins smiled and left the room.

Halloween was over. So was October. Shorter, colder days now and it would only get worse. Cross lit the crumpled paper under the logs in the fireplace. Cross and Maureen sat on the sofa, a glass-topped cocktail table in front of them. Maya sat on the other side. Her seat – a pillow on the floor. Plates of pasta with crab cakes in front of them. Cross and Maureen had wine. Maya, who had insisted on a candle, sipped grape juice. Cross thought it a strange scene. A romantic evening with a woman he was not courting and a five-year-old child who drank make-believe wine. A tea party stranger than *Alice in Wonderland*, he thought. Only thing missing was a drunken Booky Man. Oh, and maybe a door that opened to another world.

'We had a nice talk at the store, didn't we, Maya?' Maureen asked her.

Maya slurped a noodle, nodded, but had nothing else to say at the moment.

'She told me that some guy named Eddie liked putting sugar in his nose.'

'Eddie is a happy-go-lucky guy,' Cross said.

'He's silly,' Maya said.

'You know Eddie?' Maureen asked.

'I talked to him. On the phone. The pasta is delicious. So is the wine.' He sipped it.

'This reminds me of an Agatha Christie story,' Maureen said. 'A bunch of people are invited out to some remote cabin where they are killed one by one until, at the end, there is this man and woman left. They sit on the sofa eating biscuits from tins carrying on very polite conversation even though they know they are next on the murderer's list.'

'And this reminds you of that? It's funny, I was at a tea party.' Cross got up, stoked the fire.

'Maya, where is your mom's most favorite place in the world?' Maureen asked.

'Home with me,' she said.

'In Hawaii,' Cross said. 'Maui, where Eddie lives.'

'Did Eddie and your mom have a fight?' Maureen asked.

'You mean like hitting each other?'

'Did they?' Cross asked.

She shook her head.

'Did they argue?' Maureen asked.

'A lot.'

'What did they argue about?' Maureen continued.

'Eddie wanted Mommy to stay home more.'

'Did he live with you?'

'Sometimes.'

A picture of Margot's life was forming in Cross's head. She led a relatively sane and proper life in Maui. She didn't let her adult-rated work invade the home. The woman who took care of Maya didn't know why Margot traveled except that it was part of her job, one that the woman probably assumed was on the up and up. Eddie may or may not have known what Margot did for a living and may or may not have cared if he did know. But whether he did or not, he didn't like her traveling. Was he threatening her or Maya, threatening her enough to scare her, to make her leave her home and leave her child on Cross's doorstep?

Cross excused himself, went into the office area, leaving the younger and older women by the fire sipping grape juice and wine respectively. He dialed Hawaii. The point to pay attention to, Cross thought, was that Margot took Maya *away* from Hawaii, apparently not able to keep her safe there.

'Not India-no-place again,' Eddie answered.

'Yes, Eddie. Just calling to see if you heard from Margot.'

There were sounds of clinking glasses, the indistinct buzz of conversations, and music.

'And I would tell you if I did, that's what you're thinking?' Eddie said.

'Yeah, I may have to get the Maui police to talk with you. Seems the kid is missing too. That's a federal offense.'

'Wasn't my day to watch them.'

'What day was that?'

'Any day you name,' Eddie said.

'Do the cops know how much you put up your nose?' Cross asked.

For at least ten long seconds all Cross could hear was the noise of the restaurant.

'You don't want to play with me,' Eddie said finally.

'The biggest kid in the neighborhood?' Cross said. 'It's a little neighborhood, Eddie. I don't care if your nose falls off. I want to find Margot and the kid, and I don't want to have to come to the Sunset Palms Restaurant to find out what you know. So I don't mind having the police check things out for me.' He had added the kid to throw the scent off of Maya's whereabouts.

'A little advice and then I'm going to hang up. Know who a guy is before you make him your enemy,' Eddie said.

'Is that what happened to—'

A click interrupted his sentence.

'Margot.'

Cross had no way of knowing if Eddie's tough-guy routine was a bluff. If it wasn't, it might explain why Margot was hiding. He was reminded that this woman who could own his soul at will was nonetheless a pretty poor judge of character. Cross himself was proof of that.

Cross went back into the dinner party, wishing his glass of wine were something stronger. Just as well it wasn't. He had to stay respectable tonight. There were ladies present.

Twelve

'You've had a little wine, haven't you?' Shanahan said to Maureen, who had just called.

'When you get out, we'll celebrate with a fine dinner,' she said.

'Sounds like you just had one.'

'With Howie and Maya. A little dinner. A roaring fire. Some wine. How do you feel?'

'Besides jealousy which you have intentionally inspired, fine. I don't know why I'm here.'

'Because they want to run some tests. Besides, we've been thrown out of our house. I'm staying at Howie's.'

'And is Howie there now?'

'Of course. It's his house. Where else would he be?'

'Cozy.'

'We have a chaperone. She'll keep us in line. Poor Howie. He's trying to figure out who is trying to kill you and where Maya's mother went and why. On top of that, I add to the destruction of his contented bachelor life by moving in.'

'How long do you plan to stay?' Shanahan asked, not quite hiding his sarcasm.

'Tonight. Tomorrow, I'm moving back into the house whether they like it or not.'

'Whether who likes it? The police or the killer?'

'Yes.'

'Maybe you should stay at Howie's.' He thought better of it. 'No, I'll be out, we'll take a room somewhere.'

'You can if you want,' she said.

That's what he liked about her. It was also what concerned him most. She knew no fear, or if she did she was too stubborn to admit it. He was just as determined to leave the hospital. He didn't want to have Maureen at the house by herself and he didn't want Howie doing his work for him. The killer was his.

The girls, as Cross called them in his mind, were in bed. The dog had settled in the middle room. Still awake on the sofa, he had no idea where the cat had gone. The fire crackled and popped but these were its dying gasps. If he timed it right, he'd be asleep as the last ember died. Perhaps, he thought, the cat sensed the warmth had come to an end and sought a warmer place for his old bones.

Cross must have drifted off, because he felt jolted awake. It was cold and pitch black. He stayed quiet, listening.

He heard the sound of scratching. Was it the cat? No, it was metal on metal. Somebody was trying to pick the lock of his front door. He got up and moved in the dark through the living room up the few stairs and into the middle room. He went to the door to the bedroom.

He heard some clicks. It was an old lock, easy to pick.

'Maureen,' Cross said in a loud whisper close to her ear, hand over her mouth.

'Mmmnmp.'

'Dial 911. Get under the bed.'

Cross crept out of the room, went for his gun in the desk drawer. But they were in. A bright light flashed in his face.

'Stay put,' a voice said.

Casey came in. Barked. Somebody switched on the lights. In the room were two strangers. One was a big guy. Chubby. In glasses. In a suit. Looked Samoan. The other was a slender blond guy, stylishly dressed. Judging by the tan and the summery clothes, these weren't native Hoosiers.

Since they both had guns, Cross was trumped.

'You should have called first,' Cross said. 'I could have had some hors d'oeuvres ready.'

'Where's Margot?' the blond guy asked.

'You know, Eddie, if I knew where she was I wouldn't be calling you all the time, now would I?' That's what Cross hated about cellphones. You think a guy is in Hawaii and he's in your front yard.

'The kid?'

'Same, same,' Cross said. He knew they would search the

place. He listened, full of hope, for the sirens. He wanted them scared off before they found her.

The Samoan went toward the living room. He found the lights. He came back in the room. Eddie nodded in the other direction, toward bedroom and bath.

Cross heard the exchange from the bedroom.

'Who are you?'

'Just a girl trying to get some sleep.'

'Who's that?' Eddie asked.

'You heard her. Just some girl trying to get through the night.'

'Look in the closets, under the bed, everywhere,' Eddie ordered.

There was quiet. Eddie stared at Cross.

'Hey,' the Samoan came into the room. 'The gal's got a gun.'

'What's going on here?' Eddie said.

'You're not from Indiana, are you?' Maureen asked.

Eddie shook his head.

'Everybody in Indiana plays basketball and keeps a gun under the pillow. It's the way we are,' Cross said, picking up on Maureen's line.

'Don't fuck with me,' Eddie said.

'I'm a detective,' Cross said. 'I'm on an attempted murder case and I've been trying to find Margot and the kid.'

'And why is that?'

'Why is what?' Where in the hell was Maya?

'Why are you trying to find Margot? She owe you money or something?'

Cross nodded. It was as good a story as any he could make up on the spot.

'Five thousand dollars.'

'How does she owe you that?'

'Privileged information,' Cross said. 'Client privilege.'

'Your privileges have been revoked,' Eddie said, smiling.

The Samoan came in, holding Maureen's gun. Maureen followed, giving Cross a shrug. She grabbed an irritated but unfocused Casey by the collar. The dog didn't know who to go after.

'She got in some legal trouble here – you know, with her

dancing and all. She was being railroaded by some politi-
cian who wanted her to play house. He had something over
her. And the only way to get her off the hook was to get
something on him. This was a few years ago.'

'And you wait until now to collect?'

'Sure, I'm in financial trouble.'

Cross heard car doors close out in the street. Eddie and
the Sumo heard them too. He saw panic cross Eddie's face.
Not so the Sumo.

'We called the cops,' Cross said. 'I can have you arrested,
or I can bail you out. All you have to do is put your guns
away and tell me why you're after Margot.'

The two of them put their guns away. As they did, Cross
plucked his pistol from the drawer and tucked it in the back
of his pants. He hoped he wouldn't have to turn around.
Maureen took hers and moved into the bedroom. Two armed,
uniformed police came in through the door.

'I'm sorry, officer,' Cross said. 'My cousin just got in from
Hawaii, was trying to sneak into the house to scare me.'

'Not a good idea,' the nearest cop said. He wasn't believing
a word of it. But couldn't figure out what was going on
either.

'No, it isn't,' Eddie said. 'I've got this thing about practical jokes. I'm sorry, officers.'

The second cop came in, looked around.

'It's three in the morning,' the first cop said. 'You got
anything better to do?'

'Yeah,' Eddie said, 'get some sleep. Sorry, a little old for
pranks, I know. Howard and I, we have this history.'

The two cops went out of the door, but held a hushed
conversation on the porch. They were trying to decide something. Then one of them shouted, 'Stay out of trouble.'

Cross shut the door, came back in. Maureen was holding
a gun on the two Hawaiian visitors.

'So why are you so interested in Margot all of a sudden?'
Cross asked.

'You got me worried,' Eddie said. 'With your calls. We're
seeing each other. Haven't heard from her. I'm worried. Thought
maybe you were pulling a scam on her or me or her and me.'

Eddie looked around.

'Margot's a big girl. She travels a lot. Knows her way around. Why are you so worried?' Cross asked.

Eddie looked Cross in the eye, offered a sliver of a grin. 'You know. The kid,' he said. 'I worry about the kid.'

'Well, aloha, boys,' Cross said. 'I'll walk you out.' He was worried about the kid too. Where in the hell was she?

'That's OK,' said Eddie.

'Listen, I'm the host,' Cross said, pushing his .38 into Eddie's back. 'Want to make sure you get safely back to your car.'

Shanahan awoke in the darkness. For a moment he wondered where he was. Which universe? The smell of alcohol – and not the good kind – reminded him of his current lodgings. He felt the tubes, those few that remained, into his arm. There was a dim slice of light under the door. Was he under twenty-four-hour watch?

He remembered that he had had some incredible dreams either this night or during some other time. He remembered they were vivid, as real as the present moment. They were now just memories, easily recollected again, but distant in time.

What he needed to remember were things not so long ago, the precise moments that preceded the bullet. Had he seen or heard something?

He closed his eyes to an only slightly darker place and drifted. The 'EAT' sign. Big in the damp sky. He turned right on the exit ramp and then left on to Highway 37. He drove. The rain stopped. The clouds had cleared the moon, allowing it to cast a pale silver light on the landscape and water glistened on the dark asphalt. There was a hill on his left and flat land to his right.

The sound! The sound of a flat tire or of a bullet. Or the sounds were simultaneous. He braked harshly, then thought to let up. Bring the car to a stop slowly. There were few, if any, other cars on the highway. He couldn't remember oncoming headlights. But by the moon he could see the road. He got out of the car looking back and then forward to see if there was anyone or anything ahead of him.

It was as if he was thrown headfirst to the ground. He remembered that. He remembered feeling the cold, wet highway on his cheek. He opened his eyes. He could see light in the puddle where his head landed, the ripples of water settling, the ripples of light becoming still.

He heard an engine, a car approaching. He heard a door open. He heard faint footsteps.

Whoever it was shot out his tire. He or she was coming to finish him off. He tried to reach for his .45. Nope. Nothing moved. He was frozen in place.

When Cross returned he found Maya standing in the middle of the room, smiling.

'Where did you come from?' Cross asked.

'You know,' she said, grinning conspiratorially. 'The secret place.'

'You have a secret place?' Maureen asked Howie. She smiled. 'A secret place, how very interesting.'

'I do. Only Maya and I know.'

Maya was pleased. She went to the kitchen.

'Why did you let them go?' Maureen asked.

'They'd be out in twenty-four hours and pissed. This way I got a good look at their rental car. The license plate. I can find out when they got here and maybe who the big guy was. Run a check on him.'

'Mr Booky Man,' Maya said, coming back into the room.

'What?' Cross asked.

'Mr Booky Man and Eddie.'

'That was Mr Booky Man with Eddie?'

'Yes.'

'I thought Mr Booky Man was a teddy bear?'

She nodded. There was no contradiction in her mind.

'They're both Booky Mans?'

She nodded.

'I see. You named your teddy bear after Mr Booky Man?'

Maya nodded.

'So you knew him and something happened and you hid because of Mr Booky Man?'

Again she nodded.

'Right after you came in, I told her to hide,' Maureen said. 'I meant under the bed. Instead, she hid in your secret place.'

'Good thing. They don't know she's here.'

He couldn't say anything now – in front of Maya – but thought he was getting it. It was the kid Eddie was after. Margot hid Maya and then kept running so they would run after her, not Maya. He'd seen on some *National Geographic* special that some animals do that to protect their young.

But the name Booky Man was not helpful. And Maya knew him by no other name. In a few hours, he'd call the rental agencies until he found the car. And if he were lucky Booky Man would be listed as driver or co-driver. If that worked, he could call his new friend in the Maui police and find out a little more about the dynamic duo.

For now, he'd go back to sleep. Maya and Maureen had gone back to bed, though it was doubtful any of them could sleep right away. He headed to the kitchen for the tequila. He'd no sooner pulled it from the shelf than Maureen appeared.

'I could use a hit,' she said.

'Straight?'

'Please.' As he poured a generous shot into a glass, she leaned against the counter. 'You know, this whole "home is a castle" idea isn't working. Two homes . . .'

'Two invasions. That's why castles were built. To ward off invaders.' He handed her the glass and poured an equal amount into his own. 'Feeling a little vulnerable?'

'Why are you and Shanahan in this business, anyway?'

'Shanahan was army intelligence. I used to be a cop. What else can we do?'

Even with the tequila, Cross couldn't get back to sleep. He had his own autumnal 'tequila sunrise.' Cotton mouth, tired eyes falsely energized by cups of black coffee, he was on the phone to rental agencies. He started with the largest and worked his way down. No car rented by an Eddie Creek came out of Indianapolis.

This didn't make a lot of sense until he remembered that Margot flew into Louisville and drove the 110 miles to Indianapolis. If she were being followed, wouldn't Louisville be where someone, probably the big Hawaiian because Eddie was still in Maui when Cross called, picked up the trail? The car would be rented to the Hawaiian, whose name Cross wanted.

Christ, this wasn't easy.

He called the same car-rental agencies in Louisville and had them check the name Eddie Creek. As he did with the agencies in Indianapolis, he pretended to be Adam Grossler, an insurance investigator who was trying to trace a criminal whose specialty was stealing rental cars and selling them to chop shops.

He was lucky. The fourth agency down the chain had a record of a call-in, adding Eddie Creek as co-driver to a Nissan Altima rented to Kawika Anatelea. Apparently, co-drivers were free if they were renting on behalf of a corporation. The corporation listed was Sunset Palms Corp. Thank God one of them was a stickler for details.

So, it was clear. Mr Booky Man, aka Kawika Anatelea, was after Margot as she arrived in Louisville, two days before Maya was dropped off at his place. He was the advance man. He either worked for Eddie or Eddie worked for him.

That set up the call to Lonala Kielinei, the Maui cop. But it was still too early to find someone awake in Hawaii. It wasn't too early for Maya and her early morning cereal, orange juice, and cartoons.

Thirteen

Shanahan was dressed before the doctor came in to check him out, before Maureen came to visit, before he knew they would release him. For the elder detective, releasing himself was the only thing that truly mattered.

'Whoa, whoa,' said the doctor entering the room. The guy was young enough to be Shanahan's grandson.

'Now why would you whoa me?' Shanahan said, slipping on an ancient Bulova watch with a rose face. He looked at the clock on the wall, set the time, and wound the stem.

'You are under observation. You need to stay here for a few days. We need to watch you.'

'That's a problem. I don't like to be watched.'

'Mr Shanahan, there's a potential for scarring in the brain . . . and for swelling.' He paused. He was trying to find the words to explain it to a layman. 'We're not completely out of the woods. Scarring and swelling, when they happen at the same time in just the right way, can cause seizures . . . or even put you back in a coma.'

'The coma was nice,' Shanahan said. He had a few vague recollections of his various journeys. 'But I'm not in a coma now. This place is boring, the food is terrible and,' he said, pulling a bottle from underneath his pillow, 'the beer is warm.'

The doctor smiled. 'Some MRIs, then maybe we can let you go.' He took Shanahan's arm. 'We just want to be sure.'

'*Let* me go? I don't think you're getting the drift of this conversation,' the detective said.

The doctor released his arm, stepped back a little.

'The drift is coming this way. Yes, I feel the drift now,' the doctor said, smiling. 'I know this won't mean one single damn to you, but I'm obligated to tell you. If you leave

before we officially release you, we are not at all responsible for anything that happens afterward.'

'You giving the doctors trouble?' Maureen said, coming in.

'They don't want me to go,' Shanahan said. 'I mean a lot
to them.'

'Apparently,' Maureen grinned, looked at the doctor.

'It's wise for him to stay. Until we run a few tests.'

'The house is still off limits,' Maureen said. 'And there
are no vacancies where I'm staying.'

'So this is a matter of a housing shortage?' Shanahan asked.

'Yes, you have no place to go. You've got a bed, food,
servants. It's virtually free here. Plus you have a nice guard
protecting you.'

Shanahan winced.

'Any word from the police?' she asked.

'Not to me,' Shanahan said, seeing a smiling Lieutenant
Collins in the doorway.

'You're quite a guy, Shanahan,' Collins said.

'Thanks, you are too.'

'Shall I step outside so you can have a quiet moment
together?' Maureen asked.

'The people you have pissed off in this town . . . it's a big
list,' Collins said. 'Cops, corporate leaders, politicians . . .
hell, entire religions.'

'I do what I can,' Shanahan said.

'Don't know whether the city should erect a statue or put
you in a cage,' Collins said, then, changing his tone, 'We
put a team out. We're still working on it. But so far, we can't
connect any of these folks to attempts on your life.'

'You clear the house?'

'Yeah. But you're not seriously considering staying there?'

'Everybody's got to be somewhere.'

'So do I,' Collins said. 'That's where I'm going now.' He
nodded and grinned before he left. 'Somewhere,' he said,
halfway down the hall.

All those years in homicide, Shanahan thought, what does
this guy have to smile about?

'You're really checking yourself out?' Maureen asked.

'Yep.'

'Anything happen to you, I'll kill you.'

'The problem is you are not the only one with that feeling. And if I don't find the guy, who will?'

'Officer Kielinei, please.' Cross waited.

'Just a moment, I'll transfer you,' said a voice.

Muzak.

'Investigative Services Bureau,' another voice said.

'Officer Lonala Kielinei, please.'

'Just a moment.'

No music this time. Voices in the background.

'Kielinei.'

'This is Cross. I thought you always answered the phone.' He sat at his computer. Maya was cutting pictures out of a fashion magazine Maureen had given her. The dog was asleep. It was quiet. Time to get something done.

'I get around. Tomorrow I'm tasked to the Criminal Intelligence Unit.'

'These are exceptionally smart criminals you're talking about?'

'Actually, yes. A wise-guy, as you might say on the mainland. Organized crime. What's up? You find Miss Hudson?'

'No. Trying to find out about Kawika Anatelea. How'd I do?'

'Not bad for a Howlie. Accent on the second syllable. What about him?'

'You know him?' Cross asked. 'Or of him?'

'Both. Honolulu. Los Angeles.'

'Is he a smart man, this guy?'

'Flying below the radar.'

'But . . .' Howie said, encouraging Kielinei.

'But we think he's moving farther into Hawaii. He owns strip bars in southern California. And he's moving fast in Honolulu . . .'

'And he wants to open his clubs in Maui,' Cross said. 'Anything criminal in that?'

'Maybe yes. Maybe no,' Kielinei said. 'To the extent that he'll bring prostitution and then all the lovely things that come with it. Right now, the only things close to strip clubs in Maui are the Korean clubs. No stripping. Basically, you buy a girl an expensive drink, then another. After so many twenty-dollar drinks, the girl just might be so grateful, she'll go home with you for free.'

'Mr Anatelea wants to up the ante,' Cross said. 'And maybe he needs land, liquor licenses, etc., things that Eddie Creek might help him get. For the right money, Eddie is willing to cross over.'

'Beginning to sound like it.'

'So maybe we should work together,' Cross said.

'We are, aren't we?'

Cross realized the reason Kielinei was so cooperative was that he was getting important information as well. It made him feel a little stupid. On the other hand, it also meant he could count on the guy in the future.

'Glad to be of help,' Cross said.

'Don't mention it. Keep me up to date. I'll look around.'

'Please. Look around Margot's place, would you? Carefully.'

'I understand.'

'Any recent unsolved murders in Maui?'

'Nope. Other than an occasional confused shark, we're a quiet community. An occasional bar fight. Severe cases of sunburn. That sort of thing.'

Thinking of the pair that came to see him, Cross thought there were more sharks than those in the water and they were circling. Did Fast Eddie and his sumo-sized friend know more about Margot's traveling plans than he did?

Maybe not. They left Cross's place empty-handed. But they did have Anatelea's contacts with the dance-bar world. What had they learned, or could they learn, from the folks at the Palace of Gold, where Margot did the Indianapolis leg of her circuit? Would Margot stay with friends in cities where she danced? If so, they might be able to figure out which cities those were.

The more he thought about it, the surer he became that it was Maya who was in the most danger. What happened? Did she see something she wasn't supposed to see? Was she the blood in the water?

He would check the dance club out early evening before it got crowded – that is if he could find a babysitter for Maya.

'Thanks,' Howie said to the Maui cop.

'Come visit paradise sometime,' the cop said.

'I might have to.'

Shanahan and Maureen stopped by Howie's place, exchanged a few words including Cross's admonition about moving back to the house the attempted killer knew about, inside and out, picked up Casey and Einstein and headed to the Eastside.

Maureen hummed a few bars of 'These Foolish Things'.

'Remind you of me?' Shanahan asked.

'Maybe us. We're doing two really foolish things in one day,' she said as the car pulled into the driveway. 'You leaving the hospital against the doctor's advice and moving back in here against everyone's advice.'

'I know. But you were going to anyway. Even without me.'

'I didn't say I wasn't foolish.'

'You think dying together is romantic,' Shanahan said. 'I know.'

'What I picture is a gunfight. A big shootout. Guns blazing.'

'Lots of slow motion.'

'Yes. A couple of times we look into each other's eyes as windows break, lamps explode, and wood is ripped from the doorway as we duck.'

'We're looking into each other's eyes as we duck?' Shanahan asked.

'It's hard, but we can do it.'

She looked at him deeply, pretended to duck.

'Works for me,' he said, as he saw the silver baby Infiniti parked in the drive. 'You got the car back, thanks.'

'Had it towed. The tire's fixed.'

Inside was sobering. It seemed oddly quiet to Shanahan. He looked around. The place was clean. The crime-scene team, unlike cops searching for contraband, had not only been orderly, but they carefully put things back where they found them. The room, the furniture were dust free. The kitchen was immaculate.

'It's like the place isn't ours anymore,' Maureen said, as she followed Casey into the bedroom. 'The mattress is gone. We'll have to get one.'

'We'll call and have one delivered.' In the kitchen,

Shanahan noticed the wood that still covered the window that was broken during the first attempt. He had been foolish, he thought, to drive out to meet the guy that night, and to come home now. 'Where's my .45?' he asked.

'The police have it.'

'You have something?'

'The 9mm Howie lent me.'

'Keep it near you,' he said. He flipped on the light in the basement and descended cautiously.

'I know, Harry,' Cross said. 'I don't have an alternative. She can't stay with Shanahan. That's putting her in the line of fire.'

'It's not good her being here,' Harry said.

'Nobody is going to check for underage this afternoon.'

'Not just that. It's not a good environment for a little girl.'

Harry was behind the counter, looking down at Maya, who seemed quite content to be anywhere. In that way, she was easy.

'She taught you how to make a royal gin fizz, didn't she?'

'That's my point,' Harry said. 'Too much, too early in her young life. A bunch of drunks, telling dirty jokes.'

'That's not us,' said an older man, looking up from his beer. 'That's you, Harry.'

The others mumbled their agreement.

'How long you be away?' Harry asked, ignoring them.

'Couple of hours.'

Harry shook his head. 'Just don't feel right.'

'I have a joke,' Maya said. 'Why was six afraid of seven?'

Harry looked around. She had everyone's attention.

'I don't know,' Harry said.

'Because seven eight nine!' She smiled triumphantly.

Harry laughed politely as did a couple of other usually quiet drinkers at the bar. A couple of them applauded. A few moments later, one of the others laughed.

'Two hours. No more,' Harry said.

'Showtime,' Cross said, smiling.

'Kinda odd,' Harry said, head shaking again.

Shanahan descended the stairs. They'd been in the house only a few months, so the basement was without the usual stacks of history. There were a few boxes. Books Maureen couldn't part with, old photographs Shanahan had planned to send to his son in California. A tool box.

He went to the furnace room, then squeezed around behind it, locating his snub-nosed Smith & Wesson .38. It was unregistered. He'd taken it from someone who wanted to use it on him. He kept it as a weapon of last resort. It was disposable if need be. No one could track it back to him. No one knew it was there – not even Maureen.

The S&W 637 Airweight held only five rounds in the chamber, but it weighed less than a pound and was easily concealed. Also, unlike many more popular pistols, the .38 was reliable and surprisingly accurate.

Next he moved to the far wall, reached up to the narrow ledge that separated the wall from ceiling. Inside that small space was a box of Remington Golden Saber bullets. He loaded the pistol and put the box back.

Fourteen

The Palace of Gold was on the west side of town on a stretch of road that changed names every few miles. It went from Bluff Road to Southwestern on the south side to Northwestern to Martin Luther King Jr. Street, to Michigan Road to Highway 421 on the north side. The club was set back from the broad street bearing one of those names with ample parking in front.

Cross had been there many times. For fun and for business. It used to be a hangout. He'd sit at the bar with a Guinness and watch the girls from a distance. The Palace was where he first met Margot and where, in his off-and-on-again relationship with her, he became on again. It wasn't intentional. He wasn't looking to pick up where he'd left off. But he did. And soon, it was off again.

Now he was back looking for her. Was this some sort of Buddhist reincarnation dance?

He checked in with the bartender, who he didn't recognize. Could he speak with the manager? There was no business yet this afternoon, so the tall redhead left the bar to find him.

Cross looked around. There were all kinds of strip clubs. In his job checking on wayward husbands and picking up bail jumps, he'd seen them all. Small, dark, seedy places where professional dancers not smart enough to get out in time hit bottom and where beginners didn't have a chance. There were also spectacular places, luxurious spots with incredible sound systems, top-of-the-line performers, and some of the best steaks you could find anywhere. The Palace fell in the middle of the spectrum. It was clean, well lit. Empty, one could imagine a magician or stand-up comedian performing on the center stage.

The bartender came back. Trailing him was a slightly chubby man who wore a coral-colored cardigan over a starched white shirt. His hair was thin, but what he had was swept back without a part. His eyes were reptilian, lids half closed. His face expressed terminal boredom.

'My name is Cross.'

'All right.' The guy was impatient. He didn't see the need to introduce himself. 'What do you want?'

'Margot Hudson.'

The guy pulled at a stool, keeping a stool between them, sat down, leaning back against the bar. He seemed to be pondering something. His long quiet became awkward. Finally, he looked up and at Cross.

'Don't know her.'

'It took you a long time to figure that out.'

The guy nodded. 'I know of her. Only recently.'

'She danced here regularly.'

'I know. I'm new.'

'You don't look new,' Cross said.

The guy laughed. It came as a surprise. Cross didn't think the guy had a good laugh in him.

'No, I don't suppose I do. I don't know her. But her name has come up. What's your interest?'

'She's a friend,' Cross said.

'Sure she is.'

'And she's missing. You know that, right?'

The guy nodded.

'In fact, I'm not the only one asking about her. A skinny blond guy and a big Asian guy were here asking about her.'

'You have all the answers. So why do you bother me?'

'I want to know what they asked you. And I want to know what you told them,' Cross said.

'I want a world at peace,' the guy said. 'You think I'm going to get my wish?'

'I'll do what I can,' Cross said.

The guy grinned. He looked over his shoulder to the bartender, and gave the guy a nod.

The bartender poured a couple of fingers of Glenfiddich in a short, wide glass.

'Not usually a good idea for a businessman,' he said, taking a sip. 'But one in the afternoon and two in the evening eases me through the night. And I'm a tolerant boss.'

'You own the place?'

'I do now,' he said. 'One of the principles of business I hold dear is to mind my own. If you don't mind a little friendly advice, I suggest you do the same.'

'Minding other people's business is my business,' Cross said. 'I'm a licensed private investigator and a former vice cop with a lot of friends on the force.'

Half of that was true, Cross thought.

'I don't know where she is. I don't want to know where she is. And even with your formidable background, you might want to let things be.'

'I didn't get your name,' Cross said.

'No, you didn't.' He smiled. 'Come back sometime when you want to enjoy yourself. I'll buy you a drink and we can have a nice talk. I like you. I want you to stay alive.'

He slipped off the stool and headed back the way he came.

Truth was, he didn't have many friends at IPD. What few he had weren't influential. But he was pretty sure he could track down his new friend at the county clerk's office or through the Indiana Alcoholic Beverage Commission. Nobody served booze without IABC permission. He wanted to know the guy's name to see if he had any links to the Hawaiians.

He wasn't sure if it was enough, or fast enough, but he felt like he was finally making progress.

Cross checked his watch. He'd been gone an hour. He promised Harry he'd be back in two. He downed his beer and cruised around the loop to the Eastside.

The radio in Cross's borrowed old Trooper was stuck on light rock. The buttons wouldn't be pushed and the knob wouldn't be turned. This time it was 'Everybody Plays a Fool'. Fitting, he thought, Margot still on his mind. He was more fool than player.

What was he doing, anyway? Was it his job to find runaway mothers? He'd ceased believing that the world was a just place. What was he trying to do? He'd made up his mind long ago not to take on causes, to make things right. It never worked. He could do what he could. Contribute what he could, when he could, when it didn't cost too much.

Maybe Maya would be better off somewhere else anyway. Some state or social-service agency. If she was in danger, didn't that prove that she wasn't being taken care of properly? If she wasn't in danger . . . Of course she was.

Shanahan took off his shirt. He duck-taped the .38 to the small of his back, to the right, the pistol handle ready to be gripped. He slipped on his shirt and went upstairs.

They drove to Harry's for a quick drink on their way to Amici's for dinner.

'Jesus Christ, Deets,' Harry said, 'coming in here with your head all bandaged. You'll scare away the customers.'

'Your customers aren't easily scared or they wouldn't be here,' Shanahan said.

Harry fixed Maureen her rum and tonic with a twist of lemon and was about to decapitate a Miller's.

'Make it a Guinness,' Shanahan shouted.

'What?'

'A Guinness.'

'What the hell's gotten into you? I mean you were acting strange before that bullet hit you in the head. Now you're worse.'

'A guy can change his mind?'

'After fifty years?'

'Yeah.'

'You get a girl you don't deserve. You buy a new car, get a new house, and now you're changing your beer. Why?'

'Just takin' a walk on the wild side, Harry,' Shanahan said.

'I love it when you're out of control,' Maureen whispered in his ear.

'I'd say you lost your mind, but you never had one to begin with,' Harry said.

'Harry, we're talking about a beer here,' Shanahan said.

He stormed away, muttering, 'More than a beer. I've got five-year-olds and crazy old men to deal with.'

Cross came in. He looked around, looked puzzled, concerned.

'Where is she, Harry?' Cross asked, almost angrily. 'Where's Maya?'

'Now, don't you start,' he said. 'She's in the back booth, taking a nap.'

Cross went back to confirm Harry's claim, came back smiling, relieved.

'You didn't feed her your stew, did you?' Shanahan asked Harry. 'She might be dead.'

Harry glared.

'I'll have what he's having,' Cross said, nodding to Shanahan's Guinness.

'Not you too?'

'What?' Cross asked, confused.

'You drink Rolling Rock or a margarita.'

'I'm feeling like a Guinness tonight, Harry.'

Harry gave him a cold stare and went to fetch the beer.

'What's with him?' Cross asked Shanahan.

'His whole world is falling apart.'

Cross nodded. 'That kind of thing is going around, isn't it?'

Harry came back with the bottle.

'You should get this on draft, Harry,' Shanahan said.

'You want to run the bar, too?' Harry looked at Maureen and said in exaggerated gentlemanly tones, 'You like your rum and tonic?'

'Love it, Harry. You always know what I like.'

'See? I think the only mistake you ever made in life was choosing him instead of me.'

'If only I hadn't met him first,' Maureen said.

'This could all be yours,' Shanahan said, gesturing expansively to the bar.

Back at Amici's. There were plenty of nice restaurants in the city, but none so close to home and none so dark at night. The owner nodded a welcome. She kept on familiar terms without being intrusive. Shanahan asked to be seated in a dark corner. With his head bandaged, he wanted to avoid stares. He also wanted to avoid being a target.

Maureen ordered what she often did – the Alfredo and a glass of inexpensive Chianti. Shanahan had the chicken with vegetables and vermicelli and a beer. A German beer. He might have moved away from American brews, but it was doubtful he'd ever switch to Italian. Or French. Not beer.

'I wish we could have invited Howie and Maya,' Maureen said.

'I know.'

'We kind of put anyone around us in danger,' she said.

'I put you in danger.'

Shanahan could see the flames from the candles dance in her eyes. He wished he could convince Maureen to go somewhere until all of this was resolved. He might as well wish he were twenty-five again.

'It's the nature of the beast,' she said. 'You know, for better or worse.'

'We haven't struck that bargain.'

'Sure we have.'

He wouldn't go back to twenty-five even if he could. Maybe he'd go back to fifty if he could keep Maureen in the bargain. There were a lot of dark years before he met her.

The room was filled with the low hum of conversation, unidentifiable music hidden behind the tinkling of glasses. This wasn't the Olive Garden crowd. It wasn't exactly a showplace either. People who wanted to be seen didn't come here. It was quite the opposite. People came to Amici's not to be seen – celebrities who wanted to dodge autograph-seekers, lovers on the down low, romantics avoiding prying eyes.

Shanahan thought it doubtful the would-be killer was outside waiting for him. Or inside across the dark dining room. He wasn't exactly a stalker. He didn't have to know where his victim was every minute. Just some convenient moment, the next right moment. He missed twice. He'd be doubly careful. He would also be doubly determined.

'He's frustrated,' Shanahan said, taking a sip of his beer.

'You supposed to have that?' Maureen nodded toward the bottle.

'No.'

'What do you think he's doing right now?' she said. 'You suppose he's some sort of lonely lowlife, living in a dirty basement, seething with anger? Or is he some sophisticated hit man, dressed in the finest clothing, dining in the best of restaurants with an elegantly beautiful blonde across the table?'

'He wore boots,' Shanahan said.

'What?'

'He wore boots. It just came to me.'

'Cowboy boots?'

'He wore some sort of sporting or construction boots.'

'What else?'

'Nothing.'

'You mean he was naked?' she grinned.

'No. I mean all I remember is the boots.'

'About the boots, what else do you remember,' Maureen asked.

'Light brown. Clean. Surprisingly clean.'

He thought he might remember more. Patience. Then again, he didn't know when the killer would try again. It was a man, Shanahan assumed, about whom he knew absolutely nothing but the color of his boots.

She sipped her wine, lifted a forkful of creamy noodles. 'Someone that dark in your past?'

Shanahan nodded.

'What about you?' he asked. 'Any potential for nightmares?'

'Killers?' she asked. 'No. I don't know. You never know. My life is filled with people who did the unexpected.' It was a sad comment. She allowed herself only a split-second of self-pity. 'How are you doing? You don't look good.'

'Slipping,' he said. 'You can see in the dark?'

'A feeling. It's like you're getting small,' she said.

'Small? I'm getting small. Maybe it's you who has the problem.'

'We'll go.'

'No dessert?' Shanahan asked. 'What's that Italian pudding you can't do without?'

'Tiramisu. But don't worry, I'll make you pay,' she said standing. 'You'll remember these sacrifices, right?'

'Can't guarantee it,' he said. His head felt light. His body felt unsubstantial. A mild wind could blow him away. Maybe he was getting small.

Fifteen

Cross ordered a pizza from Bazbeaux's in Broad Ripple. He built a fire to kill the night chill that seeped into the living room through the walls and concrete floor. He had a beer and Maya had a glass of orange juice.

She gravitated toward the healthful. That was good, Cross thought. But he worried. This was November now. She should be in school. She should have friends her own age. She should have her mother.

It didn't seem to matter to Maya. She got through the days without complaint. She didn't ask about her mother or when she was coming back. She entertained herself when there was no one else around. She read. She watched TV. She made pictures. She was content to sit with Cross over dinner.

'I want to talk about Mr Booky Man,' Cross said.

Maya looked up, waiting for more.

'The man, not the teddy bear. OK?'

She nodded.

'You are afraid of him,' Cross said.

She nodded, but didn't seem alarmed.

'Why?'

She had taken a bite of pizza. Cross would have to wait for the answer.

'He's mean,' she said, finally, after taking a sip of juice.

'What makes you say that?'

She looked puzzled.

'Did he do something bad?'

She nodded.

'What did he do?'

'He covered a man in plastic.'

'Covered a man in plastic? What did you see?'

'Mr Booky Man showed Eddie this man wrapped in plastic.'

'Where?'

'Eddie's house.'

'There was a man wrapped in plastic at Eddie's house?'
She nodded.

'Where in his house?'

'Not in his house, silly. In his car.'

'The car was at Eddie's house?'
She nodded.

'And the man in plastic was in the car?'

'In the back.'

'In the back seat?' Cross asked.

'No, in the back.'

'In the trunk?'
She nodded.

'You saw this?'
She nodded.

'Let me get this straight. Mr Booky Man showed Eddie this man in plastic. And what did Mr Booky Man say?'

Maya shook her head.

'Did Eddie say anything?'

'He said, "Jesus Christ."'

'Anything else?'
She thought a moment.

'He said, "What in the hell are you showing me that for?"'

Cross was speechless. Maya seemed to be able to jump from kindergarten to the streets at will.

'Did they see you?'

'No.'

'How could you see them and they couldn't see you?'

'I was in a tree.'

Cross exhaled. How could he be sure what was true and what wasn't? She was in a tree. All he could think of was palm and pine, the kinds of trees one didn't climb easily.

'What kind of tree?' he asked.

'Banyan tree.'

Possible, Cross thought. If it were an older banyan, it would have very climbable, perchable branches.

'Then what happened?'

'Mr Booky Man closed the trunk.'

'That was it?'

She nodded.

'Did they know you saw them?'

She shrugged.

'Did you tell anybody?'

'I told my mommy,' she said. 'I'm going to get more orange juice.' She got up, went toward the kitchen. She stopped, turned. 'Do you need a beer?'

'Not right now, thanks.'

What a mix of old and young. The picture was forming. Maya told Margot. Margot told Eddie. Eddie told Mr Booky Man. And Mr Booky Man was not amused.

Who was the man wrapped in plastic? Why was Mr Booky Man showing Eddie?

A warning, perhaps? Maybe Booky Man, aka Kawika Anatelea, wanted to let Eddie know the consequences of not cooperating. If Eddie was wavering about engaging in business with the sumo-sized hooligan, such a display might convince him otherwise.

Maybe that's what Eddie meant when he said, 'Know who a guy is before you make him your enemy.' It wasn't just Eddie. It probably wasn't Eddie at all. It was Mr Booky Man.

'Not so tough, are you?' Maureen asked as Shanahan made his way to the sofa. 'You wanted to leave the hospital.'

He sat down. He never felt less tough. He'd never been afraid of dying. Indifferent to it during the years before Maureen, he even welcomed it from time to time. But he didn't like the idea of somebody else choosing the time, place, and method. He didn't like the idea of not knowing why.

Worse, he didn't like the way it put Maureen into jeopardy. If the killer wanted to punish Shanahan, killing her would be a more effective way.

'He'll make a mistake,' she said. Her voice revealed how much she wanted to believe it.

'He's made two. He won't make a third.' Shanahan rolled back, his head on the pillow at one end. He brought his feet up. 'I want you to go somewhere. Howie's. A hotel room. Italy.'

She took off his shoes. 'Now you're really testing my loyalty.'

'I know,' he said. 'Go to California. Stay with my son. The whole family likes you.'

'They like you too. So we'll go. We'll put Casey in that dog country club he likes with the beautiful girl. And Einstein can go to Howie's.'

'Just you. They have all this wonderful food. Wine.' Shanahan's voice weakened. 'Sunshine.'

'If you go.'

'Even if we do that without his knowing, that will just drag it out. If he doesn't find us there, he'll simply wait until we get back. I need to face him.'

'Well, that's the problem, isn't it? He knows you. You don't know him.'

'Look, wherever I go, I bring him with me,' Shanahan said. Breathing was hard. He looked at Maureen. She was worried.

'Don't go to sleep,' she said. 'I'm afraid . . .'

'I'm too tired to sleep.'

'I get that way sometimes,' she said.

'When?'

'OK, never. You want some ice cream?'

'No, but you do.'

'I'll stay here with you.' She sat on the edge of the sofa, next to him.

'Swiss Almond Vanilla in the freezer and you stay with me? You must think I'm dying.'

'No,' she said, hitting him lightly on the shoulder.

The phone rang. Maureen left, went into the kitchen. Shanahan could hear her voice.

'He's resting,' she said. 'Tell me what you found out.'

It was quiet for the next few minutes, punctuated only by short acknowledgements. 'Yes. OK. I understand.'

Maureen came back in the room.

'It was Lieutenant Collins. They're watching the house, he said. Wasn't sure how long they could keep that up. But for now, someone's out there. He said that if we need them, flash the lights a few times.' She sat back down on the sofa, put her hand on his forehead, checking his temperature. 'The blood on the mattress was from a deer. Still checking the DNA on the blood from Casey's hair.'

'Good,' Shanahan said. 'You can get some sleep.'

'Feeling better?'

'I'm fine. Just tried to do too much, I guess.'

'You're sure that's all it is?'

'Yep.'

She clicked off the lights in the living room. Because they hadn't purchased a new mattress, she found her way to the second bedroom, where there was a single bed.

He let his mind take him where it would, and it settled on Maureen. He didn't like sleeping away from her. Wasn't sure he could protect her. If he couldn't, what good was he? He thought about his brother who was lost to him years ago. How his brother just disappeared one night, and the silence that followed. It was as if he never existed. He needed to find him. There was his son and his family – a grandson he wanted to know better. This was a problem, he thought. He cared now. Cared about people. Cared about living or dying. That was supposed to be good, he thought. But it wasn't entirely. It also meant that he lost his edge when it came to his work. That didn't bode well as he faced an invisible, obsessive enemy.

Cross's goal, beginning this morning, was to find out exactly who he was dealing with, this Mr Booky Man, Kawika Anatelea. He'd put in a call to his friend at the Maui Police when the day began that far out in the Pacific. In the interim, he'd Google the guy, find out if he was in the news, perhaps find out what other holdings Mr Anatelea had, and where.

Maya was in the kitchen performing what had become a ritual of cereal and orange juice and TV. She had added fixing Cross's morning coffee to the routine and was doing a fine job of it. Though it had been slow in its revelation, Maya was also helping with Cross's attempt to find her mother. The case, if he could call it that, was moving forward. He wished he could say the same for Shanahan's. Cross had gotten nowhere. He didn't know where to begin. And it was clear that Shanahan didn't either. He would call him as well. The only thing he could hope for was that the old man's memory would return.

Google News tied Mr Anatelea to a 'gentleman's club' in
Los Angeles, thanks to a media story on zoning. In a second
story on the zoning, there were allusions to Anatelea's West
Coast holdings and 'other similar clubs in the US'. When
Cross visited the Los Angeles club's website, he noticed
there was a list of sister clubs, one each in Honolulu, San
Diego, San Jose, and San Francisco.

There were membership cards that provided special
privileges at all the clubs – a free drink and discounted access
to the VIP room, not to mention email updates of where and
when new dancers were brought in. Mr Anatelea was an
entrepreneur and an ambitious man.

Though it was only speculation, Cross thought that in order
to move quickly, Booky Man had to either buy out, partner
with, or threaten people who could expedite his startups or
acquisitions.

Perhaps Eddie did a little due diligence on his new friend,
had second thoughts about partnering with a man of such
questionable character, but was brought back in the fold with
the display of a corpse. Whose corpse was the next question. The answer could shed some light on Margot's whereabouts. Or not. It occurred to Howie that, logically, Margot
probably wasn't running from Eddie. She was running from
Eddie's partner, and Eddie probably would too if he could.

'I'm going to take a bath now,' Maya said, passing by
Cross as she headed toward the bathroom.

'Take your clean clothes with you,' Cross said.

'I am.' She said it in a tone that suggested he was being
foolish to remind her.

They were like an old married couple, he thought. Perhaps
he had finally met someone his own age. But the moment
of introspection quickly passed. He was excited. He had a
hunch. He searched for the Palace of Gold website. He found
it quickly and clicked. Similar setup as the West Coast sites.
There was the Indianapolis club and a bunch of sister clubs
– a number of them in Ohio. Cincinnati, Cleveland, Dayton,
and Toledo had sister clubs. There was also a place in
Louisville. They had a membership card setup. Even the
websites were designed similarly to those in California and
Hawaii.

Cross got the picture. He wasn't sure he liked what he saw. This was, to use the polite corporate word, a franchise. To use a less polite criminal word, this was a syndicate. It was quite possible that Anatelea wasn't top dog. Maybe the enforcer or fixer.

What Cross was imagining was a network of clubs that, at some point, could be turned into a corporation that could import product, buying at quantity discounts, and seriously controlling the inventory. There could be other groups throughout the country. In the east and south and southwest. Big, big business. Big, big crime roots.

It also explained what Margot told him about doing the circuit. She'd dance a few weeks at one club, then move on to another, usually around some big event in that city. The Kentucky Derby in Louisville, the Indy 500 in Indianapolis, and so on. She was probably on the Anatelea circuit. His clubs. Anatelea or his bosses probably had interests in all of these clubs.

Also, the friends that Margot would seek out might very well be in those circuit cities. If Cross was her contact in Indianapolis, someone with whom she invested only the time she was there, someone just to get her through the night, she probably had others – maybe a guy in each port.

Now, what would he do with this new information? Verify first. He could go back and talk with the manager of the Palace of Gold. But if he put himself in jeopardy, he'd be putting Maya there too.

'Damn.'

Cross went to the kitchen, got his coffee, went back to his desk. He heard Maya singing in the bathroom. He looked at his watch. Still too early to call Hawaii.

Shanahan felt better. The sleep had replenished him. The sunlight streaming through the blinds was encouraging. He swung his legs over to sit up on the sofa and felt light-headed. He took a moment to recover. He looked at his watch. It reminded him of something, but it slipped away. He looked again. It was 9 a.m. He'd slept in. He heard rustling sounds in the kitchen.

Maureen came into the room.

'Sleep well?' she asked, smiling, knowing that he did.

'You're all dressed up.'

'I've got clients. I've neglected them. You feel OK?'

He nodded.

'I'll get you some coffee,' she said. 'Hungry?'

'Yes. But I'll fix something. Go on.'

'I put my cellphone number by the phone. Promise me you won't be macho about your health.'

'Whatever macho I had has been leaking out for quite some time. Not sure there's any left.'

'Yeah, right,' she said.

Casey loped into the room, headed for the front door. He anticipated the knock.

Maureen started toward the door. Shanahan stopped her. 'Probably OK. Casey's not upset.' He peered through the slot. It was Collins. Shanahan invited him in.

'Can't stay,' Collins said, staying outside.

Shanahan stepped out, getting an invigorating chill from the November air.

'The human DNA from your dog . . . no match anywhere,' Collins said. 'Disappointing, but not surprising. We don't have much of a base to work from, but it will help identify him when we catch him.'

'You're confident.'

'You remember anything?'

'Boots. Hunting or construction. Clean,' Shanahan said.

'Anything else? What about his voice? He called you, right?'

'It wasn't real. He had a cloth over the mouthpiece. Talked funny. Ghostlike. Fake.' Shanahan remembered. 'He cursed.'

'What?'

'He cursed. It just now came to me. The gun jammed. He was going to make sure I was dead. But the gun jammed and he cursed.'

'How did his voice sound?'

'Not old, not young,' Shanahan said. 'Sorry, I know. It's that "medium height, average weight" kind of description. Not a kid, anyway. Probably not an old man. Definitely male.'

'Well, that's something.' He put his hand on Shanahan's shoulder. Maureen came to the door. Collins nodded toward her. 'We've got a car on you now. But that could change at any time. You may want to think about relocating. I'm up against budget and the chief is doing this grudgingly.'

'What else are you doing?' Maureen asked.

'You know what we know,' Collins said.

'That's not what I asked,' she said.

'I know. We're still tracking down possibilities with your past cases,' Collins said. 'But it's been pretty dry. What else is there?'

'So you're just waiting for him to try again, thinking maybe he'll do something wrong, leave a clue, leave a corpse?' Maureen said.

'I wish I could argue with you,' Collins said with surprising defeat in his tone. 'Talk to you later.'

'You have your gun?' Shanahan asked after Collins was out of earshot.

She nodded. 'I'm packin'. What am I packin'?'

'I can think of a few things.'

'Heat,' she said. 'Right? I'm packin' heat.'

Sixteen

Cross stood at the sink in his kitchen, washing the few dishes they had used that morning. Maya stood beside him on a box, drying them, setting the finished products on a clear counter space. Even with the box, she could not reach the cabinets.

'Did your mom ever talk about special friends?' Cross asked her. He wanted to see if he could locate either a confidante or, perhaps, someone with whom Margot would seek secret asylum.

Maya seemed puzzled.

'You know,' Cross continued, 'maybe a best friend in some other place, some other city?' It was a long shot.

Maya shook her head.

Not only a long shot, an impossible shot. Maya didn't pay attention to those sorts of things. She lived in her own world. Even if she could remember a name being bandied about, it was likely only a first name. And in what city?

'Does your mom have a sister or brother?'

Again, puzzlement.

'Do you have an uncle or aunt?'

Maya shook her head.

'Do you have a grandpa or grandma, poppy or grammy?'

She shook her head again, this time giving him that look that suggested he wasn't all there.

He wanted to say everybody had a grandmother and grandfather, but that wasn't true. It only heightened the fact that Cross knew very, very little about a woman who owned a significant piece of real estate in his psyche. He hadn't known she had a daughter, hadn't known she lived in Hawaii, hadn't known she was dealing with this level of the criminal class.

Erotic dancing, even prostitution, if they were chosen

professions, were not immoral in his mind. Though he didn't buy into much of what went for conventional morality, he felt strongly about putting little girls in jeopardy, about killing people.

He had Maya put on something warm. They'd go downtown to the mall and take in a movie. Play some games in the arcade, if she were interested. He hoped she would be. It was a little dangerous taking her out in public, but there was only so much he could do to keep her entertained at a home not at all designed for kids.

Also, he figured Slick Eddie and the sumo were on the road. And if they were still in Indianapolis, they weren't the types to be hanging out at the mall.

While she changed, he called Hawaii. After a few transfers, he was connected to Officer Kielinei.

'Don't you ever have a day off? It's Saturday.'

'From time to time.'

'You have a dead body somewhere in Paradise,' Cross told him.

'I'm sure we do. We offer happiness, but not immortality.'

'I'm talking about a body wrapped in plastic that was not too long ago carted around in the trunk of Mr Anatelea's car.'

'And you know this how?'

'A little birdie told me.'

'You have a name to go with that?' Kielinei asked.

'Not at the moment.'

'Tell me what you can tell me.'

'The car was parked at Eddie's house at the time of observation. Apparently Mr Anatelea needed to impress Eddie.'

There was a long silence.

'Crap,' said the voice in Hawaii.

Cross explained his theory about the consolidation of dance clubs to eventually create a national chain, that Anatelea was either a regional player or a national one, but that the whole thing was likely bigger than Anatelea, and certainly bigger than Eddie.

'Eddie may be in this completely against his will,' Cross said.

'Play or die,' Kielinei said.

'Did you find anything at Margot's place?'

'No. No blood, no sign of violence.'

'Little black book, maybe?'

'No, but she had a DSL connection. There was no computer. No discs.'

'Did you check her bills, see what service she was on?'

'You're not bad,' Kielinei said. 'Yeah.'

'So?'

'So?' Kielinei echoed.

'Tell me.'

'Who told you about the body?'

'I want to keep that quiet for a while,' Cross said. He wanted to say, but he came from a background that suggested that the police were not always as discreet as they might be.

'Trust is a two-way street.'

'OK. I'll tell you the truth and nothing but the truth, but this has to stay with you and you only until it's safe to do otherwise.'

'OK.'

'And I determine when it's safe.'

'OK.'

Cross filled him in on Margot, Maya, and what he'd learned so far.

Shanahan pulled the drapery away from the living-room window a few inches and peered out. A big black sedan, a Ford Victoria – a model that seemed to appeal only to government agencies and was therefore obvious – was parked on the curb in front of the house next door. In this case, the police weren't hiding. The stalker could easily see the stakeout. That wasn't the point. Protection. That was all.

He could see the man inside. A black man in plain clothes. Big, broad-shouldered. Dark suit, sunglasses. A cup of coffee on the dashboard – no doubt bored out of his mind. Shanahan was empathetic. He had spent a good chunk of his life doing the same thing. And today? Today he faced hours of similar boredom. He didn't feel well enough to do anything constructive. And he didn't feel bad enough to give in to bed and allow the day to be a wasteful blur.

He let Casey out in back, in the fenced area. He kept an

eye on him. He was glad Casey was around. He wasn't sure how much physical protection his old hound would be, but after getting a whiff of the would-be murderer, he would clearly know when the guy was near. It was an early alarm system less fallible than the electronic security systems sold to nervous luxury-home dwellers.

When Casey had finished his task, pawed a bit at the grass, and moped back inside, Shanahan locked up, rechecking windows and doors. He still felt weak. The momentary lift he felt when he chose to leave the hospital was just that – momentary. It was probably a mistake.

He had a feeling that this wasn't the only mistake he made. It was pure stubbornness that made him stay where the stalker could find him. It was a characteristic – with potentially deadly consequences – he shared with Maureen, who also wouldn't budge no matter what the threat.

He stood in the middle of the living room, turned around. There he was. For the day. The only thing left for him to do was to sift through decades of memories. Try to connect some moment in his life with what was happening now.

What else could he glean from those few moments when his face was in a puddle of water on the highway?

Boots, the sound of a weapon not firing, the obscene frustration . . .

The man wanted him dead. What had he done to this guy?

'What in the hell could I have possibly done to this guy?' he said out loud in the empty room.

Maybe not wanting to grow up was the basis for Cross's unwillingness to make a commitment. At his age, most men are married or have been. At least once. He'd read about the Peter Pan syndrome. He knew he had trouble making any promises that stretched out into an uncertain future. There were advantages, though. There were advantages to maintaining his adolescence. He could still enjoy a silly animated film and play in the arcade.

And Maya was good cover. He could avoid those looks that suggested that a guy Cross's age doing things like this meant he was a big-time loser or a midlife crash site.

'Maya, come over here, what do you think of this one?'

About commitments in anything, but particularly in relationships, what little long-term fantasizing he had done, what few long-term expectations he'd allowed himself to have, ended in trouble. Margot was a case in point.

Not only had she brought out all the insecurities he possessed but usually kept in check, she seemed to encourage him to desire what she would ultimately not give. Then . . . there was the matter of Maya. Suddenly he was her guardian. Suddenly he felt responsible for helping Margot out of danger when, in fact, Margot hadn't really asked for it. All she really implied by dropping her daughter on his doorstep was to watch over Maya, not Margot. And that's the way she was. It was the way they were together. He was second-guessing what she wanted. The chances of him being right were nil.

Finally tired of the noise and activity, Cross and Maya went to the food court. Early dinner. They could eat light tonight. Take the burden off Cross in the kitchen. She could eat healthy when her mother came back. That solved, his mind turned back, involuntarily, to Margot.

She could have called, couldn't she? All these days, she could have called. She could have mailed him a note or had a friend contact him. Wasn't she worried about her daughter?

'Chinese?' Cross asked Maya, who stood taking in the choices in the bustling atmosphere.

She smiled.

Chinese it was.

She wanted to use chopsticks and was quite adept with utensils he used with more spirit than talent. She was, it seemed, accomplished in many ways for a child her age.

'Tell me, Maya. What else do you do? You know music and mixed drinks. And you handle those chopsticks like a pro. What else do you know?'

She shrugged.

He was convinced she knew more. But she had no idea what information would help him. And he had no idea how to ask for it.

'Maya, you remember my secret place?'

Her eyes widened as she smiled and nodded.

'Does your mother have a secret place?'

'I don't know,' she said uneasily.

He took note of how uncomfortable the question made her.

'A secret friend?'

Maybe, Cross thought, there was someone she knew that she hadn't mentioned to Eddie or to anyone. Could be. He knew now they were not really close. The intimacy was sexual for him. True. Over time, though, it was more than just the sex. For her, he had finally concluded, he was just a security guard getting her through the lonely gray hours after work and before daylight.

Maya looked at him for a moment, a cloud of fear crossing her face. She poked a piece of General Tsu's chicken between her lips.

'You know something, don't you?'

She looked away. When she looked back, she took another bite, this time lifting a substantial pile of rice on her chopsticks. Amazing, he thought, before he realized she wasn't going to answer him. She was like her mother. Sometimes warm and funny, but able at any moment to slip into another, distant world.

'I want to find your mother.'

'Why?' Maya asked.

Maybe he needed to get tough.

'To make sure she's all right,' he said.

'She's all right.'

He wasn't tough enough. Story of his life, he thought.

The day passed slowly. Shanahan paced. He tried to nap. He wanted to do something, but he wasn't sure he had the strength. He didn't know where to begin. He'd washed the dishes. He'd cleaned the house. He had nothing to do. There was nothing on television. It was too late in the year to do much in the yard. Even if it weren't the killer would probably be flying over in a hot-air balloon, shooting him as he dug up the tulip bulbs.

He decided he could venture as far as Harry's bar. If he fell off the stool, at least there would be a friend who would pick him up off the floor. And Harry had cable, which meant there might be something worth watching . . . though it might be best to stay off the brew for a few more days.

Harry was embarrassed at not having provided more help in snagging the guy who put his friend in jeopardy.

'I don't know where to begin either, Harry,' Shanahan said, sipping a ginger ale. 'The police are on it. Cross does what he can. Kowalski says he's going to look into it. But until this guy tries again, I'm not sure what any of us can do.'

'Surely to God, Deets, you have an idea of who you crossed,' Harry said. 'You have either cost somebody some big money, or you've humiliated them, or they've had to do time, or you stole their woman. What else is there?'

'I've been over it,' Shanahan said. 'The police have checked out the list I gave them of my past cases. So far, nothing's lined up.'

The big television over the bar showed soccer. No one watched. Shanahan wondered why he bothered venturing out. Maybe he should have stayed home to watch one of the many TV judges make fun of the litigants, or stretch out on the sofa and stare at the ceiling.

'So is this permanent, this ginger-ale stuff?' Harry asked.

'I hope not.'

'Good, you've been making too many changes. A new car, a new house, drinking Guinness. It's not healthy.'

'Not healthy?'

'It's not normal,' Harry said, pouring himself a half a glass of draft. 'I want to help you with this. But I don't know what to do. Anyway, it's up to you. You're the only one who saw him, heard him. And as you tell it, nobody's got nothing.'

'Everybody's got nothing,' Shanahan said.

'That's what I said. Better tighten those bandages, I think the brain fluid's dripping out.'

Harry might be on to something, Shanahan thought. He had difficulty focusing. His mind seemed always to be vaguely distracted. Had the bullet scrambled his brain, and if it had, would it ever return to normal? Or had this been going on for a while? A gradual dissipation of brain function due to the progressive disease of old age or any one of its attendant illnesses?

Whew! He had at least enough coherence to discern the possibilities. Now could he go back to the night of the shooting with that clarity?

In a few moments, the dim light and lazy informality of the bar helped him relax. What could he remember? A hand. Caucasian. A little ham-fisted. The guy must carry some weight. The watchband was metallic, large like a Rolex, but not a Rolex. Something cheaper but with all the gauges of an engine room in a submarine. This was good, Shanahan thought. 'Damn,' he said. It came to him. A wedding ring. The flesh of his fingers seemed to swell at its edges. The guy would have a helluva time getting it off. Yes, the man wore a wedding ring. This was good.

He looked up. Harry was there, staring at him.

'You got something?'

'Just a little more. A hunter, I'm guessing.'

'He's hunting you.'

'That too. No. He's probably got a hunting license. He's married. He's heavy-set. He wasn't always heavy. A white guy.'

'That bullet in your head has made you psychic?' Harry said, grinning.

'No, the fat of his fingers had grown up around his wedding ring.'

'Oh,' Harry said.

'How many people have hunting licenses?' Shanahan asked.

'Not many issued to hunt humans,' Harry said.

'Deer. Seems as if the ammunition used is sometimes used to hunt deer.'

'Yes, sweetie,' Harry said.

'Deer-hunting licenses. How many does Indiana issue?'

'You're the psychic. How the hell would I know?'

'You act like you know everything,' Shanahan said, downing the last of the ginger ale. 'I thought I'd put it to the test.'

'Well, it's a good idea,' Harry said. 'Maybe a name on that list will ring a bell. Then again, lookin' at you, I'm not sure any of your bells are ringing these days.'

Seventeen

What Cross wanted more than anything at that precise moment was a hot sun, a body of blue water – lake, ocean, swimming pool, it didn't matter – and a brain-numbingly cold margarita with bits of crunchy ice. But it was November in Indiana and he had a five-year-old girl to watch over. And that was all he was thinking about. What he needed was a plan. What he needed was what was called in the business world, next steps.

He needed to drop by the dance club again, talk to the manager of the Palace of Gold about girls, syndicates, murders, and kidnappings. On the other hand, everything he did that could put him in jeopardy would put Maya in the same place. On the third hand, he thought, something has to change. Though he wasn't about to desert her, he wasn't willing to watch over her until she graduated from college.

'Are we going out for dinner?' Maya asked.

He thought they might have to. He wasn't sure he had the makings for a complete dinner for two, or one and a half in this case.

Another fine thing about Maya, Cross realized, was that she was not a fussy eater. Though he didn't try it, he suspected she wouldn't hesitate a moment if a plate of frogs' legs and snails were set in front of her.

That's not what she picked out. She ordered the chicken maque choux, pronounced they were told as 'mock shoe.' And she tasted his hunter's stew. A mix of all colors of beans and chunks of sausage.

The place was colorful and brightly lit. They walked to the place not quite a mile straight east on College Avenue. It was one of Cross's favorite places. It had enough authentic

Cajun and Creole to satisfy his yearning for New Orleans. Words like spicy and fiery came to mind. It was called Yats. Cross didn't know why and didn't ask. Inside he felt warm and happy.

The trip back was long and chilly. Maya huddled into him as they walked.

'When's Mom coming back?' Maya asked.

She sounded older than she was, using Mom instead of Mommy.

'I kind of hoped you might know,' Cross said.

She looked up at him with a look that said she knew he'd understand and shook her head. An almost fatal no.

It was after dark. Shanahan watched two Latino boxers he had taped earlier go at it on Telemundo. He had the sound off. He couldn't understand Spanish, so what was the point? Maureen sipped wine at the kitchen table, thumbing through paperwork. She had either just listed a house or shared in a sale. Shanahan had forgotten; but either way she had work to do. She also had some catching up to do after spending so much time looking after him.

Light spilled out into the quiet from the kitchen a few feet on to the dining room's wood floor. The light by Shanahan's chair formed a small circle around him while a bluer light flickered lightly on the walls from the television set. A light whistle of a wind came and went, gently rattling the windows. Shanahan wondered if there was a storm blowing in.

The sudden heavy pounding on the front door jarred him. It must have gotten to Maureen as well. She was in the room instantly. Shanahan stood, motioned for her to get back, to get her gun. He moved to the door, coming at it not directly, but at an angle. He flicked on the light, pulled a cloth covering aside, and saw Collins.

'It's all right,' Shanahan called back to Maureen, as he unlocked the door.

A chilly gust of wind followed Collins inside.

'Come in, have a seat,' Maureen said, turning on some lights in the living room.

He sat, looked up at Shanahan. 'Have a seat,' Collins said.

'I'll stand,' Shanahan said.

Collins smiled. 'If I said stay standing, would you sit?'

'Why would you think you should be telling me to do anything? Do I tell you to blink, swallow, or take a breath?'

'OK,' Collins said. He stood, still smiling. 'We've run checks on Marion County gun shops. We looked for sales of rifles that would use the shooter's ammo and we've looked at the sales slips of purchases of the ammo itself. There were cash sales, so . . . Anyway, we've got nothing.'

'Have a seat,' Shanahan said.

'I can't stay,' Collins replied, shaking his head. 'The real reason I stopped by is to tell you that a judge has been killed.'

'Ghery?' Shanahan asked. Because that would end the nightmare for him and Maureen, Shanahan felt a split second of relief, then guilt for the feeling.

'No. Another judge. A criminal judge. Happened a few hours ago. Some early takeaways from the scene: he was shot from the World War Memorial as he walked to a restaurant, .223 Rem just like you. He must have seen the piece in the paper about you, realized his mistake.'

'Got a thing for judges, you think?' Maureen asked.

'Two cases don't make a pattern . . .'

'But you're taking your guys off,' Maureen said.

Collins nodded.

'We don't know how we're going to protect every judge in the city, but we need all the resources we can muster. We don't see where either of these judges were connected to you. The perp made a mistake. He finally discovered it and moved along with his plan. You were a mistake.' Collins smiled. 'This really shouldn't be disappointing news.'

Shanahan wasn't buying it, but he wasn't going to beg for protection. He looked at Maureen, changed his mind.

'The guy would have to be an idiot. Sure, the first time he made a mistake. Not the second time. Not when he broke into the house and put deer's blood on the bed. He had to know.'

'Maybe he *is* an idiot, Shanahan. Maybe he had to read it in the papers. Remember there was nothing in the papers until after the second attempt.' Collins looked like he was holding back, a little turmoil on his brow, frustration around his mouth. 'It's out of my hands. You have a means to protect yourself?'

Shanahan nodded.

'You know the way it is,' Collins said. 'Try to get his body inside, make sure there's a weapon nearby.' He nodded, went to the door. He stopped, turned. 'There will be someone out there tonight. After that, you're on your own.'

'He's not convinced,' Maureen said after Collins left.

'No. But killing another judge adds a puzzling dimension.' Shanahan headed to the kitchen.

'Are you getting a beer?' Maureen asked, following.

'Of course not. How foolish do you think I am?' Shanahan answered.

'Are you going for the whiskey?'

'Yes. I am.'

'Is that wise?'

'You know me better than that. When have I ever let wisdom get in the way of a shot of whiskey?'

'So you are foolish,' she said, grabbing a corked bottle of sauvignon blanc from the refrigerator.

'When I asked you how foolish you thought I was, I was just curious about the degree.'

She smiled, kissed him on the nose.

'What do we do?' she asked.

'Find out more about this poor judge. See if there is a connection between the two judges.'

'Or wait for a third judge to be shot at so we can rest more easily. I don't like it.'

Cross put a wool blanket on the sofa, relit some old wood unburned from the last fire, and turned on the TV. Maya was drifting off to sleep despite attempts to remain awake.

Cross had run through his options, failing to find one that worked. He couldn't leave Maya at home alone. He couldn't leave her in the car in a parking lot while he went into a strip club. He thought about leaving her with Harry, but it was one thing to leave her there during a quiet afternoon, quite another to leave her there at night. He wasn't sure what the distinction was, but there seemed to be one.

He couldn't call on Shanahan and Maureen. He felt bad enough about not being more help in finding the old detective's would-be assassin. He couldn't ask them to do something, especially when it might put Maya in danger. He was in what his mother used to call a big predicament.

'Jesus Christ,' he said smiling. The world was good. 'Jesus Christ.'

Maya opened her eyes, looked at him with a mix of curiosity and displeasure.

'How would you like to visit a farm?' he asked.

'A what?' she responded grumpily.

'Chickens. Do you like chickens?'

She looked at him like he was crazy.

He hadn't visited home in a few years – his parents weren't happy when he left the police force – and they were 'getting on,' as they often said about themselves. Even so, he was pretty sure there was a cow or two, some chickens, and perhaps Buster, a contrary goat that refused to do anything he was expected to do, including die. The farm had been downsizing since he was a teen. Agribusiness killed the family farm . . . slowly. No room for him. Good thing, he wasn't up for a life in the cornfields.

What was left of the family farm? Last he saw of the place near Eaton, north of Muncie, Indiana, it was a bit ramshackle. His father kept a hand in, but it was a slower, shakier hand. Maya would be safe there, though. And welcomed. His parents doted on the young, damaged, or abandoned animals. He thought that could extend to a young and abandoned child. She could be the daughter he never had, or better yet, the granddaughter they never had. Cross's aversion to marriage and offspring was another on a long list of issues they had with their incorrigible son. Cross would have lunch with them, leave Maya there for a few days so he could investigate Margot's disappearance and the man who wanted his friend Shanahan dead.

It was too late to call his parents. Like most farmers, they were early-to-bedders and early-to-risers. He'd do that first thing in the morning and then they'd be off on a drive that would take the better part of two hours.

Cross had a beer, watched the news, checked on Maya. He went to bed, slept lighthearted, and dreamt of sand and waves. The dream was hot enough and real enough that he woke up craving a margarita.

'Kowalski?'

'Shanahan,' Kowalski said. 'Nobody calls this early in the morning. Too early for criminals. And that's just about the only people I talk to.'

'Where are you?'

'Matter of fact, I'm in bed.'

'I called your office,' Shanahan said.

'Well, for all practical purposes this is my office. The roof fell in downtown.'

Shanahan didn't know whether James Fennimore Kowalski was talking about a real roof or a sudden dip in finances. It didn't matter.

'I need you to find out something.'

'Is this on the clock?'

'If you want it to be.'

'For you?'

'Yep.'

'What's up?' Kowalski asked.

'Somebody killed a judge yesterday.'

'First I've heard. Your judge?'

'No. Now the police are thinking that the killer wasn't really after me but was after Judge Ghery after all.'

'So they got Ghery?'

'No. Another judge. They've concluded he's just a judge-killer.'

'You want to know which judge,' Kowalski said. 'That'll be in the news real soon. Can't keep a thing like that quiet. Probably on the news right now.'

'I want to know about him and about Ghery. What they have in common. I'll do the work, Kowalski. Just tell me where to start.'

'I'm putting you on hold,' Kowalski said before Shanahan could object.

Shanahan looked around the kitchen. Einstein slept in a spot of light coming from one of the remaining panes of the window. The others were still boarded. The refrigerator hummed. The creaking of the house in the wind was barely audible. The house seemed so empty without Maureen, who had already left for a meeting at her firm's office.

'Judge Wallace Wright,' Kowalski said. 'Big news. Sniper. This is probably your guy. I was in front of Wright a few times. Criminal judge. Middle-of-the-road kind of guy. Not one of the lunatics in robes.'

'What do you know about Ghery?'

'Civil court,' Kowalski said. 'I'll have to do some checking. I don't do civil. You should be breathing a sigh of relief. Ghery was the former owner of your house, right? The obvious conclusion, especially now, is that he got you mixed up for Ghery. Now that he knows . . .'

'That would be the obvious thing,' Shanahan said.

'Sometimes things are what they seem to be,' Kowalski said.

'Yep.'

'Then again, even the paranoids get it right some of the time. You and Maureen want to stay out here with me?'

Out there meant in Ravenswood, a river community on the north side of town, a neighborhood shut off by limited road access, inhabited by folks who liked it that way. It was a great place to hide out. Shanahan thought of Maureen.

'Maybe,' he said.

'Anytime. Bring the menagerie,' Kowalski said then hurriedly added, 'and Maureen.'

'Glad you phrased it that way.'

'Me too. She's a fine woman. You're a fortunate man.'

Shanahan said nothing.

'I'll see if I can find connections between the two judges,' Kowalski continued. 'Could be he just hates judges.'

'Think so?'

'Maybe he's a defense attorney. I could see how he might have developed his obsession.'

'You have a rifle?' Shanahan asked.

He could hear Kowalski's laughter just before the line went dead.

Eighteen

There's really nothing pretty about Indiana as winter approaches. Central Indiana is largely flat. The fields this time of year are barren. With the exception of a few pines, the trees are newly stripped and the sky begins its long, gray season. Maya was as bored with the landscape as Cross was. The desolation, he thought, was conducive to depression.

'You're going to come back and get me?' Maya asked for the third time in an hour, this time with increased anxiety.

'Of course,' he said. 'I'm going to try to find your mother and then we'll both be back to get you. This is just for a few days.'

The phone call was long and the conversation awkward. Cross's mother was suspicious. What was her son really up to? She agreed to watch Maya because Maya was five and her mother had disappeared. It was an irresistible situation for a woman who took in birds with broken wings and diseased, crazy, mangy, feral cats. She would have lunch ready, she told him when he called earlier. Though his father was not nearly so nurturing, he understood why Cross needed their help. He wanted to know what he could do.

'Will you call me?' Maya asked.

'Yes. Every day. Tell you what, I'll call you at noon every single day. You want me to do that?'

She nodded, but she still looked worried.

'Just like clockwork,' he said, trying to reassure her.

She still looked frightened.

'You'll be all right.'

Off the interstate, the roads narrowed and narrowed again. Once in Eaton, where the only landmarks were the grain elevators, he turned north. Just a few more miles. The isolation of

Eaton, like similar communities too far off the interstate throughout the Midwest and South, created a sense of going back in time, a fitting prelude to visiting home.

'Mom is a good cook. And they have cable.'

He should have thought of the farm option earlier. He was behind in his investigations. The trails were cold, but the threats were real. He would be free to do what he needed to do and Maya would be safe in Eaton. Other than the census bureau and Eaton's 1,500 inhabitants, no one knew the town existed. He knew Maya would be lonely, but the momentary anachronism of the Cross farm would do her no real harm.

The house was set back, approachable by a gravel road with little gravel left. The gravel had been dispersed or pushed down deep into the earth. The house itself was difficult to describe, a Victorian without any of the gingerbread, much like many farmhouses – plain to a fault. It was clear the place had fallen victim to benign neglect.

His father did his best. The place was clean and the small lawn had been mown before fall set in. But the gutters teetered precariously on one side. The paint was thin. The chimney looked to be missing a brick or two. The elder Cross was able to keep up with the milking, egg-gathering, and planting in the small garden enough for marginal self-sufficiency. She did what most city women of her generation didn't know how to do. She canned vegetables and fruits, made jam. She made her own soap, blankets, butter, and cheese.

Cross grabbed Maya's hand and led her to the door. As he approached the door, he was filled with dread. Visiting had always been painful to him and to them, but it was worse now. They would never admit it, but they just might need him now. Yet they disapproved of him. A man in his mid-forties, never married, no children. What kind of man could he be? If they knew more they would be mortified. They would one day be forced to accept but resent his help.

He opened the screen door and then the second door. They were both unlocked. His mother came from the kitchen, drying her hands with a towel, and he felt like he was twelve again.

Shanahan spent the morning on the phone, trying to get a list of those applying for and receiving hunting licenses. Not getting much of a response from the office that handed out deer-hunting licenses, he called the attorney-general's office. He talked his way to the top: Jennifer Bailey, whom he'd worked with before she was elected to such a prestigious office and who had paid him a brief hospital visit. She called him back within minutes. He explained what was going on. She was aware of the attacks against the two judges, but thought Shanahan had been ruled out and therefore safe. She was following the case.

'I had no idea,' she said. 'I can subpoena the records, but do you know what that means?'

'No,' Shanahan said, puzzled.

'I'm guessing there are tens of thousands of licenses issued every year.'

'Deer hunting?'

'Yes. Just hunting deer. We get involved from time to time, as you can imagine, with illegal hunting, accidents, and disagreements that end in a shooting. More than a hundred thousand deer are shot each year. The limits are one or two, depending on various things. So it could easily be forty or fifty thousand licenses with muzzle-loaders.'

He took her word for it, though he hoped she was wrong. Maybe the Division of Fish and Wildlife had a lower, more manageable number.

'Do you want me to look for a specific name?'

'I wish I could identify a name or two.'

'So this is a fishing expedition?' she asked.

'A hunting expedition,' he corrected her. 'I'm trying to find him before he finds me again.'

'But you don't think this is about judges?' she asked.

'I'm not convinced.'

'I'm afraid I could only verify a name,' Bailey said. 'I'm not sure I can release the list to you.'

Shanahan wasn't sure it made sense trying to go through a list of 40,000 names to see if one of them rang a bell. 'What if I sit in some state office and take a look?'

She was silent. He knew she was weighing the law, the ethics. He didn't always agree with her, but she meant well, always intended to do right, which was more than he could say for most politicians.

'I'll call you back. You'll be there the next half an hour or so?' she asked.

Shanahan fiddled around the kitchen, organizing the refrigerator, then the cabinets. He'd come to hate winter. Not so much because it was gray and depressing, but because he couldn't take a bottle of beer out in the yard and warm his bones. No wonder old people moved to Miami and Phoenix. The front, back, and side yards of their new place needed work. Unfortunately, it would be months before he could do anything about it.

He could complain to Casey, but it would do him no good. As the old dog grew older, he grew less interested in Shanahan's words. The cat had never been interested.

The ring of the phone interrupted his impatience. It was Maureen checking on him, making sure he was all right and inquiring about dinner. He would cook, he said. She was busy catching up on what she missed while attending to him, which seemed to underline the fact that he had nothing to do.

Jennifer Bailey called immediately after. If he could come downtown, he could sit in front of the computer screen and scan through the names of those holding Indiana deer-hunting licenses. God help him, she said, if the culprit was a hunter from Illinois.

His search for a needle in a haystack would begin in the morning. For now, he'd think about dinner.

Bringing Maya to his parents was a selfish act. So it was a pleasant surprise to see the happiness explode on his mother's face. Just as Cross had undoubtedly disappointed her over the years, he had inadvertently brought her a gift she welcomed.

Ham sandwiches, warm potato salad on the kitchen table. Though he didn't have one himself, Cross's father brought his son a beer. During past visits, rare as they were, his parents displayed a kind of passive interest in living. It was something one did until death. What Cross saw over lunch, what he saw in his parents' faces, eyes, was new energy, a light that illuminated from them through a layer of day-to-day dusty reality.

'How long is she staying with us?' his mother asked.

'I'm not sure,' Cross said. 'We can talk about the details in the other room.' He nodded toward Maya.

'Until he finds my mother,' Maya said. 'She's running away from some people.'

The elder Cross gave his son a look. Concern.

'Would you like some apple sauce?' his mother asked Maya. She nodded brightly.

'It's fresh,' Cross said.

'It's canned,' his mother said.

'But you canned it,' Cross replied.

'I did,' she said. 'So it's fresher than you'll get in the store, I guess.'

Cross remembered. Not only fresher, but she made it from green apples, so it had a bit of bite to it, like his mother.

Afterward, she asked Maya to help her.

Cross went with his father to the hen-house. There was a flutter of feathers when they walked in. The smell of hay didn't quite override the other smells, but it was tolerable. And it brought back more memories, not all of them pleasant. The rooster examined Cross for a moment, deciding whether or not to run him out of the building, deciding in the end not to.

'What's this all about?' his father asked.

'We think Maya is a witness in a murder, maybe after the fact, but a witness nonetheless.'

'Why is she with you? Where are the police?' There was accusation in his voice, suspecting as he always had, and maybe not without reason, that Cross was complicit if not in something deeply wrong, then at least foolish.

'I'm working with the police in Hawaii,' Cross said.

His father shook his head.

His father was a law-abiding man. He had confidence in the system. He believed that the reason Cross was booted off the force was because he couldn't measure up. Another in a long line of disappointments.

'I know how you feel about this,' Cross said, 'but the police can botch things up. I'm working on it in a way that will protect Maya and her mom. If Margot had wanted to go to the police she would have. She trusted me. I need to honor that as best I can.'

There were no chores to be done in the barn now. Cross's dad brought him here to talk. The cleaning and egg-gathering were done in the morning, long before most city folk had their morning coffee.

Senior Cross looked away, scratched his neck. He looked back. Though his gaze was direct, it was soft, understanding.

'She can stay with us as long as you need for her to. What you're doing is good.' He turned, quickly went to the door. Without bothering to turn back, he said, 'You be careful, son.'

Left to his own devices, Shanahan decided to drop in at Harry's place. He brought Casey with him, checking from time to time the rearview mirror as he drove the short distance to 10th Street.

Though it was against the law to bring animals into bars and restaurants, Harry looked the other way when it came to Casey. And now in his older years, the dog was content to find an out-of-the-way spot and plunk down for his ongoing nap.

'Any word on the cowardly sharpshooter?' Harry asked.

'Shooting other people,' Shanahan said. 'Collins thinks the guy is after judges. I was an error.'

'So you aren't special, after all?' Harry laughed. 'Hurt your feelings?'

Shanahan didn't answer. He looked up. There was an attractive judge on television, smiling as she dispensed justice. The sound was off. In fact, there was no sound in the place. What few customers Harry had this afternoon were quietly replaying their pasts or merely contemplating their beers.

'So what do you want?' Harry said.

'Nothing. Just came down for a few minutes.'

'Why?' He was suspicious. He was always suspicious.

'The excitement.'

Harry picked up the remote, flicked through the channels. 'You watching over Maureen?'

'As much as she'll let me.'

The front door opened. A weak light invaded the place. Harry's eyes expressed surprise.

Shanahan turned to look. It was Collins.

'Just talking about you,' Shanahan said as the tall, good-looking cop approached. 'Harry, this is Lieutenant Collins, IPD.'

Harry reached out his hand. They shook. Casey, recognizing Collins' scent, came over to acknowledge the new customer.

'The dog belongs to a blind guy,' Harry said, nervously.

'Looks just like Shanahan's,' Collins smiled. He sat at the bar, next to Shanahan. 'Maureen told me I might find you here. What are you having?' He nodded to Shanahan's drink.

'Ginger ale.'

'Sounds good to me,' Collins said, looking at Harry.

'What's up?'

'A deputy sheriff was shot.'

Harry came back with the drink, hovered. Collins gave Harry a hard look.

'I have no secrets from Harry. It's impossible.'

Collins relented. Harry remained.

'Same MO. Sniper-style. Remington. From an overpass.'

'A moving target,' Shanahan said. 'Either he's getting better or he was lucky.'

'The bullet got him, but it was the crash that killed him.'

'Not just judges. The common thread is the law?' Shanahan suggested.

'Maybe. We're running connections between the two judges and the deputy. Just wondered, though. The name, Tom Reidman, does it ring a bell?'

Shanahan thought a moment.

'Not sure my mind is running on all cylinders, but no. No, it doesn't. You have reason to believe it would?'

Collins shook his head. 'Looking for anything . . . Just in case you're in the loop after all. Hope not. Keep an eye out.'

He took half the glass in one gulp, left the rest. He patted Casey on the head as he stood. 'You're a saint, you know. All the good work you're doing for the blind. Keep it up.' He grinned at Harry.

Harry managed his sarcastic smile, which made him look like the world's oldest teenager.

Shanahan put on his glasses, took his small notebook from his jacket pocket. He wrote: Judge Bradshaw Ghery, alive.

Judge Wallace Wright, dead. Deputy Tom Reidman, dead.
None of the names meant anything to him. Had the killer
moved on?

Shanahan still wasn't convinced.

The ride back was lonely. As much as Cross thought he wanted
a little peace and quiet, it was a letdown. Seeing his parents
again caused him to remember why it was so painful to go.
The world they lived in was so remote to him, farther away
than the physical ninety to a hundred miles. It was more time
than place. Their fixed lives seemed to be disintegrating. His
dad calling him son made it even sadder. Reaching hands
would, in the end, be unable to grasp. Soon, he would be
unable to reach them at all.

His mother had followed him to the car.

'Your sister is coming to stay a few weeks over
Thanksgiving,' she said. 'Will you be able to come up?'

He nodded that he would.

When Cross hit the 465 loop around the city, he chose to
go east. He stopped by Shanahan's place, but got no response
from the knock. The fact that both cars were gone relieved
him of the notion that something bad had happened. He drove
to Harry's.

'What's this, your office?' Harry said to Shanahan as Cross
sidled up to the bar.

'I know, Harry,' Shanahan said, 'it's downright wrong of
me to bring you customers. What was I thinking?'

'What do you want?' Harry said angrily to Cross, while
winking.

'If you'll turn up the heat ten degrees, I'll have a
margarita. If not, make it that weird whiskey that Shanahan
drinks.'

'Weird?' Shanahan asked.

'It is weird, Deets,' Harry said. 'Try getting J. W. Dant
anywhere else.'

'Come to think of it . . .' Shanahan said. He could never
get it any of the restaurants Maureen picked. Or other bars,
for that matter.

'They drink it in England, you know. And a little bit here
on the East Coast and a tiny bit in Indiana. I only order it

for you. Nobody else drinks the stuff. Too much rye in it, I think. Nobody drinks rye.'

Cross took a sip. 'Good,' he said, with a trace of surprise.

'What brings you here?' Shanahan asked.

'Guilt.'

'A horrible reason to do anything.'

'I've not been much help to you.'

'Where's the kid?' Harry asked, demanded.

'In safe-keeping,' Cross said.

'Nothing to do,' Shanahan said. 'The police have it.'

'Yeah,' Cross said, unbelieving. He glanced at Harry, then back to Shanahan. 'I've got to go to the Palace of Gold, you want to come along, look at some naked women?'

'He'll do nothing of the kind,' Harry said. 'What kind of thoughts are you puttin' into that man's damaged head?'

'How about some service, Harry,' yelled the man at the end of the bar near the door.

'How about you payin' rent on the stool, McCormick?' Harry responded, grabbing a bottle from the refrigerator bin, quickly lifting the cap, and heading down toward the customer. 'One beer every two hours barely pays the taxes.'

'You're a helluva businessman, Harry,' the man said, tongue thick, but mind working. 'I got to give it to you. Because of your stellar personality there's this line out the door, all of them waitin' for my stool.'

'It's the cheer that you bring to the place that makes it so popular with the masses,' Harry said. The bottle hit the bar with a thud.

'What's going on with the little girl?' Shanahan asked.

Cross filled him in.

Shanahan asked what he could do to help.

'I should be asking you that,' Cross said. 'I've got a place to go poking around. If you want to stay at my place, please feel free; but I'm not sure who might be dropping by to see me either.'

Shanahan nodded.

Cross felt better about going back to the dance club and pushing some buttons. Maya was out of the line of fire. And who knew whether Fast Eddie and his sumo sidekick were closing in on Margot? If they were, he had to move fast, certainly faster than he'd been moving. The depression of this afternoon's ride home was giving way to a rush of energy. He hated to admit the way it was for him. The game was on, and he was exhilarated.

Nineteen

S hanahan, from time to time, checked the windows, brushing curtains aside, or peering through the slats of the Venetian blinds. He was relieved when it was time to begin dinner. He wasn't bad in the kitchen, perhaps a four-trick pony. A couple of pastas, a bean dish, and then the basic grilled something – steak, pork chop, or chicken breast – with a baked potato. This was his repertoire.

Tonight, he was using a few of Maureen's flourishes. He added fresh basil and green onions and a smattering of olive oil to his own garlic-and-butter vermicelli. Maureen was fine with what he cooked. While she experimented, she never complained about Shanahan's limited menu. Shanahan's theory was that for Maureen, food was a means to an end, the end being wine. The food simply made the wine taste better.

He waited for her, not exactly weak physically, just sketchy mentally. Uncertainty, which did not inhibit his thinking before the shooting, invaded his mind. And it was this mental tentativeness that seemed to move into his movement. Maybe the shot just pushed him further into old age.

Shanahan heard the car door shut. Casey ambled to the door, clearly identifying a known human.

'You OK?' She kissed Shanahan on the forehead.

He nodded.

'You cooking?'

He nodded.

'What do I want?' she asked. 'White or red?'

'Bits of pork sausage in garlic sauce,' he said.

'You make it difficult,' she laughed.

Shanahan could tell that her laugh was strained. It was the bunker spirit that the stalker forced them to adopt. Both

of them felt it. Every move could be their last. And no matter
how determined they both were not to let it get to them,
that they wouldn't let this stalker change their lives, let alone
wreck them, they couldn't keep all the anxiety out or stress
at bay. It wasn't so much fear as it was having to be hyper-
aware.

'A deputy was shot by our man,' Shanahan said as Maureen
poured a glass of red wine.

'You want a beer?' she asked.

'Not yet.'

'Has a thing with authority,' she said.

Shanahan nodded, checked the boiling pasta. He had fine
chunks of garlic wiggling in the oil in the frying pan. He
tossed in the chopped pork sausage. It sizzled.

'So other than a general class of targets, is it random, you
think?' she asked. 'Just finding people connected with the
legal system and shooting them?'

'I think that they all did something to him. Maybe they
were all involved in one event that changed his life.'

She sipped her wine.

'You, a couple of judges, and a deputy?'

'Or a couple of judges and a deputy or me, a judge and
a deputy. Thing is, I don't recall any of these people. I didn't
know Deputy Reidman or either of the judges.'

Cross waited until nine to arrive at the Palace of Gold. The
parking lot was nearly empty. What few cars there were probably belonged to the dancers and bartenders; the Mercedes,
he guessed, to the man who claimed to own the place. At
this time of night, they would likely be set up for evening,
but for the most part, the evening hadn't begun. He could get
some time with the guy before the customers arrived.

The man, whose name Cross found in city records was
Karl Herrmann, was in the front of the house. He talked with
another man who was seated next to one of the stage areas.
The stage was empty. Herrmann had a wide glass of whiskey,
his friend a glass of something clear, vodka, or gin. Herrmann
glanced back at Cross, obviously recognizing him, but neither
pleased or disturbed, judging by the bland expression on his
face.

Cross sat at the bar, ordered Scotch. He ordered Scotch because he was not fond of it, and he would not be tempted to down it. This was as good for the pocketbook as it was for the clarity of his thinking.

Herrmann wore a dark suit with a vest, crisp white shirt, and silver tie. There was something dandyish about him. He apparently brought some of his taste to the club. The brass rails were shinier than Cross remembered them. Huge vases of flowers, lit by spotlights, had been added. Like Herrmann, the place looked spiffy, spiffier than it was before.

Cross sipped his Scotch. He watched the stage. Despite his time with Indianapolis Police Department's vice squad, Cross felt no guilt watching pretty women dancing nearly naked. Like any other job, there were women who did it out of desperation – that was terrible – and there were women who did it because it got them through college, or it got them to the next stage of their lives, or they truly enjoyed the attention.

A few customers showed up. A group of three in suits. Out-of-towners, no doubt. Here on business, but happy to combine a little pleasure. A couple of guys going solo arrived, less well dressed, and sitting apart from each other but close to one of the small stages. In short order, a blonde with long shaggy hair began to dance – mechanically – unhappy no doubt that she had to break in the cold, nearly empty room.

Herrmann stood, shook hands with the man he was talking to. The man followed Herrmann to the back where they pushed open brass-plated double doors.

Cross took another sip, felt the warmth of the whiskey in his chest. Nothing does this like whiskey, he thought. Gin doesn't. Vodka doesn't. Maybe brandy. He watched the ice queen move about under the appropriately blue light.

'So,' Herrmann said, somehow appearing almost magically on Cross's periphery. 'Have you come to enjoy the beautiful ladies or are you determined to play the stereotypical tough private eye?'

'Oh, I'm not tough,' Cross said. 'Just a poor schnook doing his job best he can.'

Herrmann sat at the bar. A drink appeared.

'This is a professional visit?' He raised his glass.

Cross nodded.

'The woman? Is that what you're after?'

'Margot Hudson.'

'And I would know about her because?'

'Because this involves the franchise.'

Herrmann smiled, a thin smile, thin lips. His heavy-lidded eyes squinted even more.

'The franchise?'

'You don't own this place, Mr Herrmann.'

Herrmann's smile remained, but Cross guessed it took a little extra effort to keep it there.

'Well, that's news to me,' he said. 'Who does?'

'I'm not sure yet,' Cross said. He was sure he was right about Herrmann not owning the place, but he wasn't sure what place Kawika Anatelea held in the hierarchy.

'It seems to me, Mr Cross, that you are beating the bushes to see what comes out.'

'You're right about that,' Cross said. 'But whoever is running this operation, the Midwest conglomerate, the East Coast branch and the West Coast, including the expansion into Hawaii – the top dog, that is – is the one pulling the strings and the one the law is most interested in finding and, maybe, just maybe, linking to the Maui murder.'

Herrmann's face was stone. He was giving nothing away.

'Or,' Cross said, shrugging as if it didn't matter, 'doesn't know how Mr Anatelea botched a murder in Maui.'

The reptilian eyelids blinked.

'You remember that movie, *The Mouse That Roared*?' Herrmann asked, slipping off the stool, still holding his drink.

'Yes, I remember.'

'The little country bluffed its way into winning a war against a mighty country?'

'Yes, I said I remembered.'

'That was a movie, Mr Cross. And even if this were a movie, and it isn't, it wouldn't end that way.'

Herrmann clinked Cross's glass, looked at the bartender. 'We're picking up the tab for this warrior's drinks tonight.' He looked back at Cross. 'There's a thin line between bravery and idiocy. I'm terribly afraid you are about to cross it.' He took a couple of steps, stopped, looked back. 'Enjoy the girls.' He left the bar, headed toward the three men in suits, thanking them for coming, and encouraging them to have a good time – a great and charming host.

Cross, long curtailed by little Maya, felt like celebrating a little. A slender and sensuous brunette had taken the stage and why not, he asked himself, take advantage of Herrmann's generous offer? One more drink wouldn't kill him. Or would it?

Two big guys in jeans and sweatshirts came in, oblivious to the girls on stage, oblivious to the bar; they marched instead to the double brass doors and then through them. They knew where they were going. In a few moments, they came back out. They took a long look in Cross's direction and left.

Cross stayed on until midnight. It was an interesting evening and somewhat puzzling. Every other dancer was Asian. Cross liked Asian women as much as he liked women of any other origin. He was, in his way, an equal-opportunity voyeur. For him, beauty existed in all colors, shades, and hues. But it was unusual to see Asians at Midwestern clubs, let alone so many. He wasn't sure what that meant, but he did take note.

'Take care,' Herrmann said pointedly as Cross left.

Maureen was up and out early. A quick cup of coffee together and she was off to the office for a meeting. Shanahan was glad to have something to do. Because his energy was not what it used to be and the weather was uninviting, he'd taken to morning television. The local news with its endless reports of road conditions and the weather was mind-numbing. He found the network morning shows distasteful, but somehow mesmerizing. The cloying sweetness of the hostess made him more sour, and the strange and frightening ability of seduction that Regis and Kelly possessed left him depressed after watching them. Then there were the commercials, which seemed longer than the shows they sponsored. Spending the day in government offices looking at lists on a computer screen seemed downright exciting.

Shanahan was always a little surprised when he went downtown. It was very different from the Indianapolis he returned to in the eighties. It was lively, full of restaurants and shops. Condominium complexes mingled with new hotels. There was a new baseball stadium for the city's triple-A team, a new basketball arena for the Pacers, and talk of a new place for the Colts.

The offices he sought were in the new statehouse buildings built west of the statehouse. One side of the handsome, formal-looking government buildings faced Washington Street, the other the canal area. Shanahan found his way to the Division of Fish and Wildlife to meet the bureaucrat that Jennifer Bailey had contacted. In the tradition that suggests good news is always paired with bad news, Shanahan learned he could take his time going through the list, and that unfortunately the list contained not the 50,000 hunting licenses that Bailey suggested, but 200,000.

Her math was based on 100,000 deer being killed with a two-per-license limit. The truth was that at least one in two hunters failed to bag a deer. This, he thought, might be good luck for the deer, but not so good for him.

Shanahan sat in front of the screen, scrolling down, taking forever to get out of the As. How many Adams were there? And then there were the Browns. There were a number of Hunts and Hunters who were hunters as well. What were the odds that any of these names would mean anything – that he could find this or that needle in this incredibly lengthy haystack? He plowed through to the Johnsons a little after noon. Just the sheer number of Johnsons and upcoming Jones stretching out on the computer screen nagged at his willpower. It wasn't just the boredom, it was the eyestrain. He begged off an afternoon session. He would return the next morning and finish it then.

He stopped at Harry's on the way back.

'Ginger ale.'

Harry shook his head. Shanahan would get no sympathy. Fortunately he didn't expect any.

'I worry about you, Deets,' Harry said. 'You're getting' kind of . . . kind of . . . you know . . . like an old woman or something.'

'I'm getting in touch with my inner self, Harry,' Shanahan said, barely able to keep from grinning.

Harry looked confused.

'Look,' he finally said, 'if I ever say I'm gettin' in touch with my inner self, I want you to kill me.'

'It's all right, Harry. Sometimes, it's important to acknowledge your feminine side. It's OK. Really.'

'Or maybe I'll just kill you.'

'Get in line.'

'What are you tryin' to do, for Christ's sake.'

'I just wanted to see your face turn red.'

'You're treadin' on dangerous ground.'

'Seems so. Now where's my ginger ale?'

When Harry brought Shanahan his drink, he'd decorated it with a slice of orange and a little pink umbrella. Harry smirked.

'I knew it, Harry. I knew it. You do have a feminine side. Sweet. Thank you.'

Cross knew he had poked at some part of a larger, and likely very dangerous creature. Problem was he poked only the part he saw. How big and how dangerous the monster really was he had no idea.

He sat at his computer, glad he remembered to call Maya at noon, laughing when his mother told him that she had completely charmed the elder Cross, had him eating out of her hand as she had literally the mean old goat. He checked the various strip-club sites in various cities that seemed connected, waiting for a response to his perhaps injudicious probe. Would he see Fast Eddie and the sumo again? Or were they just errand boys? How much of a player was Herrmann?

It was clear to him, as it often was in his cases, that he might have bitten off more than he could chew.

He had been prepared for an ambush in the parking lot last night, but he got to his car, drove home, climbed in bed, and slept late without incident. He didn't know whether to feel good that he avoided confrontation or bad because the case was at a standstill without a reaction from them – whoever 'them' turned out to be.

He realized he needn't have fretted. If he had had the earplugs of his iPod plugged in or had the stereo on, which he often did, he wouldn't have heard the slight tinny click of his front gate as it echoed off the concrete walls of his home.

Twenty

The common perception that there are more Smiths than any other name in the US was not debunked by Shanahan's experience with hunters' licenses – Bob's, Jim's, Steve's and Bill's. He shouldn't have been surprised. Smith was Maureen's last name. Not her maiden name, but her married name – she had never divorced – and when she first told him, he thought she was trying to keep her real identity secret.

Then there were the Thompsons, Thomases, and Wilsons. Not quite so many, but enough redundancy that made him sillier and sillier as he traversed to the end of the alphabet. In the end, he had nothing, nothing at all. He left at two in the afternoon with nothing more than he had when he first started. Not a clue.

He called Maureen on her cell. She was listing a house, promised that she would fix dinner, and encouraged him to relax.

'Maybe,' she said, 'this was all a mistake.' Maybe he could help Cross with his case, she suggested. 'If you need to keep busy.'

'Do you believe that?'

'No. But if I believe something else, I'm just too scared to keep on going.'

Shanahan had scanned the neighborhood as he drove back from downtown. And even now, he periodically looked out of the windows on all sides of his house. He wanted to nap, but couldn't sleep because part of him stayed on alert. Every little sound the house or the dog made would send a little dose of adrenalin through his tired body.

Maybe they could go away. Take a vacation.

He called Swann.

'I've got nothing,' Swann said.

'How could he shoot two different people in downtown Indianapolis and nobody sees him?' Shanahan asked.

'We've been asking ourselves the same thing. Early morning, both of them, just before light. Nobody around. He's got a sight. That has to be. You think he's still after you?'

'I do.'

'What makes you think that?' Swann asked.

'I think I was too hot after he missed twice. He went on with his business and he'll come back for me when all of you lose interest. And you have, haven't you? What does Collins think?'

'Collins doesn't let anybody know what he thinks.'

'Forget Judge Ghery for the moment,' Shanahan said. 'What do the other judge and the sheriff have in common? Put me in the equation. What do the three of us have in common?'

'Oops,' Cross said to himself. He got up, peeked out of the blinds in his bedroom to see not just the two toughs from last night, but also Sumo and Fast Eddie, who was following at some distance.

Cross might have faced one or two of them with this advanced knowledge and his pistol. But not four. They were splitting up, two heading for the front door and two walking around to the back. Obviously Eddie and the sumo had told them the layout of the place. Cross had no time. He moved quickly to the secret place. He thanked Maya. He wouldn't have thought about it as a hiding place if it hadn't been for her. He hoped he slipped in before the guys at the rear glass doors could see him do it.

He pulled the wall tight, took a deep breath, let it out. It was a tight fit and the fact that he was claustrophobic wasn't helping anything, but it was better than being beaten senseless, tortured, or killed.

The glass doors in the back weren't locked. He heard them slide open. He heard them walk through the room and up the few steps to the office and the front door to let the others in.

He could hear them clearly.

'He's around somewhere,' a voice said. 'His cell is on the sofa. His computer is on.'

More footsteps. Doors closing, drawers opening and shutting. Curses.

'Hey, he vanished,' a voice Cross recognized as Eddie's said.

'Lift up the floorboards,' said a voice.

'It's a concrete floor, you idiot,' said another.

'Not up there.'

The middle room, kitchen, and bedroom were on wooden floors above a crawlspace.

'There's a shed out in the yard. Maybe he saw us coming. Also, check the crawlspace.'

Someone left.

'Herrmann's not going to like this,' said the voice Cross recognized as the sumo's. Mmmnn, Cross thought. Kawika Anatelea works for Karl Herrmann. That was good to know, though he would have thought it was the other way around. Surely the center of the syndicate wasn't Indianapolis. Maybe Herrmann was just here to settle the Indianapolis club into the fold and would move on. On the other hand, this suggested he wasn't the top either.

'Should we wait until he comes back?' Eddie asked.

'Police may be on their way,' Anatelea the sumo said. 'That's what he did the last time.'

'Maybe he saw us coming and went out the back and over the fence.'

'It's a high fence.'

'When you're scared, man,' Eddie said.

'Yeah, you'd know about that,' Anatelea said.

'You act like this is all on me,' Eddie said. 'I didn't kill Umecki. I didn't let that little brat and her mother get away.'

'If it weren't for you,' Anatelea said, 'there would be no little brat in the first place.'

'Shut up, both of you,' said an unfamiliar voice.

'Herrmann will have us all whacked,' Anatelea said.

'Shut up,' the voice repeated more firmly.

'Nothing in the shed, but a lawnmower, a pitchfork, a spade, and a really pissed-off possum. Got baby possums. Momma possum's got the ugliest teeth I've ever seen.'

'Shut up about possums, will you. What about the crawlspace?'

'Small grill over a very small hole. Nobody could get in under the house without a hell of a lot of digging. A squirrel, maybe.'

'He can't just vanish.'

'Maybe he went out for smokes and will be right back.'

'And we're all in here.'

'I say we vamoose,' the sumo said. 'If he called the police . . .'

'I agree. He's still in the city. He'll turn up. We should work both ends. We'll work Indy. Herrmann thinks Margot may be in Mexico. You speak Spanish, Eddie?'

Mexico, Cross thought. If Margot were known in many American cities and in Hawaii, maybe Mexico wasn't so far-fetched. But where in Mexico? It was a big place. If it was Mexico City and its twenty-two million inhabitants, there was no hope for the bad guys or the good guys.

He waited and waited some more – maybe twenty minutes. He heard people leave. Was everyone gone? Had they left someone behind – just in case he emerged from his hiding place. Cross waited another ten before slowly slipping out of the oppressive space. He moved cautiously from room to room. Surprisingly, they did not destroy anything. And as far as he could tell, they hadn't taken anything. It wouldn't have surprised him if they destroyed his computer, smashed his phone, and generally wreaked havoc. Instead, they left the place as they found it. He wondered if they left prints.

Maybe he could identify the two goons from the strip joint. Maybe he should pay the Palace of Gold another visit. Poke another thumb in Herrmann's eye.

Cross called his Maui police pal, Lonala Kielinei.

'The name of the dead man is Umecki,' Cross said to Kielinei when he answered. 'It's likely that a guy here, a Karl Herrmann, put in the work order. Herrmann claims to own an Indianapolis dance club. I think he's not the top dog.'

'Wow,' Kielinei said. 'You work fast. How did you get the info?'

'Beat it out of them,' Cross said.

'You did?' Kielinei said. 'How many of them were there?'

'Only four.'

'So when do you call for reinforcements?'

'Dozen. That's if they're kung-fu fighters,' Cross said. 'One at a time.'

'Anything else?'

'Isn't that enough?' Cross asked.

'It's good.'

'You know Umecki?'

'No. I'll see if I can track him down on this side of the world. You have anything on the woman?' Kielinei asked.

'Margot? No. Maybe Mexico.'

'Where's the kid?'

'Safe.'

'Are you?'

'Safe? Yes.'

'Talk to you later,' Kielinei said.

Cross clicked off the Maui call. Before he could tuck it in his pocket, the phone rang again – the soft sounds of a tune he couldn't identify. Cross thought it might be his new friend, the Hawaiian cop, calling back. It wasn't. It was Kowalski.

Shanahan had spoken with Kowalski, appreciated his offer of help, but there wasn't anything for the attorney to do. There was nothing for Shanahan to do either. He found no one on the list who had anything to do with him. He told Kowalski that Cross had offered as well – even though he had his own problems finding the mother of a little girl dropped on his doorstep.

'You're just sitting there? Waiting?' Kowalski asked.

'There's no trail,' Shanahan said. 'And the fact is, it may have nothing to do with me.' He went through what he did know about the shooter with Kowalski – chubby, wedding ring, kind of boots. Not much more.

'We have to get you some security,' Kowalski said. 'I told you. You guys need to come stay with me until this blows over. Shit.'

Shanahan liked Kowalski. Kowalski didn't much believe in authority either. But he'd rather piss them off than shoot them. So he took a job as a criminal lawyer, sometimes public defender, to keep poking at whatever powers there were. The renegade attorney who smoked cigars and rode a Harley had helped him and Cross from time to time.

'You have Cross's number?'

Shanahan, after giving Kowalski what he wanted, checked the windows. He looked at his watch, called Maureen. She had things to do, would be back late. He checked the windows and doors and went to the sofa. He felt light-headed, more light-headed than he should, he thought. He turned off the only light in the living room and settled in.

This time Cross waited until ten thirty before heading out to the Palace of Gold. The place was jumping. A different bartender, this time an attractive Asian woman. She poured him the Scotch he nursed while working. He looked around. Herrmann was playing host, moving from table to table. Both stages were occupied with scantily clad women flirting sensuously with brass poles and two-thirds of the seats were taken.

It would be a good take for Herrmann and whoever he worked for. The cover charge alone would pay for the operation. The high-priced drinks were just an extra, including the non-drink drinks the guys bought for the girls in between dances.

Cross wanted to be noticed – he wanted to upset Herrmann and his friends – but he didn't like making scenes. He'd be patient. Sitting in a strip club sipping on drinks wasn't the worst stakeout he'd ever had.

He followed Herrmann's movements. He was smooth, charming, comfortable in his role as host, chatting with this one and that one, calling a girl over for another someone at a table – introducing product to shopper. Cross had to admit that the man was as classy a pimp as he'd ever seen. In fact, he brought a little class to the place just by being there.

Could he be a bigger player than Cross thought? Was he just in Indianapolis, maybe, to bring this Midwestern club on line then move on to the next acquisition or assimilation? He could be a second-in-command.

Herrmann finally looked up at the bar. The only thing that made Cross realize he had been spotted was the slight interruption of the host's movements, his eyes lingering a second too long in Cross's direction. He turned away before Cross could wave.

Cross ordered another Scotch and headed for one of the deuces near the first stage. A slender Asian dancer, not particularly good at dancing, was nonetheless one of the prettiest dancers, perhaps the youngest, he'd ever seen at the club. Sometimes, at close range, there is a hardness to the look of the dancers. There was nothing hard about this one, just a forced, almost frightened smile. Even so, the quality, from a voyeur's perspective, was better. Another sign of new management.

Cross felt a hand on his shoulder.

'I had hoped that you wouldn't become a pest,' Herrmann said, swinging around and sitting in the empty chair.

'I'm a paying customer,' Cross said. 'The cover. The drink. I thought you'd be happy to see me.'

Herrmann gave him a thin smile. His thick eyelids stayed nearly closed, viewing Cross, it seemed, in a very narrow, possibly predatory way.

'You sorry I wasn't home for your friends?' Cross continued. 'Maybe if you'd called ahead . . .'

'You have your affairs in order? Life insurance. Will. That sort of thing?' Herrmann looked up, shook his head ever so slightly at someone Cross couldn't see from his angle.

'I'm pretty sloppy in my personal affairs. The good thing is there's not much of an estate to settle. I haven't got a whole lot to lose.'

Herrmann got up. 'You disappoint me.'

'Oh, wait, wait. I'm guessing you're much better organized than I am, you know, in terms of personal affairs. So my guess is you have a really good defense attorney on retainer?'

Herrmann put his hand back on Cross's shoulder.

'I have several people on retainer,' he said.

'The slave-traders? That's commission, isn't it?'

Herrmann sat down again.

'Maybe I've misjudged you. You may turn out to be an interesting storyteller. You have a story for me?'

'You know, the other night when I was in here, I noticed

you'd changed the dancers quite a bit. A lot of Asian girls. Hispanic girls too.'

'Is that a problem? That's not very worldly of you, Mr Cross.'

'No, I'm more worldly than you think. I worked in vice for a few years, as I'm sure you know. And I've been reading the papers. More than fifteen thousand girls are brought to the US from Mexico and sixteen thousand from Asia each year. Some of them are bought from their families and have to pay off their debt by working in massage parlors and strip clubs and others are taken the old-fashioned way. Kidnapped. They just work for free, right?'

'You have quite an imagination,' Herrmann said.

'Margot's flight was about more than just protecting the kid,' Cross said. 'She knew what was going on. And she didn't like it.'

'I think we knew different Margots,' Herrmann said.

'I thought you said you didn't know her, just of her,' Cross said. Herrmann shrugged, smiled. 'Then she realized how you guys played when she discovered that murder was part of it as well.'

'And you can make the authorities believe this fantasy of yours?'

'What I'm thinking,' Cross said, 'is that your franchise operates in – what – maybe twenty cities? So I get each of those cities to do their own investigation. My guess is that you run a pretty tight ship, but, Mr Herrmann, it's kind of hard to tie up every little detail in every little club of yours across America.'

'You're clever. I can reward clever,' Herrmann said.

'Oh, there would be hard feelings.'

'You're right, Mr Cross,' Herrmann nodded. 'For an ex-vice cop, you are pretty naive and the saddest part of your little plan is that you would rather be right than alive. I'm leaving you now. Have a nice journey.'

As Herrmann left, Cross felt the presence of others. He looked back over his shoulder. The two guys from the other night were standing beside him. They looked happy to see him.

Twenty-One

Shanahan awoke. It was dark. He had no sense of how long he'd slept. Five minutes. Five hours. He felt weak. He struggled to find the switch on the lamp on the table next to the sofa. A dim yellow light spread into the room. He looked at his watch. It was after midnight.

Maureen would have awakened him, made him go to bed. Anxiously, he tried to get to his feet, but it wasn't so easy. There were small, quick pains in his brain and the flashes of pain sent little flares that disrupted his vision.

'Maureen?' he tried to yell. 'Oh, Christ.'

Casey came into the room, studied Shanahan as if trying to determine if there was anything he could do to help. Without opposing thumbs and a little more heft, there was little the dog could do.

Shanahan managed to get to a sitting position. He was terrified. He believed she was in trouble. He wasn't sure he could do anything – *anything* – about it.

Shanahan tried to get up twice. He failed twice. He counted to ten, took deep breaths, tried to push the pain away. Fortunately, getting up was the hard part. Once he was up, he could walk, though at a snail's pace. He called out Maureen's name as he went toward the kitchen, though he didn't expect an answer.

He flicked on the lights in the kitchen and went to the phone. Cross's number was still scratched on the tablet on the wall. He dialed.

'If it isn't Pete and Repete,' Cross said, looking up at the two guys.

'Let's go outside and look at the moon,' one of them said.

'That's very sweet of you, but I haven't finished my drink.'
Cross's cellphone went off, but he wasn't allowed to answer.
One ham-fist pushed his arm away.

'We're heading out, now.'

'You want to make a scene, right here in front of all these
nice people?'

'It's a sad thing when a drunk has to be removed by force,'
said one.

'And the more you resist, the more drunk they're going
to think you are,' said the other.

'We'll talk outside, where it's quiet, right,' Cross said,
doing nothing more than trying to slow down the process so
he could think of a plan of action that didn't put him alone
with these two guys.

'Sure.'

'Let me ask you a question,' Cross said, quickly trying to
think of one.

Arms lifted him from his seat. Cross could see Herrmann,
off to the side, watching, hoping it would go well. Herrmann
gave him a look that Cross read as 'See, if you'd only done
what I told you.'

'I can walk,' Cross said. He looked from side to side to
see if there was any possibility of escape. Christ, he thought,
the sumo Anatelea was at the front door, which was where
they were headed. He figured that had to be better than the
back door.

'OK, give us the keys to your car,' the guy said.

'Nice touch,' Cross said, trying to walk sober even though
he was sober. He thought about yelling out that these girls
were part of the international slave trade; but even if he were
heard above the din, it would add to their belief that he was
in fact inebriated. 'You'll have to find them yourself. But be
careful, I'm easily excited.'

'We'll get them outside,' the other guy said.

'Tell me,' Cross said. 'In addition to dancers, you have a
whole cadre of prostitutes at massage parlors, right? And
they live in locked basements. And the real young ones? This
is all done through lucrative private contacts?'

They didn't answer.

'Come on. You're not really as dumb as you look.'

They stopped for a moment. One of the guys stepped in front of Cross. His smile was bigger than his face.

'You want your last dying wish?' He grabbed Cross and pulled him toward the door as the other pushed from behind. As they approached the front door, the sumo held it open for them.

Now the four of them moved away from the door, to the dark side of the building.

Shanahan looked. There were no messages on the answering machine. There were no papers on the kitchen table. That's where she would leave them if she were home. She would leave the laptop there as well. He went to the bedroom. Nothing had been disturbed. He went back into the kitchen, not sure how long he could remain conscious.

He called Swann's number. No answer. He called Cross. No answer. He waited for the voicemail to kick in. He wasn't sure how much longer he could stay conscious or coherent.

'He's got her,' Shanahan said, then realizing he didn't have much time and that Cross could not be of immediate help, he dialed 911.

'I think there's been a kidnapping or an accident,' Shanahan said.

'Which is it?' came the voice.

'I'm not sure.'

'Where are you?'

He gave the wrong address, then corrected himself. He felt himself losing consciousness.

'Who are you?'

'Shanahan. Tell Lieutenant Collins the guy has Maureen. Tell him that, will you?'

'This Collins is a policeman?' the voice asked.

'Yes.'

'Are you all right?'

'No.'

He said, 'Goddammit,' as he fell to the floor. He also knew who the stalker was. He *knew* him, met him. He didn't understand the guy when he said it. He understood the words, but it didn't make sense. Now it did. He wasn't the only one who knew the guy. Maureen knew her captor.

*   *   *

'Howie Cross, you old pervert you. How the hell are you?'

The group stopped the forced march. It was Kowalski.

'I haven't seen you since prison,' the attorney continued as he came up to them.

'Your friend's a little tipsy,' one of the guys said.

'Well, that's not surprising,' Kowalski said, reaching into grab Cross's shoulder. 'I'll get him home. It won't be the first time I've had to play nanny.'

'We got him,' the guy said.

Kowalski reached in his pocket, pulled out a cigar, bit off the tip, and spit it out.

'No, you don't,' Kowalski said. 'I got him.'

One of the big boys stepped toward Kowalski, who kicked him hard in the knee. Cross could hear the tendons rip and the bones break. The guy went down like a boulder.

The sumo moved around behind as the third guy reached for a weapon. Cross elbowed 'Pete' in the nose, grabbed him by his hair, and pulled his head down as Cross's knee came up. Kowalski approached Anatelea.

'You ever killed anybody?' Kowalski asked.

'You'll just be another in a long line,' the sumo said coming toward him warily.

'Good, I won't feel so guilty.' His body language implied a kick, but as Anatelea moved down to catch the anticipated foot, Kowalski head-butted him, catching him just above the eyebrows.

With two unconscious, Kowalski joined Cross, who was kneeling in front of the writhing man with the broken knee. Cross had the man's pistol.

'Who's the big boss?' Cross asked.

The man didn't say anything.

'Who does Herrmann work for?'

Kowalski squeezed the guy's knee.

'I don't know,' the man said.

Kowalski pulled the man's wallet and checked it, taking his driver's license, some little pieces of paper and cardboard, and leaving the rest. He went to the others and did the same.

'I didn't get to see much of the show,' Kowalski said.

'How long were you there?'

'Well, I was there before you were. You tend to leap before you look. And I thought, what the hell, I like naked women. What did you say that got the dandy all upset?'

'I told him I knew about his slave trade,' Cross said.

Kowalski smiled, lit his cigar.

Two customers came out. They looked over, probably disturbed, Cross thought.

'These guys got in a fight,' Cross said. 'You know, looking at these girls, they get their testosterone up to dangerous levels. We called the police. Everything will be all right.'

The conscious man moaned.

'You're not going to be safe tonight,' Kowalski said. 'Need a room?'

'I can probably stay at . . . the old man's place.' The third guy might be missing a functional knee, but he still had ears.

'Out of the frying pan . . .'

'That particular boogey man won't expect a guest, should he decide to pay a visit. And these guys don't know where to find me.'

'I'll get the background on these guys and get back to you,' Kowalski said.

'Thanks,' Cross said. He went back toward the door of the club.

'Where are you going?'

'Say goodbye to Herrmann,' Cross said. 'Say what you will, but he is a charming host.'

'Wait,' Kowalski said. The man on the ground couldn't see Kowalski's smile. 'You haven't told me what to do with these guys. You want me to kill them? It's easy enough to do.'

'No. But we know where they live if we need to,' Cross said. He went inside, saw Herrmann talking with Eddie by the bar.

'Thanks for everything, Karl,' Cross said to Herrmann. 'You have health insurance for your employees, I hope.'

Outside, Cross saw Kowalski on his motorcycle. The engine rumbled with that bass Harley sound. He had waited until Cross returned. He was laughing. 'I just wanted to make sure your car starts.'

'Or blows up.' He surveyed the damage – two unconscious

bodies and one groaning mess. As he got into his car and keyed the ignition, he thought to himself, 'Now what?'

He wasn't sure what he had accomplished this evening.

He drove out of the lot, watching Kowalski rumbling out on to Northwestern.

Shanahan drifted in and out of the corporeal world. His limbs were belted to his side. He could feel the oxygen mask. As his body was jostled about by the ambulance hitting rough patches on the road, he focused on two things: Maureen and the man who had kidnapped her. He was unable to talk, unable to tell them. Again he was powerless.

Cross felt alive. The cold night air swirled in through the crack he kept in the window of his borrowed Trooper. He had cut back east on Kessler Boulevard, taking the gentle, smooth curves that wound through Crow's Nest, once a very pricey neighborhood, and still beyond most mortals' means.

He remembered he'd had a call. He checked his phone. It was Shanahan. He didn't like driving and using the phone, but it seemed odd that Shanahan would call so late. He checked his voicemail before calling.

'He's got her.' Shanahan's voice was weak. 'He's got her.' That was it.

Instead of turning from Kessler to Westfield Boulevard to get home, he stayed on Kessler until it hit Emerson Way. At this time of night, it wouldn't take long to get to their home.

'He's got her,' Cross repeated in his mind. That could only mean Maureen. He checked the rear-view mirror. No head-lights behind him. He wondered how many thugs were on Herrmann's payroll. Probably only the two, along with the sumo. Certainly Eddie wasn't hired to break bones.

Twenty-Two

Shanahan's place was dark. Cross knocked. Waited. He heard Casey bark. Again he knocked. Quiet. He took his cell out of his jacket pocket, called Shanahan's number. It rang until the answering machine kicked in.

This wasn't good. He looked around, out into the darkness. No inspiration. He decided he'd go inside. Someone could be hurt. It took him only a few seconds to pick the lock. Inside, Casey came up to him, then turned and walked away. He wished he had a weapon. He flicked the switch he felt on the wall beside the front door.

Nothing in the living room was disturbed. Slowly he made his way around the house, checking closets. All seemed in order. The kitchen was in order. He turned on the basement light from the top of the chairs. This was where the unsuspecting in all the movies get whacked. The wooden steps creaked and the light cast shadows. He reacted so violently to the sound of his phone ringing that he nearly tumbled the rest of the way down.

He fished for his phone, flipped it open. The screen indicated a private call.

'We've got her,' the voice said.

For a split-second he was thinking Maureen. Why would Shanahan's stalker call him? How did they get his cellphone number? And the caller said *we*.

'You've got who?' Cross asked. Margot? he wondered. Maya?

'If you give us the kid, we can work things out for both of them.' The voice wasn't Herrmann's. It wasn't Eddie's. 'Not looking to do anybody any harm.'

'What makes you think I have any kid?'

'Don't toy with us. You played your last hand wrong. You

make happen what we need to have happen and we can forgive and forget.'

'So who are you?' Cross asked, moving down the steps. 'You're not Herrmann, not the sumo, not Eddie, not a member of the dynamic duo . . . so we have a new player. Where are you on the organization chart?'

Cross moved around the basement. No one here.

'Mr Cross. Do you care for Margot?'

'Are you a messenger boy or are you someone who can make decisions?'

Cross was stalling while he finished casing the basement. Shanahan's car was in the driveway. Maureen's wasn't. If Shanahan went out to find her, why was the car still there?

'You're playing with lives,' the man said.

Cross didn't answer. Seemed as if he was playing with several lives.

'You have to give me the girl.'

'I don't even know if you have Margot,' Cross said. 'Is she there?'

'No.'

'Have her call me. Let me talk to her,' Cross said.

'Leave the police out of it,' the voice said.

'It's not the police now. Not if you have Margot. It's kidnapping. A federal case. Right? You know that.'

Silence.

Cross started back upstairs. He would call Collins when he got off this call.

'I know your connections,' Cross said. 'I know what you're doing. Except for you I know who the players are – not just here but in Hawaii and across the United States. So if you harm Margot, how are you going to find the kid? If you think I have the kid and you kill me, how are you going to find the kid? Have Margot call me.'

Cross flipped his cell shut. He took a deep breath. He flipped it open again. As a former member of the force, he knew the main line to the police. He punched in the number, asked for Lieutenant Collins.

'Not on duty,' the operator said.

Of course he wasn't. It was late. He asked her to connect

him to Swann. Same story. Her tone seemed to imply, 'What did you expect? They have lives too.'

He put his phone in his pocket. He drove over to Harry's bar.

Rarely ever busy, it was certainly in decline at this hour. Allowed to stay open until 3 a.m. according to Indiana law, Harry stayed open until midnight, about an hour after the last customer stumbled out the door.

Harry sat at the far end of the empty bar with a glass of some kind of whiskey. The flickering light of the television flashed across his lifeless face. Shanahan's best friend hadn't seen him come in. He looked down into his drink, serious maybe, depressed possibly. Sad, somehow, either way.

He must have heard Cross's footsteps. He looked up.

'You're out late,' he said.

'Have a problem. A couple, actually.'

'Go on,' Harry said, getting up, lifting up the slab of bar that allowed him entry into the sacred area. 'What do you want?'

'Whatever you're having,' Cross said. 'I need to get hold of Swann.'

'OK. What's up?'

'Got a call from Shanahan saying Maureen was taken.'

Harry looked up angrily.

'And?'

'I can't find Shanahan. His car is at home. He's not.'

'What else did he tell you?'

'That's it. Short and not so sweet.'

'That stubborn old son of a bitch,' Harry said, putting the glass of whiskey in front of Cross. 'He has to do everything his own goddamn self.' He went back to the register, came back with a sheet of paper with phone numbers scrawled on it in different inks. In the middle of the list was the entry 'Swann', with two numbers, one with a 'w' and one with an 'h.' Harry pulled the phone over to Cross.

Cross punched in the numbers. After several rings, the voice of a woman.

'Lieutenant Swann, please?'

'Who's calling?'

'Tell him it's about Shanahan.'

Cross heard muffled voices, then finally, 'Yeah?'

'Maureen's been grabbed, Shanahan's missing.'

There was a long pause. 'I know.'

'You know?' It wasn't a real question. It was disbelief.

'Shanahan is in the hospital. Word's out on Maureen. We're looking.'

'Christ,' Cross said.

'I know what you're thinking. We are doing what we can. It's midnight. This is Collins' case, but I promise I'm on it. All of homicide is on it.'

'Do you have anything at all?'

'No. Just that now we know Shanahan's involved. It wasn't the killer mistaking him for a judge. We're trying to figure all this out. What's the connection? Shanahan. The judge. The sheriff. We don't know. We're focused, though. I promise.'

Murder was all in a day's work for the police. It was what they did. They had to eat, sleep, lead a life. But knowing that didn't help when it was someone you knew.

'Cross?' Swann asked.

'What?'

'What's going on at the strip club?'

'What do you mean?' Cross asked, not knowing whether or not he wanted the police involved and wanting also to know what they knew.

'I'll be straight with you. Be straight with me. You were out there. Some guys ended up in the hospital.'

'It's a case,' Cross said. Maybe he should at least get it on record. 'I'm working a missing-person case.'

'Who?'

'Margot Hudson,' Cross said. 'She used to dance there.'

'Who are you working for?'

'I'd rather not say,' Cross said.

'I'd rather you would,' Swann said.

'Me. What hospital is Shanahan in?'

'Methodist.'

'How is he?'

'Unconscious.'

'How come?' Cross asked.

'Don't know. They're trying to find out.'

Harry was waiting, leaning over the bar, inches from Cross. He was frustrated hearing only one side of the conversation.

Cross explained the situation, in between Harry's angry expletives.

'I'll be at the hospital in the morning,' Cross said. 'They're not going to let us in now.'

'You think not?' Harry said.

'Harry, it won't help, you being there and creating a scene.'

'At least I'll be doing something. Who is this asshole that kidnaps somebody like Maureen?'

Nothing to be done tonight, Cross thought, at least about Shanahan and Maureen. He called the guy who owned the car lot. He wasn't asleep, but he wasn't happy that Cross wanted something so late at night. What Cross wanted was to relinquish his Trooper in exchange for a fast but nondescript car. He wanted to do it tonight. He stopped by his home to pick up his binoculars and a few things he might need to defend himself. It was 2 a.m. before he drove off the dark lot in a 2000, slightly beat-up black Saab sedan. Cross filled the tank at a twenty-four-hour gas station on his way to the Palace of Gold.

The lot was full. He parked across the street in the parking lot of a store that had closed much earlier. He found a spot in the darkest part of the lot, where he also had an angle on the club that enabled him to see the front door and the side door. Both were lit – the front far brighter than the side, but he would be able to recognize anyone who left the club. He kept the engine running to keep warm and the windows clear.

Cross was thinking Herrmann, but changed his mind when he saw Eddie leaving by himself a little after 2:30 – a halfhour until closing. This was perfect. If Eddie was a dead end, Cross probably had time to swing back and pick up Herrmann, who no doubt had to close the bar, settle with the girls, and count the money.

Shanahan was back in his nebulous world, drifting from space to space and time to time. This time he was not so much in any of the worlds, but observing them, traveling between them at will, and bringing with him the knowledge of what brought him here.

When he went in search of Maureen, there was nothing but an endless maze of hallways as if he were in a huge old house or old European hotel. She drifted just ahead of him, slipping around a corner or up a stairway as his brother had in his dreams.

It was an impossible search, he thought. He could not see the future. And he could not see clearly, it appeared, anything he had not once already observed. He knew her abductor. He could picture him as he was when they met. Harmless then. He knew then that man had once been a decent human being who after the sorrowful loss of his son, Maureen's son, sank into despair, then violence.

By the time Shanahan met him, he had found God and abided by Maureen's wish to be with Shanahan. All Shanahan could think of was that the man found the violent side of God, the Old Testament God, and was about punishment and retribution.

But who would know this? Only Maureen and Shanahan.

The inside of Shanahan's brain lit up. A lightning storm. It was painful, startling. He could feel his body jump. In each brief flash, Shanahan saw images, his brother being carried to an automobile. A Nash, he remembered. He smelled ash, something burnt. There had been a fire in the bedroom.

Flash, damp sheets, warm body, his entering another, feeling both lost and one with her, the sensuous flow of his body into hers. Dying explosions. The scent of sweat.

Flash, the boot in the puddle, accompanied by the sound of the splash, and, oddly, the smell of pine. Flash, Maureen's face, an unknowable expression on her face, a mask. Was she dead?

'We've got him back,' said the voice, not sounding particularly victorious.

'For how long?'

'I don't know.'

'Are you thinking surgery?'

'No, that would compound the problem.'

'We wait?'

'Keep him on the meds . . .'

'Do we have a code on him?'

'No,' the voice said, then in almost a whisper. 'He goes off again, though, we let him go.'

'Crap,' Shanahan thought. He couldn't go now. He was the only person who knew who had Maureen. What he thought, though, was that this wasn't about Maureen so much as about him. He wanted Shanahan dead. The others? He didn't know.

He tried to open his eyes. It worked. He could see the dim light on the lamp over his bed. He saw the plastic tubes, felt the plastic tubes. They were everywhere. This was getting tiresome. He would tell them now. Tell them who had Maureen. He moved his head, but it would only go slowly, very slowly. Eventually he scanned the room. There was no one there. He couldn't see the hallway, but there was a deep sense of quiet all about him.

He couldn't sit up. He couldn't move his arms more than a few inches. The plastic down his throat prevented him from calling out. He was tired. So tired. He fought sleep; but it won.

Twenty-Three

Because it was late night and there were few cars on the road, the trick was not to let Eddie know he was being followed. There were dark stretches on the road that angled toward downtown. Cross turned off the headlights, hoping a cop wasn't lurking. Downtown, as the traffic picked up, he turned the lights on.

He watched as Eddie pulled into the parking lot of a somewhat refurbished motel. This was good. It was harder getting around in the high-priced hotels. Eddie got out of his Nissan Altima, tie undone. Cross thought, for a guy used to driving a Maserati and probably much better accommodation, this must be a comedown.

Cross parked on the street. At this time of night, it wasn't a problem, and he followed Eddie. The way Eddie walked suggested that while he was in some control, he probably had more than the legal limit to drink. He walked, looking forward only. Just trying to get where he was going.

Cross saw Eddie's inebriation as a plus. Generally, physical responses were slower and they talked more.

Cross didn't want a confrontation outside or in the hallways. He wanted to get the guy in his room. He doubted Margot was there. It was just where Eddie crashed. But it might also be where the sumo crashed. Cross wanted Eddie alone.

Cross waited until Eddie was out of sight. He went to the hotel lobby. There was a skinny man in glasses at the desk, putting aside a *People* magazine. He looked up, a question on his lips.

'Guy just came in?'

The clerk again posed a question without speaking. The lift of the eyebrows, the Mona Lisa smile.

'Left his lights on.'

The clerk nodded. Cross watched him punch in 209.

There were only eight floors. 209 was the room number. Cross went to the rack that held all the brochures about what to do in Indianapolis. He was by the front door and his back was to the small lobby. Eddie breezed by on his way to the parking lot. Cross used the stairway, easily found 209. He checked the door. Eddie made life easy. Maybe he was forgetful. More likely he was lazy. He didn't want to have to open the door when he returned.

Cross went inside. Only the bedside lamp was lit. An expensive-looking suitcase was on the metal stand, not quite closed. A couple of pairs of expensive shoes were on the floor, left where he had taken them off. A half-empty bottle of Gray Goose vodka was on a table by the upholstered chair. All indications were that he'd been there a couple of days. A quick glance in the bathroom made it clear Eddie was the only guest in this room.

There was nothing in the room that suggested any clues to Margot's whereabouts or more information on the business he was in. Just a book, *Blink*, about how to size up a stranger in two seconds, presumably helpful to the intimidation-impaired.

Cross had done all of this quickly and to the left of the door so he wouldn't be the first thing Eddie saw.

Eddie came in, went to the bed, pulled off his sport jacket, turned to head toward the closet, saw Cross.

'What's your first impression?' Cross asked.

Eddie blinked slowly. He was farther gone than Cross had imagined. His ability to size up anyone would take considerably longer than two seconds.

'Hi, Eddie,' Cross said, realizing he wasn't going to get an answer to his question any time this century.

'What are you doing here?'

He wasn't that upset. Merely annoyed.

'I came to get Margot,' Cross said.

Eddie shook his head.

'You don't understand.' He tossed the coat toward the chair, but it caught only the arm and slithered to the floor. He sat down on the bed.

'Explain it to me. We have time,' Cross said. But he didn't believe what he said. Eddie could pass out at any time. Cross went over, pulled him off the bed. 'Come with me. Let's make some coffee.'

Cross pulled Eddie into the bathroom, where the tiny Mr Coffee resided next to the sink. He put the pre-bagged coffee into the top, filled the well with tap water, and flicked it on.

'You guys have Margot, right. Everybody knows that, right?'

Eddie shook his head.

'Eddie, I was called on the phone – on my cellphone, Eddie. Only you had the number.' He shook Eddie by the shoulders. 'Right? And they told me they had Margot. So, let's just agree about the things we know to be true.'

The coffee pot spurted and hissed. Two small cups at the most. All for Eddie.

Eddie nodded. 'OK.'

Cross was afraid Eddie would pass out on his feet.

'And they wanted me to know where she is so I could talk to her about Maya, right?'

Eddie shook his head.

'I'm not that drunk.'

'No, I know. That's what I mean. You can make decisions. You're not somebody to be pushed around. You can decide how best to get Maya.'

'You fuckin' don't understand shit,' Eddie said.

'I understand this, Eddie. I know you care for Margot. I know you don't want to see her or the kid hurt. Right?'

Eddie nodded. Cross continued.

'I know you didn't know what you were getting into when you signed on with these guys.'

Eddie started to fade. Cross slapped him. Hard. A flash of anger crossed Eddie's face, but went sad and slack in less than a second. Cross poured coffee into a water glass. 'Drink.'

Eddie drank. His muddy, bloodshot eyes wandered.

'Eddie, they're going to kill all of you. Margot, the girl and you.'

'They promised, you know . . . they just want to have an understanding with everybody. An agreement, that's all.'

'You believe that?' Cross pushed the glass back up to Eddie's lips. He sipped.

'How can I know? It's a chance. Goddammit, it's a chance.'

'Who does Herrmann work for?' Cross asked.

'Herrmann works for Herrmann.'

'This guy? This guy, who runs a club in Indianapolis?'

'He can run things from anywhere. His son is here, working for some drug company. His grandchildren are here. He's a family man.'

'Where's Margot?'

'I don't fucking know. If I did, I'd get her out of here. I'm along for the ride. I'm here because if I wasn't I couldn't help at all.'

'I know cops here and in Hawaii, Eddie. We can put these guys away. I just need to know where Margot is.'

'Jush Margot?' he looked at Cross with a sly, drunken grin. 'You know where the kid is.' He thought for a long moment. 'I thought you did.' Now a broad smile. 'Where is shheee?'

'Why don't you get me drunk,' Cross said, dumping out Eddie's coffee and grabbing the second glass. 'You can drag it all out of me.' He guided Eddie to the bed, sat him down, poured a substantial amount of the premium vodka in each glass. After a toast Eddie gulped.

'Who's the dead guy?' Cross asked. He took a sip, placed the glass on the bedside table. Smooth. Maybe there was something to expensive vodka.

'Whah?'

'Who's the guy in the trunk in Maui?'

'Dooby.'

'Dooby who? Dobby Umecki?' Cross asked, taking Eddie's glass just in time. Eddie's chin suddenly dropped and he drifted back until gravity overcame the most minimal resistance.

Cross checked his wallet, copied down the charge-card numbers, then frisked the sport jacket. In the day planner, he found phone numbers. Karl H's work number and cell number. That could come in handy. He also copied numbers that appeared to be scrawled in the book near Karl Herrmann's.

Cross looked at his watch as he crossed the hotel lobby on his way out to the street. It was 3:15. He might still be able to catch Herrmann. It took a while to get the customers out, a little while longer to count the money.

The streets were deserted. Cross spotted a police car turning into Meridian, to cruise the Circle. As Cross left the downtown area, a Yellow Cab made its way into it with two passengers. The stragglers. Maybe Indianapolis was no longer Naptown, but if this little city in the middle of America was an all-night town, Cross never saw it. And at this time of night, it was no man's land.

He turned right on West Street, drove through its various reincarnations until he reached the club. The lot was empty except for an anonymous sedan and a big, dark Mercedes that was being driven to the front door. Cross slowed, pulled off to the side, turned off his lights.

The Mercedes stopped. Herrmann, in a long overcoat and hat, came out of the club. The driver, either Pete or Repete, whichever one didn't suffer the broken knee, got out of the car. He left the driver's side front door open. Herrmann said something to the man, got in. And drove slowly out. Cross waited to see what the other guy was going to do. Would he follow his boss like a good bodyguard?

Apparently not. He lit a cigarette and walked slowly toward the last car in the lot. Cross pulled back out on the street, letting the Mercedes get almost out of sight. This was going to be tougher. Quite likely, Cross thought, Herrmann was sober. On the deathly quiet narrow road, he could tell if someone was following him.

Then it struck him. Had he made a mistake? Followed the wrong person? If someone were holding Margot somewhere, it wouldn't be Herrmann himself. It would be someone in a lower pay grade. His moment of regret passed. Kowalski had the addresses of all the boys. He had their drivers' licenses anyway.

They hadn't gone far when Herrmann turned left on a small road, Golden Hill Drive, opposite Crown Hill Cemetery. Cross hung back. It was too intimate. A small, elite neighborhood, hidden in a not so elite neighborhood. It had narrow streets that curved back into themselves. Cross lost him. He turned off the lights and cruised through the quiet, dark neighborhood.

Off to the left he saw tail lights. They disappeared as the garage door slowly hid the car. Cross noted the house, the address on Totem Lane. He waited, uncertain what to do next. He saw the lights come on, then go off.

What the hell, he thought. He flicked on the interior light, checked for Herrmann's home phone. He flipped open his cell and punched in the numbers.

A hoarse but female voice answered.

'Karl, please,' Cross said.

'He's not here. Who is this?' she asked in a tone that bordered on outrage.

'Yes, he is. He just got home.'

'What?'

In muffled tones, 'Some man wants you. He knows when you got here. What's going on?'

Cross couldn't hear the answer. But he saw a light go on in another room and a shadow pass in front of the translucent curtains.

'I've got it, Laura,' Herrmann said. The phone clicked.

'Yes?'

'I've got your grandchildren. I'll trade them for Margot.'

'Mr Cross, I like your sense of humor,' Herrmann said. 'I just wish you weren't such a pest.'

'I'm sorry about your boys,' Cross said.

'Now you see that's why you are going to lose in this little engagement, you operate within a set of moral guidelines. It's a serious handicap.'

'Karl, that apology wasn't all that sincere,' Cross said.

'You don't understand. You see, I would go after your grandchildren. Little Maya is a case in point. And while I am fond of you – or perhaps I just find you amusing – I'll have you killed.'

'Aren't you just a little afraid that all of this is recorded?'

'No, Mr Cross. I'm not. Look out your window.'

A very large .45 was aimed at Cross's head. He heard the doors of another car close. There were two of them.

Twenty-Four

A dim light crept in through the single window in Shanahan's hospital room. He guessed it was light in advance of sunrise. The other bed in the room, the one nearest the door, was occupied by a snoring man. The bed was empty yesterday.

The machines Shanahan was attached to appeared to be working properly. He could feel the plastic in his throat. It was unpleasant. But he felt stronger, more alert. That has to be a good sign, he thought, despite the panic he began to feel as he remembered what brought him here. He felt around the bed, found a plastic device that had a button. He pushed it.

'Well, I was just coming in to see you,' she said in a voice that sounded like she thought she was talking to a puppy. Her hair was dyed blonde and blown dry in homage to the era of Farah Fawcett.

Shanahan grunted, mimed the motions of writing something down on paper. But she was preoccupied with a vase of flowers she had brought in with her.

'Look what I have for you,' she said happily. 'You are loved!'

If only he had a gun.

She put the flowers down on the wide windowsill, her back to Shanahan's gesticulations. She plucked the card from the bouquet, turned around, smiled, and read with great cheer, 'Either you die or she does.' She looked at him with horror in her eyes. 'No signature.'

He locked into her gaze and again mimed the need to write something on paper. She nodded. The air was gone from her balloon. She scurried from the room. He didn't need to have a signature. He knew who sent it.

She came back quickly.

'I called security,' she said, handing him a spiral notepad and a ballpoint pen.

'Take this thing out of my throat,' he wrote, resisting the use of the f-word as an adjective. 'Call Lieutenant Collins at IPD. Tell him that Bobby Smith has my wife.' He added 'NOW' in big letters.

She ran from the room.

Sometimes things end like this. He was walking through a field toward a barn. Off to the left was the farmhouse. It was boarded up. The barn ahead of him leaned precariously to one side. Walking beside him was Sumo. He had come to the other side of the car to take the passenger seat and direct Cross to the destination, where he was sure to be shot. Now he guided Cross to some point on the farm where, no doubt, he would be killed close to where his body would be left. Why shoot somebody and carry his dead weight a hundred yards? The thug that was at the club with Herrmann trailed a good twenty feet behind, carrying a shotgun.

They had relieved Cross of his gun, but not his knife, which was sheathed at his ankle, far enough down where an inexperienced frisk would not find it. Margot was probably here somewhere, alive or dead, he couldn't be sure. Whatever happened, Maya was probably safe. His parents would see that she was taken care of, one way or another. He hoped with all his heart that he hadn't put them in jeopardy as well.

What few trees there were no longer had leaves. They were spindly as if the forces that wore down the farm wore them down as well. The ground was strewn with old rusted tools, a roll of rusted barbed wire. The sky was a mix of grays, deep blues and blacks. It was too cold to rain, Cross thought.

'This place is enough to depress a guy,' Cross said. The ground was rough and uneven. Perhaps Sumo would trip and shoot himself . . . well, at least trip.

'No, no,' Sumo said. 'You are very lucky.'

Cross spied a rake about fifty feet ahead – off to the right. It was a risk, a big risk, but having nothing to lose boosted his confidence.

'Why is that?' Cross asked, crowding Sumo so that he would bear right.

'Because I'd like to pull off your fingernails or disembowel you; but the boss wants a murder-suicide.'

'Thinking ahead, I like that in a guy. But listen, who gets murdered?' He knew the answer before he finished the question. She was here. Somewhere close.

If he didn't get the timing right he'd be dead. So would Margot. Even if he did, it might be enough.

Survival of the fittest, Cross thought, going over Herrmann's philosophy of why Herrmann would win. It seemed as if being civil was all an act anyway. Herrmann was no different than the President, no different from the heads of oil companies. It's just that we fall for the civilized act.

They were coming to the rake. Cross let his body touch Sumo, who instinctively moved just far enough to the right. Cross looked up briefly. 'You ordered buzzards, how thoughtful.'

Sumo looked up, Cross stomped the fork of the rake, it came up like the booby-trap it was. The handle didn't strike Sumo in the middle of his face, instead landing on the side of his forehead. It didn't put him down, but it caught him enough off-guard so Cross could wrench around and with the full weight of his body jam his elbow in Sumo's face.

It wasn't enough. Sumo grabbed him, threw him to the ground, and his overweight body was instantly on Cross's chest. He couldn't breathe and it didn't help that a fat fist crashed into his nose.

'You got him?' came a call from farther back than Cross imagined. He looked back. The guy had stopped to light a cigarette.

'Under control, don't you worry your pretty little head,' Anatelea said.

Cross brought his leg around, putting his foot within reach. He pulled out the knife and plunged it one side of Sumo's lower back. He aimed for the kidney and he was pretty sure he got it.

Sumo moaned. Cross recognized the state of shock that took over Sumo's mind and body. Cross rolled him off and moved behind him, using the big body as a shield. He reached for his own weapon that was in Sumo's coat pocket, but Sumo was lying on it. He reached for Sumo's. Got it. The guy who wasn't supposed to worry fired. The shot cracked the sky like thunder. Cross heard the pellets hit Sumo's well-padded flesh and the fluttering of crows' wings as they escaped the trees.

Cross looked up, then ducked. It was a double-barrel. He was right to do so. The pellets hit again. This time he felt the sting on the top of his head. Now it was time, Cross rose up, aimed his weapon as the guy tried to pull his out from a shoulder holster.

Cross fired. The guy dropped to one knee, lifted his pistol. Cross fired first by a split-second and apparently hit the guy's weapon. It exploded in his hand.

Cross walked over. The guy's hand was gone.

'Just kill me,' the guy said. 'Just fucking kill me.' He pulled off his jacket. He ripped his shirt to try to create a tourniquet. He looked up at Cross. He was looking for help. He wasn't looking to die.

'Won't be long,' Cross said. The blood gushed out faster than gasoline at the pump. Cross looked away.

The doctor came, removed the impediment to Shanahan's speech and explained that because the healing process had begun, there was the natural scarring of the tissue.

'This is good. Unfortunately there is also swelling near the scarring,' he said, again searching for layman's words. 'I was worried about that, if you remember. I didn't want you to leave; but you did.'

'I don't have time for this,' Shanahan said. His throat hurt. Each word seemed to scratch it as it came out. Even swallowing was painful.

'There's only so much room in there, Mr Shanahan.' He pointed to Shanahan's head. 'We've given you something to reduce the swelling. If it continues to work, you'll remain conscious. If we can keep the swelling down long enough, you will likely recover.'

'If not?' Shanahan asked, catching Collins' arrival in the corner of his eye.

The doctor shook his head.

'You need to disconnect me.'

'I'm afraid you're going to have to stay,' the doctor said. 'You saw what happened last time.'

'I can't,' Shanahan said. 'Give me the medicine, I'll take it.'

The doctor looked perplexed, turned, then turned back. 'Actually, I can make you stay.' He left, dodging the tall, sharply dressed cop.

'Every time I see you,' Collins said, 'you're in your pajamas.' It must have been Shanahan's look. 'I'm sorry, now's not the time for cute.'

'Bobby or Robert, I'm not sure, but a guy named Smith is the shooter. He has Maureen.'

'And you know this how.'

'It could only be him,' Shanahan said, trying to move too far, forgetting for a moment he was still attached to the machines in other places. He reached over, grabbed the remote, buzzed her. 'Because all of this is over Maureen. He's her husband.'

Collins eyebrows rose in unison.

'She's legally separated,' Shanahan said. 'She had a restraining order out on him. He moved out of our lives. We thought that was it.' Shanahan knew he was rushing the explanation, but right now how he knew it was Bobby wasn't important. Explaining was a waste of time. 'Check out Robert Smith against Judge Wright's cases in the last few years. Then see if that poor deputy sheriff was the one assigned to deliver either the separation papers or the restraining order. Bobby's out to kill anyone he thinks took Maureen away from him.'

Collins nodded. 'Especially you.'

Shanahan picked up the remote again, buzzed.

'Let us handle it,' Collins said.

'You haven't handled it. Find out where Smith lives, works.'

'Bob Smith,' Collins said quietly, shaking his head.

'Bob Smith, Robert Smith, Bobby Smith, all of them,' Shanahan said. 'I want to know where he is.'

Collins nodded.

'If you have trouble working up a sweat on this one . . .'

'I won't. And with kidnapping, we've called in the FBI.'

'Don't get her killed,' Shanahan said in a dismissive tone. He found the remote and buzzed. He wanted out of there.

The silver sky glistened. The sun nearly penetrated the clouds. Cross found his weapon. He wiped his prints off of Sumo's gun, put it in the big guy's still warm hand, and squeezed off another round. He looked around the ground to see if he left anything. Nothing. Not even footprints. The ground was too cold, too hard.

Cross went inside the barn. It hadn't been used in years, but it still smelled of straw and manure. There were half a dozen stalls, probably for dairy cows. He stomped the earthen floor to see if there was a trapdoor somewhere. He found nothing. Engine parts were strewn about, and there was an old tractor in the corner. He climbed a rickety ladder to check out the loft. Nothing.

He checked the back of the barn. There was an old well. More farm implements, broken and rusted. The wind had stopped. It was cold and quiet.

The smallness of the barn and the smallness of the house indicated that this was never a rich man's farm. Just some folks getting by, pretty much like his parents. It wasn't uncommon to see these abandoned farm houses. A big agri-company bought the productive farm for the land, leaving the house to be reclaimed by nature.

The doors and windows were boarded up – plywood covered the opening and then was held firm by one-by-fours crisscrossing the panel. The nails were rusted in place. Cross went around the back. There was what some called a storm cellar – and others a root cellar – with doors that opened almost at ground level. The door was padlocked. But the lock still had its metallic sheen. The keyhole in the lock was shinier still from recent use. The lock was new.

He didn't want to shoot it off because you could never tell which way the bullet would go and if it went straight down it could hurt what was below. It was a good lock. He wasn't sure he could pick it. He remembered seeing a rusted tire iron in the barn. He headed back, his curiosity putting a little speed in his step. He walked by the boys. Sumo had

stayed dead. And the other guy had given up the ghost. The
eyes were open and completely blank. Cross was glad the
suffering was over. He just didn't want the guy to live. Would
he pay for that lack of charity?

He found the tire iron. He went back to the lock. After
ten minutes of fruitless labor that had him perspiring in the
cold, he had to give up. He had gained new respect for the
lock manufacturer. Cross walked back to his car, driving it
to the back of the house, backing it up close to the cellar
doors. He took the snow chain from the trunk of the Saab,
wrapped it through the door handles, and connected the hooks
to the mainframe underneath the car's back bumper.

He got in, put the gearshift lever in low, slowly but firmly
pulled forward. Cross could feel the jolt when the chain went
taut, then the strain as the car seemed to inch forward. At
one point the car stopped, then lurched forward. In the
rearview mirror, he could see the cellar doors fly off their
rusty hinges.

Twenty-Five

S hanahan put on his reading glasses and, needle by needle, disengaged himself from the tubes that delivered medicine and food. Removing the tube that ran up his penis was particularly uncomfortable, physically and psychologically.

He didn't believe for one moment that the doctor could legally keep him there unless he could prove to the court that Shanahan was a danger to others. Of course, Shanahan thought, given the situation and his mood, he was a danger to Bobby Smith. He hoped he was, anyway.

He had just found his clothes in the small closet and began dressing when the doctor returned. He left immediately. Shanahan thought he'd be coming back with orderlies. The doctor returned alone, carrying an opaque plastic bag.

'Your belongings,' the doctor said. He set the bag on the bed and continued talking as Shanahan dressed. 'You know, you are in good shape for a man of seventy. But you are a man of seventy. Your body doesn't recover as quickly as it did when it was twenty or forty or even sixty. You understand?'

'I have to do this.' Shanahan's anger provided the energy.

'You may feel good now,' the doctor said, 'but . . .'

'I have to do this,' Shanahan repeated.

'Before you put your shirt on, let me apply an antibiotic on the needle punctures.'

Shanahan relented.

Afterward, as Shanahan finished dressing, the doctor removed Shanahan's .38 from the bag. He held it with two fingers at the tip of the handle to avoid contamination.

'With your personal belongings,' the doctor said. 'We removed it from your back. Haven't seen a growth like that before.'

Shanahan looked warily.

'We don't know what to do with it, so you'll have to take it with you.'

Shanahan nodded a thank-you.

'Why aren't you letting the police handle this?'

'They don't seem to be getting the job done. And now the killer has . . .' It was always awkward. Maureen wasn't his wife. He felt odd saying lover or even partner. And girlfriend seemed decidedly teenage. 'Has someone I care about.'

'In your bag is an envelope containing some antibiotics and anti-swelling pills. Follow the directions. Monitor your body. If you need to rest, rest. Be a hero, but don't be a fool. Otherwise you will not accomplish what you set out to do.'

Cross could see the particles of dust settling even in the cold light. He stepped down and the wood gave some. He would have to move slowly. He hadn't thought to bring a flashlight. Each step he took into increasing darkness he took tentatively. The danger he faced was in the darkness. The place smelled of rotting wood. Cold, yet damp.

With the padlock on the outside, if Margot was here, she was likely here alone.

'Margot?' he called out.

Nothing. This was foolish. It was too bad he no longer smoked. He would have had his trusty Zippo. He climbed back out of the hole and into the light. Maybe there was a flare in the Saab. If not, maybe there was one in the other car. He went over to the Saab. Nothing inside. Nothing in the trunk that would bring light to dark places.

Then he remembered the poor guy whose hand was shot off was a smoker. He had to have some form of fire to light up.

'Sorry, old man,' Cross said, feeling around in the coat pockets of the still bleeding corpse. He found a cheap pink butane lighter. He looked around. In the goon's rented car were fast-food sacks and cups. He squashed several of the sacks, nudging them down inside the cups. He found a long stick and pierced the bottom. When the dense paper was lit, he would have a torch.

Pleased with himself, he went back, waited until he was most of the way inside before he created the fire.

Low ceilings. Shelves. Plenty of them. Empty. The room full of the strange dancing shadows created by the flame. He saw a wooden door. It was latched and locked, with the same brand of lock as the one earlier.

'Margot?' he called out. If she was here, she was behind the door. 'Margot, it's Cross.'

He heard a knock on the door.

'Howie?'

The voice was faint, fearful.

'Get back from the door,' Cross said. 'I'm going to break it down.'

Closer investigation told him it would do no good to kick it in. The door opened into the room he was in. He had to think about it.

'Maybe not,' Cross said.

The flames flickered, faded, died.

The chains wouldn't reach this door. He took out the little pink lighter. He struck it. He ran the tiny flame around the edges of the door then down the door and along the wall. The wall was made of field stone. The lighter flickered. There wasn't much gas left. He searched the wall with his eyes and hands to find a stone that would give. He found it. The cement that held it was turning to dust. He pushed and pounded the stone – about the size of his foot and about five or six inches thick. It dislodged and fell at his feet. He could put his hand through the opening.

The scent of excrement that was evident in the cellar now escaped and nearly overwhelmed him.

'Margot?'

'I haven't gone anywhere,' she said.

Cross tried to pull another stone free. It wouldn't give so easily. He reached in and pulled at the stone next to the one that fell free and it too crashed back. He stroked the lighter again and let it shine in the opening.

He saw her face. Only briefly until the flame went out for good. Her eyes were tired. She looked like an old woman. That's what he saw in that instant. The light keeps dying, he thought. You have to work hard to keep the light going.

'Is Maya OK?' she asked.

'Yes.'

Cross used both hands on the stone that refused to budge before. He pulled it free, and then the one next to it. He continued until he had a hole large enough to pull her through. She was barefoot, but wore an overcoat several sizes too big.

She was almost without weight. Though he could only make out her shape in the darkness, he could tell she could barely stand. He led her toward the light and walked beside her up the steps into the cold air.

'She's OK? Where is she?'

'Safe. In good hands,' he said.

He moved her to the passenger side of the Saab. He opened the door, guided her in. He got his first real glimpse. She was drawn, pale, with hollow, ashen eye sockets.

He started the engine, turned the heat up as high as it would go. He backed up until he had room to drive forward. He drove over the lawn and past the bodies.

'How long did they have you?' he asked as they pulled on to the road. She had glanced toward the carnage and looked back with a question. 'Forget it,' he said. 'How many days were you locked up?'

'I have no idea. There was no day. It was all night.'

'Who took you there?'

'An Asian guy and two big guys.'

'You knew the Asian guy, right?'

'Yes. Kawika Anatelea.'

'He knew your daughter saw the murdered man?'

She looked surprised. 'You know about that?' She shook her head. 'I'm sorry I got you into this. I just meant for you to watch over Maya. That's all.'

'Maya's OK.'

'These people,' she said, pausing, searching for words, 'you have to be careful.'

'How many are involved?' he asked. They were now on the back road that would lead to the highway.

'Just the three of them, I think. I don't know.'

'You know a Karl Herrmann.'

She nodded. 'That's who I was coming to see. I thought he could straighten this out. That's why I came here. I dropped Maya at your place in case I couldn't strike a bargain.'

'You couldn't?'

'No.'

'So there's four, not three, and that still doesn't count Eddie.'

'Eddie doesn't know what he's doing.'

'He does now, Margot.'

'Where are we going?'

'My place. Get you cleaned up. Get you some food, then we'll get you into a hotel, where you can lay low.'

'Can I see Maya?'

'Soon.'

Cross still wasn't sure they were out of trouble. Herrmann, even though his only other henchman was significantly disabled, could easily call in more of his goons if he had them. Who knew what kind of army he had?

'What was that about? Back there?' Margot asked.

'You know Anatalea got pissed at the big guy and they had a shoot out. They killed each other.'

She looked at him. He couldn't read her face.

'Forget all about it. Did you leave anything in the room? Anything that would identify you?'

She didn't answer for a long time. He thought maybe she didn't hear him.

'No. They took everything. Even my clothes.' She grabbed her coat. 'Just this. They gave me this.'

This may have been her time to die as well. They bring him out, shoot him, use his gun to shoot her. Who knows?

The heat in the car was kicking in.

She moaned in pleasure. She leaned back against the seat and window. Asleep in moments.

Shanahan had met Bobby Smith once. He came by the house looking for Maureen. This was a few years ago. He behaved. He was in his 'God is Love' phase then. Apparently his beliefs evolved into the views of the vengeful Old Testament God – an eye for an eye. He was making everyone pay. Every person who he thought stood in the way of getting her back. Shanahan was high on the list. But after two misses, he took out some minor players and was now back, focusing on his first target.

Shanahan was ready to go. He didn't know where, but he couldn't just stand still. The only thing that changed was that – now – he knew who was after him. But the where-abouts of Bobby Smith, the stalker, was still a mystery. Yet it was clear that Smith had no such problem with Shanahan. He knew where to find him whenever he wanted. The flowers found the right hospital at the appropriate time. The stalker was still stalking.

Did Smith have all the advantages? Shanahan thought the stalker held most of them, but not quite all. Knowing that Smith knew his every move meant he could predict, with some accuracy, that Smith would respond to Shanahan's move home. Shanahan wouldn't gamble with Maureen's life. Certainly hers was, in many ways, more valuable. But he couldn't contact Smith. Smith would have to contact him. Smith knew that. And if Smith wanted to be sure that Shanahan was dead – if it wasn't in the news – he'd have to see the corpse himself. Up close and personal.

Shanahan would go home. And wait.

Cross left Margot in the warm car while he went into Target on West 38th to buy some essentials. He marveled at playing the same role for her as he had for her daughter. Clothing, shoes. He did it the easy way with sweatshirts, jeans, tennis shoes. Toothbrush, makeup. What else did women need?

She woke up when he opened the door. He tossed the bags in the back seat.

'I didn't give you up,' she said.

'I know. I called Eddie.'

'You what?'

'I was trying to find you.'

'How did you know about Eddie?' She was both worried and surprised.

'I know many things about you now. I was trying to find you. I knew you were in trouble. Figured you needed help.'

She went quiet.

'When can I see her?' Margot said.

'When we're sure we're not followed,' Cross said, as he pulled his Saab along the curb. Margot followed as Cross moved somewhat cautiously up the steps, across the small front yard, through the gate, and to the front door.

'How's she handling it?' Margot said, once they were inside and Cross was sure the place was secure.

'She's definitely your daughter,' Cross said. 'You know where everything is. Get cleaned up, we'll get you some food and a place to stay.'

'Why not here? I need to sleep.' Her tone was zombie-like. She asked. She wanted the answers, maybe. But expectation was low.

'Here isn't safe. I think we'll be all right for an hour or two until Herrmann learns his men are dead.'

'What did you mean she is definitely my daughter?' she asked as she headed toward the bathroom.

'Independent. Charms the birds out of the trees and then gives them the cold shoulder. Like you, she can handle anything.'

'Except being by myself,' she said and shut the door.

That was probably the worst torture of all, Cross thought, Margot locked in a room – all by herself – in the dark.

Cross heard the water running.

Now what does he do about Herrmann? The police? He went into the kitchen to put on some coffee. He looked at his watch. It was barely mid-morning, yet it seemed as if the day should be ending. It occurred to him he hadn't slept in – what, forty hours? He hadn't eaten in nearly that long. He wasn't hungry. He wasn't tired.

He was impatient for the coffee so that he could add caffeine to the testosterone of killing and adrenaline of fear that coursed through his body.

Maybe he should just kill Herrmann. Then it would all be over. It wasn't a reach in logic to think it would be in self-defense. But Cross knew enough about the law to know that it didn't work that way. The law required he go to them. And Cross knew enough about the law to know that wouldn't work either.

Cross's cellphone emitted an identifiable tune. He looked down. It was a private call. He didn't answer. He'd wait to read the message. It could be Herrmann. Unable to reach his lieutenants, he could be calling to see if the intended victim picked up. Cross didn't want him to have that information yet.

Cross dialed his parents. They would have been up for hours. His mother answered. After some polite inquiries about the day, he asked to speak to Maya.

'I'm calling early, sweetheart,' Cross said, 'because I may not be able to check in at noon. Is that all right?'

'Sure.'

'Are you having a good time?'

'I gathered eggs this morning and I fixed them for breakfast,' Maya said.

'You fixed them?'

'Yes. It's easy, silly.'

'Good.' Cross moved toward the bathroom, opened the door. Margot was soaking in the tub. Her body seemed so thin, so pale. Still she was beautiful. Her eyes were closed. 'I have a surprise for you,' he said to Maya. He gave the phone to Margot, left the two of them to talk. He went out, closed the door.

The coffee should be ready, or ready enough.

Karl Herrmann. Karl Herrmann. Karl Herrmann, Cross thought. If we can make him gone, all is back to normal.

Twenty-Six

Getting Casey and Einstein food and water was first on the agenda after letting the old dog out. He again checked the rooms to see if anybody had been there, tested the locks on the windows and doors. He checked his watch as if he expected Maureen to come home at a certain time.

How was Smith treating her? Was she already dead? No, Shanahan didn't think so. He wanted her back. He didn't want to kill her at least until he showed her what he did to those who kept her away from him. He believed that. He wanted to believe it.

He paced until he was tired. He sat on the sofa, impatiently waiting for the killer to come get him. Instead, the phone rang. He moved to the kitchen, pulled the receiver from the wall unit.

'Yeah?'

'This is Collins.'

'What do you have?'

'We're on our way out West Washington Street. We have a tip that your man is holed up there with a woman. Thought you'd want to know.'

'Thanks,' Shanahan said. 'How far out?'

'Almost in the next county,' Collins said. 'Listen, we've got all the pros out on this one. The SWAT team. Top medical team. We're doing it right.'

'That's good.'

'We'll keep you up to date. We'll be careful, I promise.'

'OK,' Shanahan said. 'I'm going now.'

He went into the living room. He checked his .38. It was still loaded.

'If you don't mind, I need to get some sleep too,' Cross said. She had already climbed in bed. He was taking off his shirt.

They grabbed a bite at a downtown eatery earlier and regis-
tered as a Mr and Mrs in the same hotel where Eddie stayed.
He didn't tell her that. 'Sleep, Margot, that's all. You're safe.'
'I don't want to be safe,' she said. 'Not that way.' Her
smile was weak. 'More than sleep. Please.'
'You need to rest.'
'You think you're being noble? You schnook. I need you
here in bed close to me. I need to feel you. I need to have
a body next to me.'
'Shhhhh,' he said, knowing she meant more than just two
bodies touching. 'Later. Maybe. If you want to.'
'This isn't about you,' she said. 'It's never been about you.'
'You did say a body, didn't you?'
She nodded. 'Don't feel bad. Not just any body.'
He went into the bathroom, showered. When he came back
into the bedroom, he thought she was asleep. He climbed
in, naked, beside her. She moved toward him, her warm
naked body pressing back against him. It wasn't until she
was in a deep sleep that he was able to untangle himself,
roll over, and find sleep for himself.

Shanahan waited. It had been roughly ten minutes from
Collins' phone call when he heard the lock to the back door
being picked. He moved, not quickly, but surprisingly steadily
to the stairway, seeing Smith's cameo against the shade of
the back door. Casey followed.
    Downstairs, Shanahan put Casey in a storage room. He
stood in the middle of the basement. Above him he heard
the lock finally give. He heard Smith move across the floor
above him. He was walking softly, but the wood floor creaked
his location. It was clear he was checking each room.
    He would be down soon. Shanahan moved toward the back
of the basement. He had a clear view of the steps. There
would be no discussion. In Shanahan's mind, this wasn't
going to be a negotiation.
    Shanahan had been in a war. He had killed before. But it
was only now that he understood what it meant for blood to
run cold – to be a cold-blooded killer.
    'You weren't fooled for one moment,' said the voice at
the top of the stairs. 'You know, I thought you were the kind

of guy that would meet me head on. That's the kind of guy
Maureen would leave me for. A *High Noon* kind of guy who
would walk down Main Street . . .'

Shanahan lifted the .38. He steadied his aim with his other
hand. He could see Smith's boots on the landing. He recognized them. If he needed more proof, he had it.

'. . . not hide in the cellar like a rat.'

There was a silence. Smith took one step down. Waited.

'Oh, I see,' Smith said. 'Fool me once, fool me twice, that
sort of thing. Well, listen, old man. I could have some dyna-
mite, just toss it down there. It would all be over.'

Another step.

'Shame is: If I should die, you wouldn't know where to
find Maureen. Or Maureen's body, if you don't find her in
time. So we have to talk, you and I. Maybe we can find
some reason not to kill each other. That's what you want,
isn't it? To kill me?'

Another step. Shanahan could see Smith's knees.

'You sure you want to play cat and mouse with her life?
Maybe you don't love her.'

Smith was a third of the way down stairs.

'You know,' he continued, 'I don't need to be the one to
actually kill you. I just need you dead. You could shoot yourself. Or maybe I'll just go upstairs and start a little fire.
Maybe pour some gasoline down the stairway.'

Shanahan felt the gun in his hand go off.

'Jesus fucking Christ,' Smith said. His legs went out from
under him. He slid halfway down the steps on his back. He
turned in flailing desperate movements to crawl back up the
steps. Shanahan had hit him somewhere in the leg. Shanahan
fired again, catching Smith in the shoulder. Smith couldn't
use his legs to propel himself. Now he couldn't use his arms.

Shanahan moved toward Smith, who moaned, turned,
raised his gun, but his arm couldn't stay up, the gun fell
from his hand.

'A man like you who found the Lord, should you be cursing
like that?' Shanahan asked.

'That was another foolish thing. You put your trust in
something. A woman. God. You believe in something with
all your heart . . .

'So you just needed to get even?' Shanahan said.

'Nature. Survival. Territory. Wanted what was mine. Had to win it.'

'You lost it a long time ago,' Shanahan said.

'What if you'd been me? What if Maureen left you for me? You would just let her go?'

'Where is she?'

Smith shook his head. 'No, you can't have her either.'

Shanahan shot him in the other shoulder.

'Jeeeeezus. You are a tough old man. I didn't think you had it in you. You know, we're more alike than I thought. Look, I don't care if I die,' Smith said. 'I just knew one of us had to. And you don't have her either. You'll live the rest of your life without her.'

'All of this because she didn't want to be with you? Get beat up?'

'She did want to be with me. I was getting back on my feet, getting better. She would have come back, but you poisoned her mind. You and them, you . . .' The words he would speak were apparently too disgusting to utter. His mouth clenched shut.

Shanahan pulled up a wooden crate. Sat down, looking at Smith, who was stretched uncomfortably on the wooden steps.

'I've got all the time in the world,' Shanahan said.

'No, you don't,' Smith said. 'You don't. You really don't. You know, if I met you under different circumstances, I'd like you.' His face brightened, morphing into some young guy on a lark. Almost innocent. Not meaning harm. 'We could have been pals.'

'I wouldn't have liked you. Guys who beat up women . . . *you know* . . . just not my idea of a man.'

'Listen, old man, I was born all screwed up and life just screwed me up a little more. Losing the kid to God, losing Maureen to you.' The other, angry Smith was back.

'Where is she?'

'An awful lot of blood,' Smith said looking down at his leg.

Shanahan nodded. 'Back's bleeding too. You'll be gone pretty soon. And if you're not going to talk, I might as well just cut out your tongue. I see you got a hunting knife right there on your belt.' Shanahan stood, leaned down, took Smith's gun, slid it across the basement floor. Felt his pockets, removed the cellphone. He felt a wave of dizziness. But he plucked the knife from its sheath. 'Quite a hunter. Prepared for anything. Were you going to skin me after you shot me?'

'I was going to mount your head in my den.'

'That would be about the scariest thing anybody had on their wall.' He leaned in toward Smith.

'You wouldn't,' Smith said as Shanahan got closer.

'What are you? Not even fifty?'

Smith didn't answer.

'Doesn't matter how old you are. Some guys are old at sixteen. And you, however old you are, you're just a kid. A punk. A worthless bag of baby ego. Cut out your tongue? Easy. What I've seen in my time . . . Not a problem. Cut it out. Feed it to the dog.'

'She's in the garage.'

'What garage?'

'Your garage.'

Shanahan got up, grabbed Smith by his boots, pulling him down the steps amidst loud screams and protests. Once off the steps, Shanahan grabbed Smith's gun and went up to the landing and out the back door, through the short yard between house and garage, and through the door. He looked around, listened.

'Maureen?'

He looked up, saw the cord that pulled down the ladder to the storage space above. He reached up, grabbed the cord, pulled it down. He unfolded the wooden ladder, and climbed up into the darkness. He bumped his head on the low ceiling. His hand found a chain that connected to a fixture that held a naked sixty-watt bulb. It clicked on, almost blinding him. In a second or two, he found her.

Maureen was tied like a rodeo calf. She was on her side, a tarp beneath her. She was blindfolded and her mouth was sealed with duct tape. She didn't move. For a mind-numbingly horrid moment, he thought she was dead. He knelt down. When he touched her, she moved.

Shanahan undid the rope. She squirmed. Hope returned. He took off her blindfold. Her eyes opened wide, no doubt unable to see who this was in the first light she had seen in a long time. He pulled the tape off her mouth.

'Well, you sure took your sweet time,' she said, getting her breath. As always, she wanted to keep it light. But it had to be a struggle. For them, being intimate meant losing the intimacy.

'There was a game on. I thought I'd wait until there was a break in the action. Anything hurt except your pride?' he asked. It was an effort; but he was able to contain his feelings.

'Where is he?' she asked, slowly rising up to a sitting position.

'In the basement.'

'Dead?'

'Bleeding. Did he hurt you?'

'Look, it's like I've slept in these clothes.' It was a rare, vulnerable, embarrassed Maureen. She had done more than slept in them.

'When was the last time you ate?'

'We'll get to that. I need to clean up.'

He reached for her.

'Oh, about the food. Priority number one and a half.'

He helped her up. She was unsteady at best. And he wasn't much better off.

In the kitchen, Shanahan called 911 and then Lieutenant Collins. Maureen went to the bathroom. Shanahan went to the basement. Smith was still conscious. He hadn't moved. Probably couldn't.

'Are you going to kill me?' he asked.

'I was. You're lucky she's alive.'

'Lucky isn't a word I'd choose.' Breathing was an effort. 'Would you have cut out my tongue?'

Shanahan went back up the stairs without answering.

'We found his SUV,' Collins said. He stood in Shanahan's living room. Maureen had poured herself a second glass of wine. She sat on the arm of the overstuffed chair Shanahan occupied. A fire was in the fireplace. Casey had plopped his bony body down in front of it. 'We found the rifle.'

Shanahan nodded. He knew there was something else on Collins' mind. He wasn't in a celebratory mood.

'Why don't you say what you came to say?' Shanahan asked him.

'Glad Maureen's all right.'

'Keep talking,' Shanahan said.

'Smith's pistol wasn't fired, yet he has three wounds. One that went into the front of his knee, the other two in his back.'

Shanahan nodded.

'Every bullet very carefully placed to minimize bleeding,' Collins said.

'Yes. No need to make a mess.'

Collins smiled. 'He was trying to get away from you.'

'Wouldn't you?' Maureen asked.

'Did I mention he was shot in the back?' Collins pressed.

'Maybe he was shooting over his shoulder,' Maureen said.

'Were all these shots in self-defense?' Collins asked, not taking his eyes off of Shanahan.

'Defending my house and the people in it,' Shanahan said.

'I know,' Collins said. 'I'm not sure how it's going to look.'

'He shot a cop and judge. He tried to kill me twice. He kidnapped Maureen and seemed willing to let her die. You think I care how things look?'

'I'll do my best,' Collins said.

'How are you doing on reducing the city's murder rate?' Shanahan asked.

'You don't know the half of it,' Collins said, shaking his head. 'Two bodies out on a farm just inside the county line. A couple more yards and it would have been on some other county's stats.'

Twenty-Seven

It was dark when Cross woke up. A dim light was on in the chair by the window. Margot sat, looking at a newspaper, smoking. She was naked, but had the extra blanket from the closet draped over her shoulders.

'You haven't gone out, have you?' Cross was worried. He hadn't planned on sleeping later than Margot. What if she'd gone out and run into Eddie? That was going to happen, but he wanted to control the situation.

'No,' she said, indifference in her tone.

Shock maybe, Cross thought.

'How long were you in that room?' Cross asked.

'How could I tell? No sunrises. No sunsets. When can I have Maya?'

'When it's safe.'

'How do we make it safe?'

Cross got out of bed, reached for his jeans. Maybe it was the distance he perceived between him and her that prompted this touch of modesty.

'By locking up or eliminating Karl Herrmann.'

She looked down. Uninterested.

'He's the top of the food chain, isn't he? The chief slave owner?'

She laughed, not that she thought it was funny, but that it was absurd in some fashion.

'Tell me,' Cross said, fastening his jeans at the waist and grabbing his shirt.

'I appreciate your helping me out with Maya. And for getting me out of this mess. It's time for me to move on, Howie. Where's Maya?'

'Not so easy.'

'Why is that?' she asked.

'It's all about you. I know that. But now I'm worried about Maya. And, not to be too selfish. I'm worried about me. Stayin' alive, as the Bee Gees said.'

She looked up. Her eyes showed no life; but Cross didn't doubt for a minute that she was checking the angles and hiding places, like a cat in a new house.

'Let's go talk to Eddie,' Cross said.

'What?'

'Let's talk to Eddie.' Cross looked at his watch. 'It's nine. My guess is he's still in his room.'

She looked up at him. The first real expression he saw on her face was surprise. Or was it curiosity. He thought she might have almost smiled.

'Get dressed,' Cross said.

'A new side of you,' she said.

Cross slipped on his shoes. He put his pistol in his belt at the back.

'We're going together?' she asked.

'Sort of.'

She dressed. He noticed her taking odd glances at him, as if trying to figure something out.

Before they left the room he told her she would knock on the door. It was recessed so it was possible for Cross to remain out of sight, but well within hearing distance and close enough to intervene. He told her not to go in. Cross was sure Eddie wasn't smart enough to check the hallway.

'What do you want me to say?' Margot asked.

'Doesn't matter. Just talk.'

Cross wanted to know how involved Eddie was. Was he some poor pigeon in over his head or was he a player?

Except for a dim light over the door of each room, the hallway was dark. Eddie's room was on the same floor, the other end. Cross walked closely behind her. She looked back once, her face asking if he really wanted to go through with this. He nudged her forward.

'This isn't like you,' she said in a loud, hoarse whisper.

At Eddie's door, she looked at him again, giving Cross one last chance to change his mind.

Cross nodded for her to go on.

She knocked.

A muffled 'Who is it?' could be heard.

'Open up, Eddie,' she said.

There was a long, long pause before the door opened.

'Margot!' Eddie said. 'Get in here.'

'Can't make that commitment, Eddie. Not until I get some answers.'

'I went along for the ride to protect you,' he said. 'I was the one who kept you alive.'

'I thought Maya was the one who kept me alive. The witness, remember? Anyway, it's over. Herrmann's boys are dead and somebody is about to drop a dime on his head.'

'Not you. You've got a dime on your own.'

There was a long silence and Cross figured there had been some nonverbal communication going on. He walked into the doorway behind her.

Eddie looked up. He wasn't surprised. Cross was right. Margot gave him away.

'Eddie, Eddie,' Cross said, his gun out, his body language instructing both of them back into his room. 'You really should have stuck to feeding happy tourists. Why don't you guys sit down?'

Margot found the same chair in the same place as the other room and sat. Eddie remained standing. Cross used his foot to shut the door.

'Sit on the bed, Eddie.'

'I'll stand.'

'No, you'll sit, now.'

'What are you going to do, shoot me if I don't sit on the bed?'

'I think he will,' Margot said, looking at Cross, a thin smile on her face. 'He's not been himself lately.'

Eddie looked confused, but he sat on the edge of the bed.

'What's this "dime" Eddie's talking about, Margot?'

She shrugged. 'I'm a prostitute, Howie. I'm not exactly in good standing with the law.'

Cross looked at Eddie. Eddie kept a poker face.

'There's more than that, isn't there?' Cross continued.

'Look, I keep bad company, present company excluded.'

'Is he expecting you tonight?' Cross asked Eddie.

'Who?'

'Jay Leno.'

Eddie looked at Margot.

'Karl Herrmann,' Margot said.

Eddie glared at Cross.

'Yeah.'

'When?'

'Between ten and eleven,' Eddie said.

'Why?'

'Why what?' Eddie said, getting increasingly frustrated.

'Why does he want you around?' Cross asked. 'What in the hell can you do for him?'

He looked at Margot.

'I'm here because of her,' Eddie said.

She gave him a long look.

'Because she knows something, right,' Cross said. 'She's dangerous.'

Eddie looked at Margot again.

'You guys are holding back,' Cross said. 'It's not just Maya seeing the dead body, is it?'

That caught Eddie's attention. And Margot's.

Margot got up, went to the door, opened it.

'Where do you think you're going?' Cross asked.

'It's not what I think, Howie,' she said in her flat, indifferent voice that suggested boredom and superiority. 'You can shoot me or not shoot me. I don't give a fuck. It's time for me to disappear one way or another, sweetheart.'

'And Maya,' Cross said.

'She's yours, Howie.'

The door shut.

Her look would haunt him. He knew it immediately.

'When the doctor says you can travel, we should go to Hawaii for a few days. Lay around.' Maureen hadn't bothered to pick up her book as she always did when she climbed in bed.

'You just want to go to the nude beach,' Shanahan said.

'No, you just want to go to the nude beach.' She was quiet for a moment. 'I'm all right, Shanahan. He's a bastard, but a bastard I know. He didn't hurt me.' She rolled toward Shanahan. 'He hurt you. He had no right to do that.'

'I'm not getting naked, you know?'

'Yes. And you'll stare at the ocean and nothing else because you are a morally upright person.'

'It's not necessarily a matter of morality. If you look around, sometimes you see things you really don't want to see. I only go there for you.'

'Is that right?'

'Because you are a secret exhibitionist.'

'It's a secret?' She smiled. 'How do you feel?'

'I'm taking the pills.'

'We could go to the Canary Islands?'

'They have a naked beach?'

'Canaries, I think.'

'Naked canaries?' Shanahan asked.

'I'm sure of it. Interested?'

Twenty-Eight

On the ride over, Cross questioned Eddie about the operation. This was after Eddie was softened up by Cross's offering a choice. Eddie cooperates or Cross implicates him in murder and kidnapping.

'Whose side do you want me to be on, Eddie?'

'You don't know these guys,' Eddie said.

'Sounds like there are a lot fewer guys and I've already talked with the Maui police. I can help put you away here or there. Doesn't matter. Or maybe you can get a suspended sentence and get on with your restaurant business.'

'I'll lose my license.'

'Cut your losses, Eddie.'

The car's heater was on. Frost would be on the pumpkin tonight, Cross thought as they cut through the quiet streets.

'There were feeder systems in place,' Eddie said.

'Illegals?'

'Yes. Girls can come up from Mexico through the southwest clubs. Russians and Eastern Europe products come in through the East Coast. Asian girls through the West Coast clubs. California mostly.'

'Product,' Cross repeated.

'Girls,' Eddie said as if Cross didn't understand what he meant by product.

'But that's where you come in,' Cross said, 'set up clubs in Hawaii too.'

'Yeah.'

'How many girls come through these clubs?'

'Hundreds at a time.'

'You set up a brand with the clubs so traveling salesman know what they can get at each club?'

'Right,' Eddie said. He looked away, out of the window.

He knew he was damned if he cooperated, damned if he didn't. It was a lose–lose situation.

'And they could get quite a bit at Herrmann's clubs.'

'Man, there was a training manual at all entry points. What to do, what not to do. How to talk to the john. How to talk to the police. It was like a fuckin' McDonald's. Anyway, you know it all,' Eddie said. 'What do you need me for? A witness to use against Karl, right?'

'Yeah. Herrmann's doing all this out of little ole Naptown?'

'That's the beauty of it, really,' Eddie said.

'And Margot?'

'Playing both sides I found out, trying to figure out which one was going to come out on top.'

Cross and Eddie were no sooner in the front doors than Karl Herrmann was coming up to them. Starched shirt, expensive tie, dark suit probably European. The tip of a white hand-kerchief peeked out from its pocket hiding place. He wasn't smiling, wasn't frowning. If he knew what happened to his goons, he wasn't sweating their deaths. He looked fresh, unworried, relaxed.

Inside, the club mirrored the parking lot. Half full. It was a mellow crowd.

'We can talk in my office,' Herrmann said, 'but not before I get you something to drink. Scotch, Mr Cross?'

Cross nodded.

'And I know yours, Eddie.' Herrmann moved toward the bar, stopped for a moment, looked back at Eddie. 'Have you switched sides?' The tone was casual. He might well have asked him if he'd seen any good movies lately.

'No, stuck somewhere in the middle.'

'Most dangerous place of all,' Herrmann said, continuing to the bar. Eddie looked at the floor, no doubt weighing Herrmann's threat against any other option he could think of.

Herrmann's office was windowless. Just a box, but a well-dressed box. Persian rug. Big mahogany table as desk. A big, soft-looking sofa. A couple of chairs. The richness, warmness of the interior was only compromised by a big old safe and a wall of flat video screens that monitored the club's front door, back door, dance floor, bar, and three VIP rooms. In one of them a birthday party was going on and the Indiana law requiring all nipples to be covered was broken six times.

Herrmann sat at his desk, where he could see the screens but also relate to anyone sitting on the sofa, where Eddie settled in. Cross remained standing.

'The two of you represent the biggest mistakes I've made in my life,' Herrmann said. He was amused. 'Eddie, I needed your connections and in my eagerness I overlooked your shallow, cowardly nature. And you, Mr Cross . . .'

'Save it for your memoirs,' Cross said, to slice up the pomposity.

Herrmann laughed. 'You know how hard it is to get good help? You would be so much fun to work with. Tell me why you're here.'

'It's my ego. I just had to come by and tell you . . . show you, I'm alive and you're in trouble. I wanted to deliver the message myself.'

Herrmann rose. 'Well, there you are, then. Go on out, finish your drink, enjoy the girls. You've delivered your message.'

'There's a second part to the message.'

Herrmann nodded, sat down.

'I suspect your slave-trafficking is in its final hours and you should think about what you want to pack for your little trip to prison.'

'Thank you for your concern. I have lawyers, Mr Cross. I'll die of old age before this even gets to court.' If Herrmann's confidence was an act, he had mastered the craft. 'I would like to comment on your noble pursuit. You're a knight. Saving the fair lady. Except the lady is not Juliet. Not even Desdemona. She's Lady Macbeth. And your crusade? Save the world from the so-called sex-slave trade? America's ingrained prudishness creates the market. Other countries, most notably in Southeast Asia, have no such sexual hang-ups. Repression breeds prostitution.'

'I don't need a sociology lesson,' Cross said.

'Mr Cross, many of these girls were sold by their parents

for a small amount of money. Had they stayed they would
have been sold to some old tubercular drunk and lived un-
happily in servitude the rest of their lives or spent every day
of their lives as a slave, yes a slave, to some corporate giant,
chained to a sewing machine until they died or were too
feeble to work.

'They come to me. The pretty ones dance for a few years
and turn a trick or two as they choose. The less pretty ones
give erotic massages for a while, then they marry some
average forty- or fifty-year-old shy white guy who thinks he
hit the jackpot. He treats her like royalty and before long
they live in a nice three-bedroom home in the suburbs. She
drives their Toyota SUV to pick up the kids at Little League.
Unlike her peers back home, wherever home is, she knows
the price. She was happy to pay it.

'And your Margot. Oh, Mr Cross. She worked for my
partner, an uncivilized, crude man who by comparison makes
me a candidate for sainthood. He was going to snuff me out.
That's the man in the trunk of the car that little Maya saw.
Margot and her lover – sorry, Eddie, you had to know that
– were out to take over the franchise. Outright theft. They
did nothing to build it.'

'That makes you man of the year.'

'Where do I stand in rankings of all-time evil? Am I on
a lower rung than, say, the energy company that stole the
life savings of their employees? You accuse me of murder.
What about America's corporate security squads in Third
World countries with carte blanche for enforcement for the
sake of Wall Street? What of our soldiers dying for oil-
company profits? Thousands of them. Do you know what's
going on out there?' Herrmann nodded his head toward the
world outside his little club. 'I provide a little pleasure to
lonely guys. That's all.

'Take a good look around and when you do, tell me I am
a criminal? And if I were, am I worth all the effort, all of
your hatred? And where are you, Mr Noble? Are you out
there trying to save the mother who's been bombed while
searching in the rubble of her village for her family? Are
you out there to protect the little girl before she's blown to
bits by a power she never offended?

'Yet you choose me to get all righteous about? How do you come by your priorities, Mr Cross?'

'I guess mine are closer to home,' Cross said.

'Have I missed something? Perhaps all your work in the soup kitchens, building houses for the poor.' Herrmann shook his head. 'I'm not judging you, Mr Cross. I just don't think you should be judging me. It's nothing personal.'

'All I know,' Cross said, 'in my little corner of the universe is that you kidnapped a woman, tried to kill me, and threatened a five-year-old girl. I'm taking all of that personally. What do you think, Eddie?'

Eddie shook his head. He wanted no part of this or anything.

'I didn't murder anyone, Mr Cross. Maybe, just maybe, a good prosecutor can shut me down here – though I doubt it. Even so, each club is a separate corporation. Each club has a separate board of directors. We're an organized business, Mr Cross.'

'Mafia,' Cross said.

'No, we're better than that. We're big business. We have lobbyists. People who know people in high places. We're connected in ways that those in your little corner of the universe don't begin to understand.'

'What if I have all this taped?' Cross asked.

'You don't. You are carrying a handgun, Mr Cross, and a cellphone. Eddie's carrying an iPod, but it's not on.' Herrmann glanced up at his machine. 'We look at you as you go through the door.' He stood up again. 'Well, this has been nice. If you ever want a real job, Mr Cross . . .'

'Never did,' Cross said. He looked at Eddie. 'You need a ride back?' Eddie looked confused.

'Christ, guys,' Eddie said.

'Nobody's offering you a choice between good and evil,' Cross said. 'Just bad and worse. Compared to Herrmann, you're a little fish. You'll get eaten first. Stay here and you're up for murder. Come with me, tell the police what you know, and you might get off on probation.'

Eddie was frozen. Herrmann appeared amused.

'Decisions, decisions,' Herrmann said.

Cross started toward the door. He looked back. 'You coming?'

Eddie didn't move.

'On the other side of that door,' Herrmann said, glancing up at his monitor, 'is a very tall black man in a nice suit.' When Cross opened the door, Lieutenant Collins was on the other side.

'My God, Cross, you're everywhere,' Collins said.

'You and Herrmann go to the same tailor?' Cross said, noting the cop's fresh-pressed look.

Collins stepped in, introduced himself.

Cross started out.

'Stick around,' Collins said. 'Mr Herrmann, you have two employees working for you. A Mr Anatelea and a Mr McClintock.'

Herrmann nodded. 'Security.'

'You know where they are?' Collins asked. He sized up Eddie as he posed the question to Herrmann.

'No. They were supposed to report in, but they haven't.' Herrmann looked at Cross.

'They're dead, Mr Herrmann. Found out on a farm north-west of here.'

'You don't say,' Herrmann said. 'How did they die?'

'Gunshot wounds. Preliminary look suggests they shot each other,' Collins said with a smile that wasn't exactly happy. Herrmann remained quiet. Eddie had already gone to a corner, staying as far away as possible from the conversation. But he looked scared.

'You know anything about this, Cross?' Collins asked.

'I came out here looking for a dancer. She used to work here. She's missing.'

'How is it that you are in the middle of my business again?'

'Somebody's got to do the work,' Cross said.

'You're going to need me one of these days.' He turned toward Eddie. 'And you. What's your name?'

'Eddie Creek.'

'What are you doing here?'

'That girl he's looking for,' Eddie said, nodding to Cross, 'is my girlfriend.'

'So you hired Cross?'

'He's helping me out.'

Collins looked around the room. 'Is there anything anyone wants to tell me?'

'Nice suit,' Cross said. 'But fishing for compliments isn't a classy thing to do.'

'So, Mr Herrmann, you have no idea what two of your employees were doing at an abandoned farm this morning?'

'No, I'm sorry. What's this world coming to?' Herrmann was good. If he hadn't known they were killed, then he was doubly good. 'You'll let me know what you find out.'

Collins looked at Cross, no doubt trying to catch a revealing expression. Cross did his best poker face by thinking about scrubbing the bathroom floor.

'If you don't mind,' Cross said including both Herrmann and Collins in his gaze, 'I'm going to head home. I need to put in a call to a really great cop in Maui. He's working on some murder case I'm interested in. You coming with me, Eddie? Or are you staying here?'

'Can I bum a ride back to the hotel?' Eddie asked. 'I'd appreciate it.'

'You be careful, Eddie,' Herrmann said. 'The world's a dangerous place.'

Twenty-Nine

Cross didn't feel safe going home and he'd already paid for the room at the hotel. He drove back the way they came, a borderline-catatonic Eddie in the passenger seat. No doubt Eddie was feeling the squeeze and knew it could easily be a deadly one.

Once they got back to the hotel, Cross invited Eddie into his room for a goodnight drink and some information gathering. Unfortunately Cross found little intelligence to mine. If there was an organization higher than Herrmann's, Eddie had no clue about it or in this state of shock no clue about much of anything.

Cross cut the conversation short, and made sure Eddie was settled back in his own room. While Eddie took a quick pee Cross opened a window, the one by the fire escape. It was open, but not enough to notice. When he was sure Eddie was about down for the count, Cross went downstairs and asked to switch his room for another – said he was sure someone had smoked in it recently and he'd specifically asked for a nonsmoking room for that reason.

The guy at the desk clearly didn't care. Cross asked for the room next to Eddie's and got it. He transferred his gear over and, as he had done in Eddie's room, opened the window, the one that accessed the same fire escape as Eddie's. He opened it wide.

Cross wasn't sleepy. A combination of the adrenaline he got from the endgame, the cold November air coming in through the open window, and the fact that his body time was all off anyway contributed to a high state of alertness. He turned off all the lights and flicked on the TV. He muted the sound.

He'd bet Herrmann and his remaining boy would go to

Cross's house tonight; and after finding no one, would come after Eddie, the turncoat. Herrmann might have fine lawyers, but it would help a lot if the list of witnesses were whittled down. And, now, could he trust anyone other than himself to do the job?

The sounds outside came in. Soon, his ears were gathering distant car doors shutting, the flutter of wings – bats or birds. Television – all the slicers, dicers, juicers, and cookers mail-order geniuses could design – lit the walls in flickering light. This kind of cold calm, rarely with him, was there now.

He heard scratching. As before at his house – probably the same idiot and same tactic – it was metal on metal. Someone was picking a lock. Cross was sure it was Eddie's door, not his. Cross moved to the window. He heard the sound of the door unlatching. He heard whispers, not the words, just breathy urgency. Eddie was not really asleep. He was passed out.

He pulled his gun from its uncomfortable spot between belt and lower back and climbed out on the fire escape. He looked in. The light was on in the bathroom. It spilled out sharply on the carpet just beyond the door and dispersed enough for Cross to see the human shapes moving in the room. Two of them. The remaining big boy, walking strangely, one leg inside metal struts. He was the one with the pillow. And Herrmann, there to observe, supervise, stood beside the goon who was pushing the pillow down on Eddie's face.

Shanahan woke up in a fright. It took him a few moments to figure out where he was. He heard Maureen's comforting regular breathing. The blue numbers on his clock radio said 5:05. He slipped out of bed and went through the darkness to the kitchen. He flipped the switch and the harsh light was less friendly than the darkness. He saw the boarded-up window forcing him to remember how this nightmare began.

He went to the cabinet, plucked the bottle of J. W. Dant from the shelf and poured himself two fingers. He took a deep breath and swallowed it all, welcoming the slight burn in his throat and the warmth that moved through his body and out to the limbs. The boarded-up window was so apt, he thought. Patched up. Not back to normal, but simply patched up.

Maureen was back. Tough as she was, she was no doubt shaken. Then again, he thought, she'd weathered a lot in her life. She would do all right. Shanahan crawled back into bed, both bitter and grateful. Still asleep, she moved toward him. Their bodies touched. He kissed her hair. Her scent invaded him, her warmth gave him refuge. Sleep overtook him.

Out on the fire escape, the night was cold and clear. Cross could see the stars even in the heart of the city. He was ready to lift the window, tell them to stop, and shoot them if necessary, when the goon lifted the pillow. The gasping, sputtering Eddie Creek came to consciousness. A couple of hours' sleep, Cross thought. Maybe Eddie could think coherently. Maybe not.

'Eddie?' Herrmann said, turning on the table lamp, and moving toward the bed. 'I have some questions for you. Your continued existence depends on your answers.'

Eddie was still gasping for breath and dealing with the sudden horror in his alcohol-addled mind.

'Do you understand, Eddie?'

Herrmann unbuttoned his long black cashmere overcoat and pulled the scarf from his neck. Perhaps Herrmann was too hot. More likely he wanted to suggest that the scarf might be more effective than a pillow.

'Yes,' catapulted from Eddie's mouth.

'What happened to Dwight and Mr Anatelea?'

'I don't know. I was with you that day, remember?' Eddie said feebly.

Herrmann nodded. 'Cross told you nothing?'

'No.'

'All right,' Herrmann said patiently, seemingly satisfied. 'Where is the child?'

Margot's words, 'She's yours,' crept into Cross's mind.

'We never found out. We thought Cross had her,' Eddie said. 'Like I told you, we surprised him in the middle of the night. The girl wasn't there. It seemed as if Cross didn't know where she was either.'

'This is the truth?' Herrmann played with his scarf. The man enjoyed messing with minds, Cross thought.

'God's honor.'

'God's honor?' Herrmann was amused. 'Margot, then? Where is she?'

'She was in the basement. It was all locked up. I haven't gone out there. It's a crime scene. I don't know where she went. Maybe the police have her.'

'You don't know much of anything, do you?' Herrmann said. 'What possible use are you to me? You are a debit in my book. You can bear witness against me, but have nothing to offer me.'

'Access to Hawaii.' Eddie tried to be tough, but it was too late.

'That's the very least of my worries. It will be years before I can consider expanding anywhere. Thanks to you and Mr Cross, I'm in a preservation mode. Not just my business.'

'She was here,' Eddie said.

'Where is she, Eddie?' Herrmann asked.

'She was here. She's gone. Ooooh,' Eddie sighed. He knew he'd made a mistake. She was here then she was gone. His face said it all. What good was that? 'Margot told Cross that the girl was all his.'

'I don't know what that means,' Herrmann said. 'What does that mean?'

'I don't know. Cross has Maya, I guess.'

Herrmann smiled. 'And Cross?'

'I can give you Cross,' Eddie said. 'I know where he is.'

'Where is he?' Herrmann asked almost too casually.

'Do I have your word? You'll let me live?'

'You're not in a position to bargain.'

There was a pause in the non-negotiations.

Eddie, Eddie, Eddie, Cross thought. You're dead either way.

'Let me put it this way,' Herrmann said. 'You are about to be eliminated. Perhaps I'll reconsider based on your assistance in this matter. Where is he, Eddie?'

'Room 214.'

'Here?' the goon asked.

Eddie nodded.

'Use Eddie to get him to open the door,' Herrmann said. 'Then bring both of them back here. Don't wake anybody.'

Herrmann followed them to the door, then pushed the door nearly closed, before turning around to see Cross, gun in hand.

'Close it all the way. Put on the security lock.'

Herrmann didn't move. 'You're not going to shoot me.'

'I'd love to shoot you. How do you think your friends ended up dead?'

Herrmann nudged the door shut, secured the night lock, turned back.

'Now what do we do?' he asked, smiling. 'Spend the night together?'

'We leave,' Cross said, nodding toward the window. 'After you.'

As they descended the fire escape one floor to the parking lot, Cross used his cellphone to call 911. He told the operator there was a man with a bum leg and a gun who was threatening people on the second floor of the hotel. Downtown, at night, the response should be quick.

'I wish we'd met under different circumstances,' Herrmann said.

'Yeah, the problem seems to be the circumstances. How do we get you to stop terrorizing women and children?'

'It's a market opportunity. If I get out of the business, someone else will come along.'

'Get in,' Cross opened the driver's door on the Saab. 'You're driving.' He got in the back seat. 'Got a place I want to show you.'

It wasn't yet light when they got there. Just a sliver of gray light on the horizon suggested day was coming, another one without the sun. But there was enough light for them to see where they were going. With the exception of the yellow police do not cross ribbons flapping in the cold wind, it could have been the morning when the goons brought Cross out there to kill him.

The ground was hard. Crows screeched in the naked trees. Somehow, in some way, the world changed for Cross. For the first time he understood the madness that hovered in the outer reaches of his mind. He was also centered – maybe for the first time in his life.

Cross reached his parents' place in full dismal daylight. They were up. She was clearing the table, but interrupted her work to fix him some eggs and bacon. His father read the paper. He had looked up, acknowledged his son's arrival, and went back to the paper. Both of them could read him and they knew that when he was troubled, he didn't like questions. He liked quiet.

Cross looked at Maya, trying to find himself or his mother in her. All he could see was Margot.

'What?' she asked.

'You gather the eggs?' he asked.

She nodded.

'Your mom has some things to do,' Cross said.

'She can stay here for as long as it takes,' Cross's mother said.

'You mind?'

She gave him a 'what is there to mind?' look.

'In spring we'll put in a garden,' Cross's father said.

'Can we grow sunflowers?' Maya asked.

'Yep,' the older man said. 'And tomatoes and cabbage, sweet peas and lima beans.'

'Can we grow pickles?' Maya asked.

'Now there's a farm girl for you,' Cross said. 'Can you grow pickles, Dad?'

'Sure can. You OK?'

Cross nodded. It was good. His parents were with him.

Thirty

It was late evening. Harry had a few more customers than usual, even if you didn't count Shanahan, Cross, Kowalski, and Maureen sitting in one of the booths playing dirty clubs.

Shanahan was dealing when Collins came in.

'Swann said I'd probably find you here.' He addressed Cross first, but his glance went around the table. 'Didn't know all the players would be here and gambling at that. I'd arrest you, but I'd have to call for reinforcements.' He smiled. 'How are you doing, Maureen? Sorry you guys had to do this on your own.' He nodded toward Cross. 'You and I need to talk.'

'Why is that?' Cross asked.

Collins was obviously weighing whether or not he should discuss this in public.

'How about outside?'

'Got a game going,' Cross said.

'You might need a lawyer,' Collins said.

'He's got one,' Kowalski said. 'Make your point and go away, or go off duty and have a drink with us.'

Collins smiled. 'You always travel with an attorney, Cross?'

'Doesn't hurt. Got framed once by you guys.'

Collins nodded. 'There is a farm way out west on the county line.' He waited. Not getting any response, he continued, 'It was where those two guys supposedly shot each other.'

'Clubs are up,' Shanahan said, after he finished dealing five cards to each player and turned up the top card on the stack of remaining cards.

'That means you have to play clubs whether you like it or not, doesn't it?' Collins said.

'You know dirty clubs?'

'Yeah. It's a variation on euchre,' Collins said. 'Flunked out my freshman year playing euchre and drinking lime vodka. Some kid from Wisconsin taught us dirty clubs.' He shook off his memories. 'So where was I?'

'On a farm,' Maureen said.

'Right. Sent the medical examiner and some uniforms back out to the scene to see if there was anything we missed.'

'You miss anything?' Kowalski asked, tossing down the ten of clubs. He must have had a couple of clubs but was fishing, willing to give up one trick to get the big clubs out on the table. It worked. Kowalski had at least three tricks coming, easy.

'No, but something turned up,' Collins said. 'Karl Herrmann, chained to a wall in the storm cellar. Been there a couple of days.'

'Alive?' Cross asked.

'Nice of you to ask. Yeah. Crazy as a loon. Kept saying you destroyed his cashmere coat.'

'Crazy, huh?' Cross said.

'This isn't the end of this,' Collins said. He stood there watching them play.

'You have something else to say?' Kowalski asked him.

'Got a call from some cop in Hawaii. Says Herrmann is operating a sex-slave gig. Big time.'

'I'll be damned,' Cross said.

'You know all the players here. The Maui cops' got an Eddie Creek willing to testify,' Collins said. 'I remember Eddie. So do you.'

'Small town,' Cross said.

'Just like Mayberry. What do you think, Ace?' Shanahan said.

'So maybe this guy Herrmann is playing crazy,' Cross said.

'Have a good game,' Collins said, and left.

'You look older,' Shanahan said to Cross.

Cross looked back at Shanahan, nodded. The two sets of eyes rested there a moment. The meaning was conveyed.

Biography

An Indianapolis native, Ronald Tierney has lived in South Bend, Font Wayne, and Bloomington, Indiana. He currently lives in San Francisco where he is at work on several fiction projects. *Asphalt Moon* is the eighth novel in the *Deets Shanahan* mystery series.